The Sentence Is Death

ALSO BY ANTHONY HOROWITZ

The House of Silk

Moriarty

Trigger Mortis

Magpie Murders

The Word Is Murder

Forever and a Day

The Sentence *Is* Death

A Novel

Anthony Horowitz

HARPER LUXE

An Imprint of HarperCollinsPublishers

Originally published in the United Kingdom in 2018 by Century Penguin Random House UK.

HarperCollins books may be purchased for educational, business, or sales promotional use. For information, please e-mail the Special Markets Department at SPsales@harpercollins.com.

FIRST HARPERLUXE EDITION

ISBN: 978-0-06-291207-7

HarperLuxe™ is a trademark of HarperCollins Publishers.

Library of Congress Cataloging-in-Publication Data is available upon request.

19 20 21 22 23 ID/LSC 10 9 8 7 6 5 4 3 2 1

In memory of Peter Clayton,
20th June 1963 – 18th June 2018.
The best of friends

1
Scene Twenty-seven

Usually, I enjoy visiting film sets. I love the excitement of seeing so many professional people working together – at a cost of tens of thousands of pounds – to create a vision that will have begun perhaps nine or ten months ago inside my head. I love being part of it all.

But this time it was different. I'd overslept and left home in a hurry. I couldn't find my phone. I had the beginnings of a headache. Even as I got out of the car on that damp October morning, I knew that I'd made a mistake and that all in all I would have been better off staying in bed.

It was a big day. We were shooting one of the opening scenes in the seventh series of *Foyle's War* – the

2 · ANTHONY HOROWITZ

first appearance of Sam Stewart, Foyle's driver. Played by Honeysuckle Weeks, she had become a stalwart of the series and she was one of my favourite actors. When I wrote lines for her, I could always hear her saying them. The new season would find her married, out of the police force, working now for a nuclear scientist. I had decided to give her a big entrance and I wanted to be there to show my support.

This is what I had written.

27. EXT. LONDON STREET (1947) DAY.

SAM gets off a bus, carrying shopping. She has just had bad news and
she pauses for a moment, thinking of
the implications. She is surprised to
see ADAM waiting for her.

SAM
Adam! What are you doing here?

ADAM
Waiting for you.

They kiss.

ADAM (CONT'D)

Let me take that.

He takes her shopping and together
they begin to walk home.

On paper, it may not look like much but I had known all along that it would be a major headache. My wife, Jill Green, was the producer and those two words – LONDON STREET – would have been enough to make her groan. Shooting in London is always a horrible business, prohibitively expensive and fraught with difficulties. It often seems that the entire city is deliberately doing everything in its power to stop the cameras turning. Planes will fly overhead. Pneumatic drills and car alarms will burst into angry life. Police cars and ambulances will race past with their sirens blaring. No matter how many signs you've put up warning people you're going to be there, someone will have forgotten to move their car or, worse still, will have left it there on purpose in the hope of being paid. There's a natural assumption that TV and film producers have deep pockets but sadly this is far from true. Tom Cruise may be able to shut down Blackfriars Bridge or half of Piccadilly without a second thought, but that's not the case for most British television, where even a short scene like the one I'd written can be almost impossible to achieve.

Leaving the car, I found myself entering a time warp. This was 1947. The production had managed to get hold of two streets of Victorian houses and had worked hard to turn them into a perfect reproduction of post-war London. Aerials and satellite dishes had been covered with ivy or plastic roof tiles. Modern doors and windows had disappeared behind frames that would have been measured and constructed weeks before. Street signs and lamp posts had been camou-flaged and yellow lines covered with sackloads of the powder known as Fuller's earth. We had brought in our own props: a bright red telephone box, a bus stop and enough debris to simulate the sort of bomb damage that would have been familiar to Londoners years after the war. Ignore the people in Puffa jackets, the lights, the dollies and the endlessly snaking cables and it was indistinguishable from the real thing.

There was a whole crowd of people standing around me, waiting patiently for filming to begin. Along with the crew there were about thirty background artists all in costume with period haircuts. I examined the action vehicles, which were being manoeuvred into position by the second assistant director. They included an Austin Princess, a Morgan 4/4, a horse and cart and, the hero of the scene, an AEC Regent II double-decker bus from which Sam Stewart would emerge. Honeysuckle was standing with her screen husband across the road and, seeing me, she raised a hand. But she didn't smile. That was when I knew things weren't going well.

I looked for the camera and saw Jill deep in conversation with the director, Stuart Orme, and the rest of the camera crew. None of them were looking very happy either. I was already feeling guilty. The script that I had written for this episode, 'The Eternity Ring', had opened in New Mexico at a test for the nuclear bomb. (Stuart had managed to shoot it on a beach at the crack of dawn, stealing the scene in the two hours before the tide came in.) From there it had moved to the Russian embassy in London, the Liverpool docks and then to Whitehall and the headquarters of MI6. It had been a huge amount to ask and Scene 27 might have been one step too far. Sam could have walked home. She could have just turned up at her front door.

Stuart saw me and came over. He was only one year older than me, although with his white hair and white beard I found him slightly intimidating. But we had already worked together on one episode and I was glad he had come back for a second. 'We can't shoot the scene,' he said.

'What's wrong?' I asked, fighting an irrational worry that, whatever had happened, it would turn out to be my fault.

'A lot of things. We had to move two cars. We've had issues with the weather.' It had only just stopped raining. 'The police wouldn't allow us to start shooting before ten o'clock anyway. And the bus has broken down.'

I looked round. The AEC Regent II was being towed out of shot. Another bus had arrived to replace it. 'That's a Routemaster,' I said.

'I know. I know.' Stuart looked harassed. We both knew that the first Routemaster hadn't appeared on London roads until the mid-fifties. 'But that's what the agency sent round,' he went on. 'Don't worry, we can CGI it in post-production.'

Computer-generated imagery. It was very expensive but at times it could be our greatest benefactor. It gave us views of a bombed-out London. It allowed us to drive past St Paul's when we were nowhere near.

'What else?'

'Look, I've only got ninety minutes to shoot the scene. We have to be out of here by twelve and right now there are four set-ups. I can't do it. So if it's all right with you, I want to drop the dialogue. We'll just film Sam getting off the bus and we'll pick her up meeting Adam when she gets home.'

In a way, I was quite flattered. As I've mentioned before, the writer is the one person on a set who has nothing to do and it's one of the reasons why I usually stay away. I have a bad habit of always being in the wrong place. If a mobile goes off during filming, it will almost certainly turn out to be mine. But here was the director actually asking for my help and I saw at once that what he was suggesting wouldn't make any material difference to the episode.

'That's fine,' I said.

'Good. I hoped you wouldn't mind.' He turned and walked away, leaving me with the realisation that he had actually made the decision long before I arrived.

Even without the dialogue, though, it was going to be a close-run thing. Stuart was going to have one rehearsal and then try for the take but it was still a complicated set-up. A twenty-metre track had been built, allowing the camera to glide along the first street as the bus came rumbling towards it at right angles down a second. The bus would turn the corner and come to a halt. The camera would continue its journey, reaching the stop just as two or three passengers got out, followed by Sam. At the same time, other vehicles, including the horse and cart, would pass in both directions. Children would play on the pavements. Various pedestrians would walk past: a woman pushing a pram, a couple of policemen, a man with a bicycle and so on. It would involve very precise timing if it was all going to be captured in a single shot.

'Positions, everyone, please!'

The actor playing Sam's husband was sent back to his trailer, none too happy. He would have been up since the crack of dawn. The driver of the Routemaster was given his briefing. The background artists took their places. I went over and stood behind the camera, making sure I was out of the way. The first assistant director glanced at Stuart, who nodded.

'Action!'

The rehearsal was disastrous.

The bus arrived too soon and the camera too late. Sam got lost in the crowd. A cloud chose that moment to block the sun. The horse refused to move. I saw Stuart exchange a few words with his director of photography, then briskly shake his head. They weren't ready to film. They would need a second rehearsal after all.

It was already ten past eleven. That's the thing about film sets. There are great stretches of time when nobody seems to be doing anything, followed by brief bursts of highly concentrated activity when the actual filming takes place. But the clock is always ticking. Speaking personally, I find the stress almost unbearable. When Stuart said he had to be done by twelve o'clock, he meant twelve o'clock on the dot. There were two real policemen holding up the traffic at the far corner. They would want to leave. The owners of the houses had given us permission to shoot for an exact amount of time. The locations manager was there, looking worried. I was already wishing I hadn't come.

The AD picked up his megaphone and barked out fresh orders. 'First positions!' Slowly, stubbornly, the passengers climbed back on board and the Routemaster reversed. The children were led to their positions. The horse was given a lump of sugar. Fortunately, the second rehearsal went a little better. The bus and the camera met at the corner exactly as planned. Sam stepped down and walked away. The horse set off exactly on cue although it did rather spoil things by veering off the road and mounting the pavement. Fortunately, nobody was hurt. Stuart and the cameraman muttered a few words, then decided they were ready. Jill was looking at her watch. It was now eleven thirty-five.

Because this was a big scene with so much production value involved, we had our own stills photographer there along with a couple of journalists who were planning to interview Honeysuckle and me. ITV had sent down two senior executives who were anxiously watching over the entire operation along with health and safety people and paramedics from the St John Ambulance. In addition, there was the usual army of sparks, gaffers, first, second and third assistant directors, make-up artists, prop masters . . . a whole crew of them standing there, waiting to see a sequence that we now had less than thirty minutes to shoot.

There were final checks, glitches, a silence that seemed to stretch interminably. My palms were sweating. But at last I heard the familiar litany that comes with every shot.

'Sound?'

'Sound rolling.'

'Camera?'

'Camera rolling. Speed . . .'

'Scene twenty-seven. Take one.'

The snap of the clapperboard.

'Action!'

The camera began to glide towards us. The bus rattled forward. The children played. Obediently, with a spring in its step, the horse set off, pulling the cart.

And then, out of nowhere, a vehicle appeared, a modern, twenty-first-century taxi. It wasn't even a black cab, which might have been adjusted, along with the bus, using CGI. It had been painted white and yellow with an advertisement for some new app in bright red and the legend 'GET £5 OFF YOUR NEXT RIDE' across the front and back doors. Just to add to the merriment, the window was rolled down and the driver was playing Justin Timberlake at full blast on the radio. It stopped, right in the middle of the shot.

'Cut!'

Stuart Orme was usually a pleasant, easy-going man. But his face was thunderous as he looked up from his monitor to see what had happened. It was impossible, of course. The police should have blocked off the traffic. We had our own people at each end of the street, keeping back pedestrians. There was no way any vehicle could have come through.

Already, I was feeling sick inside. I had a bad feeling about what was about to happen.

And I was right.

The door of the taxi opened and a man got out. He seemed completely unconcerned by the fact that he was surrounded by a large crowd of people, many of them in period dress. He had a sort of cheerful self-confidence that was actually quite cold-blooded, utterly focused on his own needs at the expense of everyone else's. He was not tall or well built but he gave the impression that, by whatever means necessary, he would never lose a fight. His hair, somewhere between brown and grey, was cut very short, particularly around the ears. His eyes, a darker brown, gazed innocently out of a pale, slightly unhealthy face. This was not someone who spent a lot of time in the sun. He was dressed in a dark suit, a white shirt and a narrow tie, clothes that might have been deliberately chosen to say nothing about him. His shoes were brightly polished. As he moved forward, he was already searching for me and I had to ask myself – how had he even known I was here?

Before I could duck down behind the monitor, he found me.

'Tony!' he called out, amicably – and loudly enough for everyone on the set to hear.

Stuart turned to me, quite furious. 'Do you know this man?' he asked.

'Yes,' I admitted. 'His name is Daniel Hawthorne. He's a detective.'

The camera crew was staring at me. The two women from ITV were muttering to each other in disbelief. Jill went over to them, trying to explain. Everyone in the street had frozen in their positions as if they had suddenly turned into one of those 'Historical London' postcards. Even the horse looked annoyed.

They did manage to do a second take before time ran out and at the end of the day they had just about enough footage to cut a sequence together. If you ever watch the scene, you can see the telephone box, the horse and cart, the two policemen (in the far distance) and Sam walking away. Unfortunately, the camera missed most of the background artists, including the woman with the pram and the man with the bicycle. Sam is carrying a shopping bag, but you don't see that either.

And in the end we ran out of money and when we got to post-production there was nothing we could do about that bloody bus.

2

A Murder in Hampstead

I left Hawthorne in my office – actually a Winnebago trailer parked halfway up a side street – while I went to get us both coffees from the catering truck. When I returned, he was sitting at the desk, leafing through the latest draft of 'The Eternity Ring', which rather annoyed me because I certainly hadn't invited him to read my work. At least he wasn't smoking. These days, I hardly know anyone who smokes but Hawthorne was still getting through about a packet a day, which was why we usually met outside coffee shops, sitting in the street.

'I wasn't expecting you,' I said, as I climbed back inside.

'You don't seem too pleased.'

'Well, as a matter of fact, I'm quite busy . . . although

you probably didn't notice that when you drove straight into the middle of the set.'

'I wanted to see you.' He waited until I had sat down opposite him. 'How's the book going?'

'I've finished it.'

'I still don't like the title.'

'I'm still not giving you any choice.'

'All right! All right!' He looked up at me as if I had somehow, and for no good reason, offended him. He had mud-brown eyes but it was remarkable how they still managed to appear so clear, so completely inno-cent. 'I can see you're in a bad mood today, but you know it's not my fault you overslept.'

'Who told you I'd overslept?' I asked, falling into the obvious trap.

'And you still haven't found your phone.'

'Hawthorne . . . !'

'You didn't lose it in the street,' he went on. 'I think you'll find it's somewhere in your flat. And I'll give you a word of advice. If Michael Kitchen doesn't like your script, maybe you should think about hiring another actor. Don't take it out on me!'

I stared at him, playing back what he had just said and wondering what evidence he could possibly have for any of it. Michael Kitchen was the star of *Foyle's War* and although it was true we'd had a lot of discussion about the new episode, I hadn't mentioned it to anyone apart from Jill, who knew anyway. And I certainly hadn't brought up my sleeping patterns or the fact that I had been unable to find my phone when I got up that morning.

'What are you doing here, Hawthorne?' I demanded. I had never once called him by his first name, not from the day I had met him. I'm not sure anybody did. 'What do you want?'

'There's been another murder,' he said. He stretched out the last word in that odd accent of his. *Another murrrr-der.* It was almost as if he was relishing it.

'And?'

He blinked at me. Wasn't it obvious? 'I thought you'd want to write about it.'

If you've read *The Word Is Murder*, you'll know that Detective Inspector Daniel Hawthorne was first introduced to me as a consultant on a television series I was writing: *Injustice.* He had once worked for Scotland Yard but that had come to an end following an incident in which a suspect, a man dealing in child pornography, had taken a tumble down a flight of concrete stairs. Hawthorne had been standing right behind him at the time. As a result, he had been fired and since then had been forced to earn a living on his own. He could have gone into security like many ex-detectives but instead he'd turned his talents to helping film and television companies producing dramas about crime and that was how we met. But, as I soon discovered, it turned out that the force hadn't quite finished with him after all.

He was called in when the police got what they called a 'sticker' – that is, a case which presented obvious difficulties from the start. Most murderers are brutal and unthinking. A husband and wife have an argument. Perhaps they've been drinking too much. One of them picks up a hammer and – bang – that's it. With fingerprints, blood splatter and all the other forensic evidence, the whole thing will be solved within twenty-four hours. And these days, with so much CCTV, it's hard even to escape a crime scene without leaving a cheerful snapshot of yourself behind.

Much rarer are the premeditated murders, where the perpetrators actually put a bit of thought into their crimes, and curiously, perhaps because they rely so heavily on technology, modern detectives find these much harder to solve. I remember a clue I put into an episode of *Agatha Christie's Poirot* when I was writing it for ITV. A woman's glove embroidered with the letter *H* is left at the crime scene. Modern detectives would be able to tell you where and when it was made, what fabric was used, what size it was and everything it had touched in the last few weeks. But they might not recognise that the *H* was actually the Russian letter for *N* and that it had been deliberately dropped to frame somebody else. For these esoteric insights, they needed someone like Hawthorne.

The trouble was, they didn't pay him a great deal and after we had finished *Injustice* he got in touch with me, asking me if I would be interested in writing a book about him. It was a straightforward commercial proposition. My name would go on the cover but we would share the proceeds fifty-fifty. I knew from the start that it was a bad idea. I make up stories; I prefer not to follow them around town. More to the point, I like to be in control of my books. I had no wish to turn myself into a character, and a secondary one at that: the perennial sidekick.

But somehow he persuaded me and even though, quite literally, it had almost killed me, the first book was now finished, although it had yet to be published. There was a further issue. My new publisher – Selina Walker at Random House – had insisted on a three-book contract and, urged on by my agent, I had agreed. I think it's the same for every writer, no matter how many books they have sold. A three-book contract represents stability. It means that you can plan your time, knowing exactly what you're going to be doing. But it also means you're committed to writing them. No rest for the insecure.

Hawthorne knew this, of course, so all through the summer I had been waiting for the telephone to ring, at the same time hoping that it wouldn't. Hawthorne was undoubtedly brilliant. He had solved the first mystery in a way that made it seem like child's play though I had missed every one of the clues that had been presented to me. But on a personal level I found him extremely trying. He was dark and solitary, refusing to tell me anything about himself even though I was supposed to be his biographer. I found some of his attitudes disconcerting to say the least. He swore all the time, he smoked and he called me 'Tony'. If I had chosen to pluck a hero from real life, it certainly wouldn't have been him.

And here he was, stalking me again just weeks after I had finished writing *The Word Is Murder*. I hadn't shown it to him yet and he didn't know what I'd written about him. I had decided to keep it that way for as long as possible.

'So who's been murdered?' I asked.

'His name is Richard Pryce.' Hawthorne stopped as if he expected me to know who he was talking about. I didn't. 'He's a lawyer,' he went on. 'A divorce lawyer. He's been in the papers quite a bit. A lot of his clients have been well known. Celebrities . . . that sort of thing.'

As he spoke, I realised that I did know the name after all. There had been something about him on the radio as I was being driven to the set but, half asleep, I hadn't really listened. Richard Pryce lived in Hampstead, which is somewhere I often go when I'm walking the dog. According to the report, he'd been attacked in his own home, hit with a wine bottle. And there was something else. He'd had a nickname. Was it 'Steel Magnolia'? No. That was Fiona Shackleton, who had famously represented Sir Paul McCartney in his acrimonious split from Heather Mills. Pryce was known as 'the Blunt Razor'. I had no idea why.

'Who killed him?' I asked.

Hawthorne looked at me sadly. 'If I knew that, mate, I wouldn't be here.'

He was right about one thing. I was overtired. 'The police want you to look into it?' I asked.

'That's right. I got the call this morning. And immediately I thought of you.'

'That's very kind of you. But what makes it so special?'

To answer my question, Hawthorne pulled a stack of photographs out of his inside jacket pocket. I steeled myself. I've often seen crime-scene images as part of

my research and I can never quite get over how shock-
ingly violent they are. It's the artlessness of them, the
fact that everything is presented without any sen-
sitivity. There's something about the lack of colour
too. Blood looks even more horrible when it's dark
black. The dead bodies you see on a television screen
are just actors lying on their sides. They have almost
nothing in common with real corpses.

The first picture was all right, though. It was a
posed, portrait shot of Richard Pryce taken while he
was still alive and showed a handsome, rather debonair
man with an aquiline nose and long, grey hair sweep-
ing back over a high forehead. He was wearing a jersey
and half smiling as if he was pleased with himself, and
certainly had no inkling that he was about to find himself the subject of a murder investigation. His left hand
was folded over his right arm and I noticed a gold band
on his fourth finger. So, he was married.

In the next shots, he was dead. This time his hands
were stretched out over his head as he lay on a bare
wooden floor, contorted in a way that only a corpse
can be. He was surrounded by fragments of glass and a
large quantity of liquid that looked too thin to be blood
and which would turn out to be blood mixed with wine.
The photographs had been taken from the left and from
the right and from above, leaving nothing to the imagi-

nation. I moved on to the other images: jagged wounds around his neck and throat, staring eyes, claw-like fingers. Death close up. I wondered how Hawthorne had got them so quickly but guessed that he had received them electronically and had printed them at home.

'Richard Pryce was struck with a full wine bottle on the forehead and frontal area of the skull,' Hawthorne explained. It was interesting how quickly he slipped into officialese. 'Struck' instead of 'hit', for example. And that 'frontal area', which could have come straight out of a weather forecaster's lexicon. 'There are severe contusions and a spiderweb fracture of the frontal bone, but that wasn't what killed him. The bottle smashed, which means that some of the energy was dispersed. Pryce fell to the ground and the killer was left holding the jagged glass neck. He used it as a knife, stabbing at the throat.' He pointed at one of the close-ups. 'Here and here. The second blow penetrated the subclavian vein and continued into the pleural cavity.'

'He bled to death,' I said.

'No.' Hawthorne shook his head. 'He probably didn't have time. My guess is he suffered an air embolism in the heart and that would have finished him.'

There was no pity in his voice. He was just stating the facts.

I picked up my coffee meaning to take a sip but it

was the same colour as the blood in the picture and I put it down again. 'He was a rich man living in an expensive house. Anyone could have broken in,' I said. 'I don't see what makes this so special.'

'Well, quite a few things, actually,' Hawthorne replied cheerfully. 'Pryce had been working on a big case . . . a £10 million settlement. Not that the lady in question got very much of it. Akira Anno. Ring any bells?'

For reasons that will become apparent further down the line, I've had to change her name, but I knew her well enough. She was a writer of literary fiction and poetry, a regular speaker at all the main festivals. She had been twice shortlisted for the Man Booker Prize and had actually won the Costa Book Award, the T. S. Eliot Prize, the Women's Prize for Fiction and, most recently, a PEN/Nabokov Award for achievement in international literature, which cited 'her unique voice and the delicacy of her prose'. She wrote – mainly on feminist issues and sexual politics – for the *Sunday Times* and other broadsheets. She was often on the radio. I had heard her on *Moral Maze* and *Loose Ends*.

'She poured a glass of wine over Pryce's head,' I said. That story had been all over social media and I remembered it well.

'She did more than that, mate. She threatened to hit

him with the bottle. It was in the middle of a crowded restaurant. Lots of people heard her.'

'Then she killed him!'

Hawthorne shrugged and I knew what he meant. In real life, it would have been obvious. But in the world that Hawthorne inhabited – and which he wanted me to share – an admission of guilt might well mean the exact opposite.

'Does she have an alibi?' I asked.

'She's not at home at the moment. No one's quite sure where she is.' Hawthorne took out a cigarette and rolled it between his fingers before lighting it. I slid my polystyrene cup towards him. It was still half full of coffee and he could use it as an ashtray.

'So you've got a suspect,' I said. 'What else is there?'

'I'm trying to tell you! His house was being redecorated and there were a whole lot of paint pots in the hall. Of course, he didn't go in for ordinary stuff like Dulux or anything like that. He had to have those poncey colours from Farrow & Ball. Eighty quid a tin with names like Vert De Terre, Ivy and Arsenic.' He spat out the names with evident distaste.

'You made up the Arsenic,' I said.

'No. I made up the Ivy. The other two are on their list. The paint he had chosen was actually called Green Smoke. And here's the thing, Tony. After the killer had bludgeoned Mr Pryce and left him bleeding on his posh American oak floor, he picked up a brush and painted a message on the wall: a three-digit number.'

'What three digits?'

He slid another photograph forward and I saw it for myself.

'One eight two,' Hawthorne said.

'I don't suppose you have any idea what that means?' I asked.

'It could mean lots of things. There's a 182 bus that runs in north London, although I don't suppose Mr Pryce was the sort who had much time for public transport. It's the name of a restaurant in Wembley. It's an abbreviation used in texting. It's a type of four-seater aircraft—'

'All right,' I stopped him. 'Are you sure it was left by the killer?'

'Well, it might have been the decorators but I doubt it.'

'What else?'

Hawthorne stopped with the cigarette halfway to his mouth. His dark eyes challenged me. 'Isn't that enough?'

'I don't know,' I said.

That was true. I was already looking at the murder of Richard Pryce from a writer's perspective and the awful truth was that, at this stage anyway, I wasn't sure I cared who had killed him. Akira Anno was obviously the prime suspect – and that was interesting because although I hadn't ever managed to read any of her books, I was aware of her name. What mattered more, though, was this. If I was going to write a second book about Hawthorne, it would need to run to at least eighty thousand words and I was already wondering if there would be enough material. Akira had threatened him with a bottle. He had been killed with a bottle. She did it. End of story.

It also troubled me that it was a divorce lawyer who had been killed. I've got nothing against lawyers but at the same time I've always done my best to avoid them. I don't understand the law. I've never been able to work out how a simple matter – a trademark registration, for example – can end up eating months out of my life and thousands of pounds. Even making my will was a traumatic experience and there was considerably less to leave to my children once the lawyers had finished with me. I had enjoyed writing about Diana Cowper, the blameless mother of a famous actor, but what sort of inspiration would I get from Richard Pryce, a man who made his living out of other people's misery?

'There is one other thing,' Hawthorne muttered. He had been watching me closely as if he could see into my thoughts – which, as he had already demonstrated, he actually could.

'What's that?'

'The bottle of wine. It was a 1982 Château Lafite Rothschild, Pauillac.' Hawthorne spoke the foreign words as if each one was an insult. 'Do you know anything about wine?'

'No.'

'Me neither. But I'm told this one would have cost at least two thousand quid.'

'So Richard Pryce had expensive tastes.'

Hawthorne shook his head. 'No. He was a teetotaller. He never drank alcohol at all.'

I thought for a moment. A very public threat from a well-known feminist writer. A mysterious message in green paint. An incredibly expensive bottle of wine. I could just about see all that on the inside flap. And yet . . .

'I don't know,' I said. 'I am quite busy at the moment.'

His face fell. 'What's the matter with you, mate? I thought you'd be jumping at this one.'

'Can you give me time to think about it?'

'I'm heading over there now.'

I let that hang in the air for a moment.

'I was just wondering,' I muttered, almost to myself. 'All that stuff you just said. About Michael Kitchen – and my phone. How did you know?'

He saw which way I was going. 'That was nothing.'

'I'm just interested.' I paused. 'If there's going to be another book . . .'

'All right, mate. But it couldn't be simpler.' I wasn't moving and he knew it. 'You got dressed in a hurry. The second button of your shirt is tucked into the third buttonhole, which is sort of classic, really. When you shaved this morning, you left a bit of hair under your nose. I can see it right there, next to your nostril, and it doesn't look very nice, to be honest with you. You've also got a smudge of toothpaste on your sleeve, meaning you got dressed *before* you went into the bathroom. So you woke up, jumped out of bed and got dressed straight away, which sounds to me like your alarm didn't go off.'

'I don't have an alarm.'

'But you've got an iPhone and you might have set it if you had an important meeting – like a set visit – but for some reason you didn't use it.'

'It doesn't mean the phone is lost.'

'Well, I rang you twice to tell you I was coming today but there was no answer. Also, if you had your phone, your driver would have been able to ring you to say he was on his way or he was waiting outside and you wouldn't have been in such a panic. Nobody else answered it, by the way, although it didn't go straight to voice message so that means it's still turned on. The chances are it's on silent and you'll find it somewhere at home.'

Hawthorne hadn't been on the set when I arrived. He couldn't possibly have known how I'd got there. 'What makes you think I had a driver?' I demanded. 'I could have just taken the Tube.'

'You're a big-shot writer on *Foyle's War.* Of course they'd send someone. Anyway, it was pissing down this morning until just an hour ago, but you're bone dry. Look at your shoes! You haven't walked anywhere today.'

'And what about Michael Kitchen? Have you been talking to him?'

'I didn't need to.' He tapped his fingers on the script, which he had closed when I came in. 'The pink pages are the latest revisions, aren't they? I just had a quick glance through and every single one of them relates to scenes that he happens to appear in. It looks like he's the only one who's not happy with your work.'

'He's perfectly happy,' I growled. 'I'm just fine-tuning.'

Hawthorne glanced in the direction of my waste-paper basket, which was piled high with balls of crumpled paper. 'That's quite a bit of fine-tuning,' he remarked.

There was no reason to hang around the set. And after what had happened, I didn't want anyone seeing Hawthorne and me together.

'All right,' I said. 'Let's go.'

3
Heron's Wake

Richard Pryce's home was in Fitzroy Park, one of the most exclusive streets in the whole of London, nestling on the edge of Hampstead Heath. Actually, it hardly looks like a street at all. When you enter it from the Heath, particularly during the summer months, you pass through an old-fashioned gate that could have come straight out of Arthur Rackham, with so much vegetation on all sides that it's hard to believe you're anywhere near the city. Trees, bushes, roses, clematis, wisteria, honeysuckle and every other climbing plant fight for space in the north London equivalent of Never Land, and the very light is tinted green. The houses are all detached and make a point of bearing no resemblance to each other at all. They range in style from mock Elizabethan to art deco to pure Cluedo – all chimneys and sloping eaves and gables – with Colonel Mustard mowing the lawn and Mrs Peacock taking tea with Reverend Green.

As if to contradict all this, Pryce's house was aggressively modern, designed perhaps by someone who had spent too much time at the National Theatre. It had the same brutalist architecture, with stretches of prefabricated concrete and triple-height windows more suited to an institution than to somebody's home. Even the Japanese-style bulrushes in the front garden had been planted at exact intervals and grown to the same height. There was a wood-fronted balcony on the first floor but the wood was Scandinavian pine or birch, unrelated to any tree growing in the immediate area.

The house wasn't huge – I guessed it would have three or four bedrooms – but the way it was constructed, all cubes, rectangles and cantilevered roofs, made it seem bigger than it was. I wouldn't have wanted to live there. I've got nothing against modern architecture in places like Los Angeles or Miami but in a London suburb, next to a bowling club? I felt it was trying too hard.

Hawthorne and I had taken a taxi from Bermondsey, climbing up Hampstead Lane towards Highgate before suddenly turning off and heading steeply down and away from reality into this fantastical *rus in urbe*. The hill brought us to a crossroads with a sign pointing to the North London Bowling Club straight ahead. We turned right. Pryce's house was called Heron's Wake and it was easy enough to spot. It was the one with the police cars in front of it, the plastic tape across the front door, the forensic officers dressed in white moving in what looked like slow motion around the garden, the uniformed policemen and the gaggle of journalists. Fitzroy Park had no pavements and no street lights. Several of the houses had burglar alarms but there were surprisingly few CCTV cameras. All in all, you could hardly have chosen a better location to commit murder.

We got out and Hawthorne instructed the driver to wait for us. We must have made an odd couple. He was looking smart and professional in his suit and tie while it was only now that I realised I had come straight from the set and that I was wearing jeans and a padded jacket with FOYLE'S WAR embroidered on the back. A couple of the journalists glanced my way and I was afraid I would end up on the front page of the local newspaper so I went in sideways, keeping the back of my jacket away from them, wishing I'd had time to change.

Meanwhile, Hawthorne had forgotten me, marching up the driveway as if he were a long-lost son returning to the family home. Murder always had this effect on him, drawing him in to the exclusion of everything else. I don't think I'd ever met anyone quite so focused.

He stopped briefly to examine two cars, parked side by side. One was a black S-class Mercedes coupé; a solid, executive car. The other, sitting there like a younger, snappier brother, was a classic MG Roadster, dating back to the seventies. It was a collector's car: pillar-box red with a black hood and gleaming wire wheels. I saw him place a hand on the bonnet and hurried over to join him.

'It hasn't been here long,' he said.

'The engine's still warm . . .'

He nodded. 'Got it in one, Tony.'

He glanced at the passenger window, which was open a couple of inches, sniffed the air, then continued towards the front door of the house and the constable who was guarding it. I thought he would go straight in but now his attention was drawn to the perfectly rectangular flower beds beside the entrance. There were two of them, one on each side, with bulrushes standing dead straight, like soldiers on parade. Hawthorne crouched down and I noticed that, to the right of the door, a few of the plants had been broken, as if someone had stumbled and stepped on them. The killer? Before I could ask him, he straightened up again, gave his name to the constable and disappeared into the building.

I smiled vaguely, nervous that I would be stopped,

but the policeman seemed to be expecting me too. I went in.

Heron's Wake wasn't built like an ordinary house. The main rooms weren't divided by walls and doors. Instead, one area seemed to morph into another with a wide entrance hall opening into a state-of-the-art kitchen on one side and a spacious living room on the other. The back wall was made almost entirely of glass, giving lovely views of the garden. There were no carpets; just expensive rugs of various sizes artfully strewn over American oak floors. The furniture was modern, designer-made, the art on the walls mainly abstract. It was obvious that a great deal of care had been lavished on the interior, even if the overall impression was one of simplicity. All the door handles and light switches, for example, were brushed steel, not plastic, and whispered of Paris or Milan. I could imagine them being carefully chosen from catalogues. Most of the house was white but Pryce had recently decided to add a few splashes of colour. There were paint pots and brushes arranged on dust sheets in the hall. An open doorway led into a cloakroom that had become an eye-catching canary yellow. The windows in the kitchen were now framed in terracotta red. I had assumed that the lawyer was married, but the house had the feel of a very expensive bachelor pad.

I caught up with Hawthorne just as a large, unattractive woman appeared, elbowing her way out of the
kitchen, dressed in a bright mauve trouser suit with a
black polo-neck sweater. What made her unattractive?
It wasn't her clothes or her size, although she was over-
weight with round shoulders and a face that was thick
and fleshy. No. It was mainly her attitude. She hadn't
spoken a word to us but she was already scowling. Either her spectacles were too big or her eyes were too
small, but she had managed to make herself look mean
and hostile, peering at the world with a malevolence
that she wore like mascara. What struck me most about
her, though, was her hair. I'm sure it was real but it resembled one of those cheap wigs worn by department-
store mannequins, jet black and as glossy as nylon. It
didn't seem to belong to her head. She had a gold necklace around her neck and below that a lanyard resting
horizontally on an ample chest identified her as DI
Cara Grunshaw of the Metropolitan Police. She moved
quickly, aggressively, like a wrestler entering an arena.
If I were a criminal, I'd be afraid of her. I hadn't done
anything wrong but she still made me nervous.

'Hello, Hawthorne,' she said. To my surprise and
despite her appearance, she was quite jocular. 'They
told me you were on your way.'

'Hello, Cara.'

They knew each other. They seemed to like each other. Hawthorne turned to me. 'This is Detective Inspector Cara Grunshaw,' he said, unnecessarily. He didn't tell her who I was. Nor did she seem particularly interested.

'They sent over the details?' She had come straight to the point, without any small talk. Her voice was heavy and emotionless, with no particular accent. 'Initial report? Photographs?'

'Yes.'

'They didn't waste any time! He was only found this morning.'

'Who found him?'

'The cleaner. Bulgarian. Mariella Petrov. You can talk to her if you want to but you'll be wasting your time. She doesn't know anything. She'd only worked for Pryce for six weeks . . . came through a good agency in Knightsbridge. Lives in Bethnal Green with a husband and two kids. Her first job was to come down from Highgate, bringing in fresh bread and milk for his breakfast. She went into the kitchen and got everything ready. Then she walked into the study and that was where she found him. We've moved the body but you can take a look if you like.'

'Sure.'

'Here . . .' She had produced plastic shoe covers

and handed them to us casually, like serviettes before a meal.

I was a little disappointed. In the back of my mind, I had been hoping that the investigating officer would be DI Meadows. He was the detective I'd met when Diana Cowper was murdered and later on the two of us had even had a drink at my club. I had been interested in his relationship with Hawthorne. The two of them had worked together and there was clearly no love lost between them. I wanted to know more about Hawthorne and although Meadows had been both reticent and expensive (he had charged me for his time), I was sure he had more information he could have given me.

More than that, he would have been a useful character if I really was going to continue writing about Hawthorne. Holmes has Lestrade. Poirot has Japp. Morse often tussled with Chief Superintendent Strange. It's a simple fact of life that a clever private detective needs a much less clever police officer in much the same way as a photograph needs both light and darkness. Otherwise, there's no definition. I'm not saying that Meadows was unintelligent, by the way, but he did think Mrs Cowper had been killed by a burglar and in that he was most certainly wrong.

Given a choice, I would have been happy to bump into

Meadows at every crime scene I visited, but of course there are more than thirty thousand police officers in London and the chances of his turning up in both Chelsea (the scene of the first murder) and Hampstead were non-existent. As I followed Grunshaw through the living room, I had already decided that she was going to be less useful to me. She was completely businesslike and seemed to know what she was doing. She had shown no interest in me at all.

We went through the living area and down two steps to the study, which, with its wooden floor and minimal decoration, actually had the appearance of a conference room. There was no desk. Instead, four white leather and steel chairs had been arranged around a glass table framed by bookshelves on one side and windows on the other. Another glass panel ran the full length of the ceiling, allowing the light to flood in. There were two cans of Coke on the table, one of them open.

The body had already been removed but there could be no doubt that this was where Richard Pryce had died. A sticky, dark red pool stretched out across the floor; a mixture of red wine and blood. Rather horribly, I could make out the lawyer's head, his shoulders and one outstretched arm in the shape left behind when the body had been removed. The broken bottle, parts of it still held together by the label, lay in the middle of the mess.

My eyes were drawn to the wall between two of the bookshelves. There was the three-digit number that Hawthorne had shown me, daubed hastily in green paint: 182. The paint had trickled down, as if in a poster for a horror film. The digits were crude and un-even, the eight quite a bit larger than the one and the two. The brush that had been used to write them had been left on the floor, leaving a green smudge on the wood.

'He was killed between eight o'clock and eight thirty. He was alone in the house but we know he had a visitor just after five to eight. A neighbour, Henry Fairchild, was walking his dog and saw someone coming off the Heath. I'm sure you'll want to talk to him. He lives at the other end of the street. It's a pink building . . . Rose Cottage. The houses round here don't have numbers. They're too fucking posh for that.' She smiled very briefly. 'It's all just fancy names . . . like Heron's Wake. What does that even mean? Anyway, Mr Fairchild is retired. He's a charming man. I'm sure you'll enjoy talking to him.'

'Was Pryce alone in the house?'

'He was last night. He was married but his husband

was away. They have a second home in Clacton-on-Sea. He got back about an hour ago and found us all here, which must have been a bit of a shock for him. He's upstairs now.' That explained the red MG with an engine that hadn't had time to cool down. 'He's not in a good way,' she went on. 'I only spoke to him for a few minutes and he didn't make much sense. He was crying his eyes out so I got someone to make him a cup of tea.' She paused and sniffed. 'He asked for camomile.'

I was listening to this with a sense of dread. I remembered well that one of Hawthorne's less endearing traits was an unapologetic homophobia, which he had expressed after we had visited a suspect together during our first case. And from the way she had pronounced that last word, Cara Grunshaw might have had similar feelings. But then again, maybe it was just Hampstead folk that she didn't like.

'The husband's name is Stephen Spencer,' she went on. 'I can't tell you very much more about him yet. I haven't had a chance to talk properly to him. But it's fairly certain that he was the last person to speak to Pryce before he died.'

'He phoned?'

'At eight o'clock last night.' She watched as Hawthorne digested this. 'Yes. The killer must have been just outside the house, maybe approaching it, when the call took place. The neighbour, Mr Fairchild, saw someone going in at more or less exactly that time, although he can't provide any description. It was too dark. He was too far away. Pryce ended the call and let them in – it looks like it was someone he knew. He offered him a drink.'

I glanced at the two cans of Coke on the glass table.

'They didn't drink any of the wine, then,' Hawthorne said.

'The bottle hadn't been opened. You saw the report? It came with a price tag of two thousand quid!' Grunshaw shook her head. 'That's what's wrong with this country. You've got food banks in the north and down here in Hampstead there are people who don't think twice about spending a fortune on a fucking bottle of wine. It doesn't make sense.'

'Richard Pryce didn't drink.'

'According to Spencer, it was a present from one of his clients. I managed to get that much out of him. The client was called Adrian Lockwood.'

'Akira Anno's husband,' I said. I remembered the name from the report I'd heard on the radio.

'Her ex-husband. Pryce represented him in the divorce and apparently she wasn't too happy about the outcome.'

She had threatened to hit him with a bottle of wine. It seemed an extraordinary coincidence. And yet, if she had made such a declaration in public, in a busy restaurant, surely it would have been completely mad to follow through, using exactly that method to kill him.

Meanwhile, Hawthorne had turned his attention to the green figures painted on the wall. 'What do you make of that?' he asked.

'A hundred and eighty-two? I haven't got the faintest idea.' DI Grunshaw sniffed. 'You should be happy about that, Hawthorne. That was why you were called in. We've obviously got some tricky bastard who thinks he's having a laugh.' She folded her massive arms across her chest. 'There are two possibilities, the way I see it. One is that Pryce painted it himself, trying to leave some sort of message. But it would have had to be before his head was smashed in. Or more likely, the killer did it after the event. But to be honest, that doesn't make any sense. What sort of killer leaves an obvious clue? He might as well have signed his initials.' She paused. 'I did wonder if it might relate to the wine.'

'A 1982 Château Lafite,' I said.

'It's the same figures, minus the nine.' Grunshaw glanced at me as if noticing me for the first time. Her small eyes rested on me for a moment, making me feel distinctly uneasy. Then they flickered away. 'I'll leave you to work that one out, Hawthorne,' she continued. 'Personally, I don't like murder when it comes with all these fancy bells and whistles attached. I leave that sort of thing to Mr Foyle's War here.'

She had noticed the back of my jacket even though I had done my best to keep it concealed from her. I wondered if Hawthorne had told her who I was.

'Fingerprints?' Hawthorne asked.

She shook her head. 'Sod all. Everything has been wiped down, including the unopened Coke can. Pryce was the only one who had any. We've got his DNA on the can and there were traces of the liquid on his lips.'

'So what are your thoughts?'

'You really think I'm going to share them with you?' Detective Inspector Cara Grunshaw looked Hawthorne straight in the eyes but there was no real malice in her voice. 'I'll leave you to earn your daily rate,' she went on. 'If they feel they need you, which, incidentally, I don't, they might as well get their money's worth.'

She stood there, her fingers drumming against the side of her arm. Then she seemed to relent.

'It looks to me as if Miss Anno is going to be our first port of call. We haven't been able to locate her yet – her mobile is switched off – but I'll let you know when I've tracked her down. I'm going up to talk to Pryce's husband and you can join me. After that you should have a word with the neighbour. If you need me, you've got my mobile, but here's the deal, Hawthorne.' She jabbed a stubby finger in his direction. 'I want to know what you know. All right? You keep me informed if there are any developments and I want to be the one who makes the arrest. If I find you've been undermining me, I'll rip your testicles off and use them as conkers. Is that clear?'

'You don't need to worry about me, Cara,' Hawthorne said, with an innocent, almost beatific smile. 'I'm only here to help.'

I didn't believe him. Hawthorne was a lone wolf if ever there was one. I was sure that DI Grunshaw would only know there had been an arrest when she read about it in the newspapers.

'Let's do it, then.'

Grunshaw marched off. I was happy to follow her. I had become aware of the sickening smell in the room, the mixture of blood and wine. I was beginning to feel queasy and knew I would be in all sorts of trouble if I actually managed to throw up at the scene of the crime. I couldn't wait to get out. But Hawthorne was still lingering.

'I'd watch out for her if I were you,' he muttered.

'DI Grunshaw?'

'Do me a favour and don't say anything in front of her. Take my word for it. She's not a nice human being.'

'She seemed all right to me.'

'That's because you don't know her.'

We went upstairs.

4
Last Words

The stairs leading up the first floor were white slabs, jutting out of the wall with no visible means of support. A steel bannister swept alongside, something to hold on to as you went. Cara Grunshaw stumped up to the top with Hawthorne padding more quietly behind, and we finally arrived at a galleried area with a view down to the living room and, on this floor, a series of doors leading off to the left and right.

There was another detective waiting for us, leaning against the colonnade that prevented visitors from plunging into the living room. He was thinner and smaller than Grunshaw, with tufts of sand-coloured hair and a moustache. He was wearing a brown leather jacket that might have been inspired by an old television series; Hutch to her Starsky, or perhaps the other way round.

'He's in there, ma'am.'

'Thank you, Darren.'

Grunshaw went first, ignoring the paintings on the wall, which were very different from the ones downstairs. I studied art history at university and recognised a watercolour by Eric Ravilious and a series of wood engravings by Eric Gill. A collection of Erics. The top floor of the house was altogether more formal. The floor was carpeted, the layout more enclosed. Grunshaw knocked at the door Darren had indicated and without waiting for an answer went into a room that turned out to be a library, filled with floor-to-ceiling shelves separated only by two windows looking out over the front drive, and a widescreen TV mounted on the wall. There were two white leather sofas, several glass tables and a fake – or perhaps I should say *faux* – zebra-skin rug on the floor.

Stephen Spencer was hunched up at the end of one of the sofas, surrounded by framed photographs of Richard Pryce, himself and the two of them together. He was wearing a crumpled linen shirt, pale blue corduroys and loafers. He must have been in his early thirties, about ten years younger than his husband, and would have been good-looking if his eyes weren't swollen with tears, his cheeks red and his fair hair flattened down and damp. He was very slim with a swan-like neck that emphasised his Adam's apple. He was holding a handkerchief in one hand and I noticed he wore a gold band on his wedding finger, identical to the one I had seen in the picture of Richard Pryce that Hawthorne had shown me.

The room had become quite crowded with the five of us in it. DI Grunshaw plumped herself down on the other sofa, her legs apart. Hawthorne went over to the window. I stood next to the door with my shoulders against the wall, deliberately hiding the embroidery on the back of my jacket. Darren had followed us in. He was standing in a very casual sort of pose, ostentatiously holding a notebook and pen.

'How are you feeling, Mr Spencer?' Grunshaw asked. She was trying to be sympathetic but her words were forced and condescending, as if she were talking to a child who had just fallen over and scratched his knee in the playground.

'I still can't believe it,' Spencer said, his voice thick with grief. He clutched the handkerchief tighter than ever. 'I saw him on Friday. I said goodbye to him. I never dreamed—' He broke off.

Darren scribbled all that down.

'You have to understand that we have to talk to you

now,' Grunshaw went on, none too delicately. 'The sooner we can get the answers to our questions, the sooner we can begin our investigations.'

He nodded but said nothing.

'You said you'd just come back from Suffolk . . .'

'From Essex. Clacton-on-Sea. We have a second home.' He gestured at a photograph. It showed a white, pocket-sized building, 1930s in style with curving balconies and a flat roof. It didn't look real.

'Why were you on your own?'

Spencer swallowed. 'Richard didn't want to come. He said he had too much work. Also, he had someone coming to the house on Saturday afternoon. I was visiting my mother. She's in a nursing home in Frinton.'

'I'm sure she was pleased to see you.'

'She has Alzheimer's. She probably doesn't even remember I was there.'

'When did you leave?'

'After breakfast. I cleaned the house and locked up. I suppose it must have been about eleven o'clock this morning.'

'You didn't call Mr Pryce before you left?'

Darren had been scribbling the details down in his notebook but now he paused with the pen over the page. Meanwhile, I'd taken out my iPhone – Hawthorne had been right about that, by the way: I'd picked it up from my flat on the way over – and quietly turned it on. I wondered if it might be illegal to record a police interview. I supposed I'd find out in time.

'I did try. Yes. But I got no answer.' Spencer brought the handkerchief up again, screwing it into the corner of his eye. 'He should have been with me. We've been together for nine years. We do everything together. We bought the house together. I can't believe that anyone would do this to him. I mean, Richard was one of the kindest men in the world.'

'Do you always take Monday morning off?' Grunshaw's voice was unemotional now. Everything about her – the way she sat, her heavy plastic spectacles, her black, pudding-basin hairstyle – could have been designed to remove any sense of empathy.

Spencer nodded. 'We never take the A12 on a Sunday evening. There's too much traffic. If Richard had been with me, we'd have left at the crack of dawn. He was always focused on his work. But I'm my own boss. I have an art gallery in Bury Street, just round the corner from Christie's. We specialise in early twentieth-century art.' That explained the Gills and the Ravilious. 'We're open Tuesday to Saturday so on Monday I work from home.'

'You spoke to Mr Pryce last night.' Grunshaw picked up the thread again.

'Yes. I rang him at about eight o'clock.'

'How can you be so sure of the time?'

'It was the twenty-seventh yesterday and the clocks had gone back. I'd just finished going round the house and I rang on my mobile.' He took it out and thumbed a few buttons, checking his call register. 'Here you are!' he exclaimed. 'Eight o'clock exactly.'

'Get a decent signal in Clacton?' That was Hawthorne, speaking for the first time, on the edge of hostile. But there was nothing new about that.

Stephen Spencer ignored him.

'Can you tell us what your husband said during your conversation?' Grunshaw asked.

'He asked me what I'd been doing. We talked about the weather and about Mum . . . the usual sort of thing. He sounded a bit down. He said he was still worried about the case he'd been working on.'

'What case was that?'

'It was a divorce case. I'm sure you've heard that Richard was a divorce lawyer, a very successful one. He had just represented a property developer called Adrian Lockwood. His wife was that writer . . . you know . . . Akira . . .' Her second name had slipped from his mind.

'Akira Anno,' I said.

'That's right.' His eyes widened as he suddenly remembered. 'You know that she threatened him. She came up to him in a restaurant and she threw wine at him. I was there!'

'What exactly happened?'

'I should have told you immediately. I don't know why I didn't. But coming home this morning and finding the police here and Richard . . .'

He paused, collecting himself, then continued.

'We were having dinner together at The Delaunay in Aldwych. This would have been last Monday, a week ago. It was Richard's favourite restaurant and we often met there after work . . . it was sort of convenient for both of us and then we'd get a taxi home. Anyway, we'd just finished eating when I saw this woman coming over, passing between the tables. She was short, Japanese-looking, and I didn't recognise her. There was another woman with her, just behind.

'Anyway, she stopped at our table and Richard looked up. Of course, he knew who she was at once but he didn't seem particularly disturbed. He muttered something polite, "Can I help you?" or something, and she looked down at him with this weird little smile on her face. She was wearing tinted glasses. "You're a pig!" Those were her opening words. She said something about the divorce, how unfair it had been. And then she reached down and picked up my wine glass.

I'd been drinking red wine and we'd finished the meal but there were still a couple of inches left. For a crazy moment, I thought she was going to drink it but instead she threw it all over his head. Richard had wine on his face and on his shirt. It was outrageous. I thought we should call the police but he didn't want to make a scene. He just wanted to leave.'

'What else did she say?'

'Well, that's the thing. Immediately after she'd thrown the wine she put the glass down and said something about how really she wished she could hit him with a bottle.' Spencer stopped as the significance of what he had just described caught up with him. 'Oh my God! That was how he was killed, wasn't it!' His hands flew out, one on each side of his head. 'She told him she was going to do it!'

'We're not jumping to any conclusions, Mr Spencer,' Grunshaw said.

'What do you mean, you're not jumping to conclusions? She confessed. She admitted it. There were a dozen witnesses.'

'Did he mention her name when the two of you were on the phone on Sunday night?'

Spencer thought back. 'No. He didn't say her name. But he did refer to her. I knew the case had been on his mind . . . he'd talked about it a bit when we were at The

Delaunay, although he was very discreet; he never gave me any details. Anyway, one thing he did say when we were on the phone was that he'd spoken to Oliver. That's Oliver Masefield. They were both senior partners at the firm . . . Masefield Pryce Turnbull. I was going to ask him about that when the doorbell went.'

'The doorbell here?' Grunshaw asked.

'Yes. I heard it at the end of the line. Richard stopped in the middle of a sentence. "Who can that be?" he said. He wasn't expecting anyone. He told me to hang on a minute and he put his phone down.'

'He was also on his mobile?'

'Yes. He must have put it on the table in the hall. There was a long pause and then I heard his footsteps on the wooden flooring and I think I may have heard the door open. Then I heard him speak. "What are you doing here?" That's what he said. He sounded surprised. "It's a bit late."'

Darren had been writing all this down too. He paused. 'His exact words?' he asked.

This time Spencer didn't hesitate. 'I'm certain of it. "It's a bit late." That's what he said.'

'And then?'

'He came back to the phone. He said he'd call me back later and he hung up.'

'He didn't tell you anything else about his visitor?'

Darren had a way of ensuring his questions sounded aggressive and intimidating. He could have made you feel nervous just wishing you a good morning. 'You didn't hear them say anything else?'

'He didn't say anything more. I told you. He just hung up.' The tears welled up again. 'I waited for him to call me again but when I didn't hear from him I thought he must have been busy or something. He was often like that. He would get absorbed in what he was doing. I drove back this morning and when I got to the house I saw all the police cars and I still had no idea . . .'

Hawthorne had been listening to all this with his shoulders half turned towards the window. Now he looked back. 'Nice car,' he said. 'Does it have electric windows?'

'What?' Spencer was so thrown by the question that he briefly forgot his tears. I was less surprised. From my experience of Hawthorne, I knew he had a way of firing off seemingly irrelevant observations. He wasn't being deliberately offensive. It was just that offensive was his default mode.

'It's a classic model,' Hawthorne went on. 'What's the date?'

'Nineteen sixty-eight.'

Spencer was tight-lipped now, looking to DI Grunshaw to take back control. She obliged. 'You know that your husband was attacked with a bottle of wine. It was a Château Lafite Rothschild. Was that the same bottle of wine given to him by Adrian Lockwood?'

'I can't be certain – but yes, I think so. Richard had said it was very expensive. It was also a waste of money because he didn't drink.'

'He was a teetotaller.'

'Yes.'

'So there's no alcohol in the house,' Hawthorne said.

'Actually, there's quite a lot of stuff in the kitchen – whisky, gin, beer and so on. I'll have a drink now and then. But Richard didn't like alcohol. That's all.'

Cara Grunshaw smiled at Hawthorne. It didn't make her look any more attractive. I was becoming aware of an edge of malice behind her good humour. 'Do you have any other questions?' she asked.

'Just one.' Hawthorne turned to Spencer. 'You mentioned that Richard was expecting a visitor on Saturday afternoon. Did he say who it was?'

Spencer considered. 'No. He just said there was someone coming. He didn't say who.'

'I think you've probably got enough,' Grunshaw cut in, daring Hawthorne to disagree. 'Why don't you run along now while I take a full statement from Mr Spencer?'

'Whatever you say, Cara.'

I still half admired the way she'd handled herself. She was the complete opposite of Meadows. She wasn't going to allow Hawthorne to get under her skin and she had made it clear that she was the one in charge. The two of us left, taking the stairs back down and passing through the front door. The moment we were outside, Hawthorne lit a cigarette. While he was doing that, I examined the broken bulrushes a second time, looking for a footprint. Sure enough, there was a small, quite deep indentation in the soil. It might have been made by the tip of someone's shoe or, more probably (I thought), a woman's stiletto heel.

'What a tosser,' Hawthorne muttered.

'Grunshaw?'

'Stephen Spencer.' Hawthorne blew out smoke. 'Christ! I couldn't have stood in that room a minute longer. If his wrists had been any limper, his hands would have fallen off.'

'You can hold it right there,' I said. 'I've already told you. You can't talk about people's sexuality like that. I'm not having it and I'm not putting it in the book.'

'You can put what you bloody like in the book, mate. But I wasn't talking about his sexuality. I was talking about his acting technique. Did you believe any of it? The tears? The hanky? He was lying through his teeth.'

I thought back to what I had just seen. It didn't seem possible. 'I thought he was genuinely upset,' I said.

'Maybe he was. But he was still hiding something.' The MG was right in front of us. Hawthorne pointed with the hand holding the cigarette. 'There's no way that's just driven down from Essex or Suffolk or anywhere near the coast.'

'How do you know?'

'That house he showed us in that photograph didn't have a garage and there's no way this car has been sitting by the seaside for three days. There's no seagull shit. And there's no dead insects on the windscreen either. You're telling me he's driven a hundred miles down the A12 and he hasn't hit a single midge or fly? I reckon he was somewhere much nearer and he wasn't alone.'

'How do you know?'

'I don't know. I'm guessing. The passenger window is open a few inches and the windows aren't electrically operated. I'd say there's an even chance it was actually opened by the passenger. If he'd been driving alone, he'd have had to lean all the way across and why would he do that?'

'Is there anything else?' I asked.

'Yes. There is one thing. Richard Pryce's last words. "It's a bit late." Don't they strike you as a bit odd?'

'Why?'

'It was eight o'clock on a Sunday evening. He'd had an unexpected visitor but it was someone he knew. He invited them in and he gave them a drink. Now, it may have been dark – winter time had just started – but it certainly wasn't late.'

'Do you think Stephen Spencer was making it up?'

'I doubt it. He's probably telling the truth about what he heard. But it's still a strange thing to say and maybe Pryce wasn't actually referring to the time. Maybe he meant something else.'

We had been walking down Fitzroy Park while we were having this conversation, leaving the police cars and all the forensic activity behind us. The taxi that had brought us here was still waiting, the meter running. The driver was reading a newspaper. We passed the turn-off we'd come down when we arrived. The far side of Hampstead Heath with the women's pond and the other lakes was visible ahead of us. A few steps later, we reached Rose Cottage, which was indeed pink and pretty, set back in its own little world and half smothered in shrubs and flowers, although all the roses had been cut back for the coming winter. Hawthorne walked up and rang the front doorbell, which immediately set off a dog barking somewhere inside.

After a long wait, the door was opened by a man in

his eighties, wrapped in the sort of cardigan that might have been knitted with rolling pins. Even as he stood there, he seemed to be shrivelling inside it. He gazed at us with watery eyes. He had straggly hair and liver spots. There was no sign of the dog, which was locked up somewhere, still barking on the other side of a door.

'Mr Fairchild?' Hawthorne asked.

'Yes. Is this about the murder?' He had a high-pitched voice that not only questioned everything but seemed to be suspicious of it too. 'I've already told the police everything I know.'

'We're helping the police and I'd be very grateful if you could spare us a couple of minutes of your time.'

'I'll talk to you but I won't invite you in, if you don't mind. Rufus doesn't like strangers.'

Rufus, I assumed, was the dog.

'Apparently you saw someone heading towards Heron's Wake last night.'

'Heron's Wake?'

'Richard Pryce's house.'

'Yes. I know where he lives.' The old man cleared his throat. 'He came off the Heath just as I got home. I always take Rufus out after supper and before I go to bed. We don't walk very far. Just down to the bowling club and back. It gives him a chance to do his business . . . you know.'

'So what did you see?'

'I didn't see very much at all. It was dark. There was someone coming out of the Heath, holding a torch.'

'A torch?' Hawthorne was surprised.

'Can't you hear me? I just said. He was holding a torch. That was the main reason why I couldn't see him. The light got in my eyes. He was quite a distance away.' He pointed in the direction of the gate, on the other side of Heron's Wake. 'I did think it a bit odd, someone walking on their own at that time of night. No animal or anything like that. At least, I didn't see one.'

'Are you sure it was a man?'

'What? I don't know if it was a man or a woman. I couldn't see because of the torch.'

'You just said *he* was holding a torch!' Hawthorne was annoyed. I could tell from his eyes and from the way his lips had narrowed until they were almost a straight line. To be fair, there was something extremely irritating about Henry Fairchild. When DI Grunshaw had described him as 'charming' she was most definitely being sarcastic.

'I don't know if it was a man or a woman and there's no point asking me what colour he was or anything like that. I've already told the police. I noticed him just as I was going into the house and I didn't think anything more about it until I woke up and saw that all hell had

broken loose with murder and the police and everything else.'

'You didn't hear anything?'

'I'm sorry?' Fairchild cupped a hand to his ear, in-
advertently answering Hawthorne's question.

'Never mind. Just one last thing. Are you sure about
the time?'

Fairchild looked at his watch. 'It's ten to three.'

'No.' Hawthorne raised his voice. 'I'm asking you
about the time when you went out with your dog. You
said it was about five to eight. Are you sure about that?'

'It was definitely five to eight. I always go out after
supper and I didn't want to miss the beginning of
Antiques Roadshow so I looked at my watch just as I
reached the door.'

'Thank you, Mr Fairchild.'

'I suppose they'll have to sell the house now. I must
say, I don't like all this disturbance . . . all these people
here and everything. I like peace and quiet.'

Somewhere behind him, Rufus was still barking his
head off.

'Yes. It was very inconsiderate of Mr Pryce getting
himself murdered,' Hawthorne agreed, at his most poi-
sonous.

We walked back down the path. I thought we'd get
back into the taxi but we continued, once again passing

in front of Heron's Wake. 'I'll tell you something that doesn't make any sense,' Hawthorne muttered, as we made our way. 'Let's assume that Fairchild was telling the truth, even if he is deaf and half blind too. It was a full moon last night.'

'Was it?'

'Yes.' Hawthorne looked around him. 'It probably gets quite dark down here, but not that dark. And Fairchild wasn't carrying a torch – at least, he didn't say he was. So why did this mysterious visitor need one?'

'He didn't know the houses,' I said. 'He had to read the names!'

Hawthorne considered. 'Well, that's one theory, Tony.'

We reached the gate and the entrance to Hampstead Heath. This was where the mysterious visitor had appeared. Ahead of us, the grass stretched into the distance with a few walkers braving the damp October air. I'd had a dog myself for thirteen years and had occasionally come this way. Kenwood was over to the left or you could continue straight ahead up to Hampstead Lane, the main road that connected Hampstead and Highgate. It had rained heavily in the past month and there was a large puddle blocking our way. Whoever had come through with their torch would have had to tread carefully and I was surprised that they hadn't left muddy footsteps at Pryce's house. Perhaps they had taken off their shoes?

I wasn't sure if Hawthorne had come to the same conclusion. He was deep in thought and clearly had no intention of sharing any of it with me.

'What now?' I asked.

'That's it for today. You can drop me off at Hampstead station. We can meet tomorrow at Masefield Pryce Turnbull. That seems the best place to start . . . at least until Akira Anno turns up, and my guess is that Grunshaw will want to speak to her straight off the mark.'

'Actually, I've got a meeting at the Old Vic,' I said. 'Why don't I pick you up at your place around ten o'clock? Then we can go to Masefield Pryce Turnbull together.'

Hawthorne considered it. I could see he didn't like the idea but then he relented and shrugged. 'All right. Whatever . . .'

We walked back to the taxi. I noticed that the charge had crossed the £60 barrier. As usual, I would have to pay. When it came to cabs and coffees, Hawthorne was always slow reaching for his wallet. But I didn't mind. The truth was that, to my surprise, I was already hooked. What was the significance of the numbers on the wall? Why had Stephen Spencer been lying? I genuinely wanted to know who had killed Richard Pryce and why.

So far I had missed three clues and misconstrued two more.

Things were only going to get worse.

5
Masefield Pryce Turnbull

The Old Vic has a special place in my affections. It's the most beautiful theatre in London and I've been going there since I was a teenager. Even now, I can remember queuing up to get standing tickets to see Maggie Smith in *Hedda Gabler*, Laurence Olivier in *The Party* and Diana Rigg in the world premiere of Tom Stoppard's *Jumpers*. Long before I published my first children's book, I wanted to write plays. I found the draw of the theatre quite magical and when I was asked to join its board, I accepted at once – even though I didn't know anything very much about finance, health and safety or charity law.

But I didn't have a meeting there on that Tuesday morning. I had said that to give myself an excuse to drop in on River Court, which was where Hawthorne lived and which was only ten minutes from my own flat, on the other side of Blackfriars Bridge.

I wanted to know more about Hawthorne. I wanted to know why he had destroyed his career by pushing a paedophile down a flight of stairs and how he had come to be living on his own in an empty flat, caretaking for the owners who were in Singapore. He had told me that he had a half-brother who was an estate agent but it still seemed an unusual arrangement. I also knew that he was separated from his wife and that she lived in Gants Hill with an eleven-year-old son who didn't read my books. Apparently, the two of them were still seeing each other from time to time. Hawthorne had two hobbies. He liked constructing Airfix models, mainly from the Second World War. If this wasn't unlikely enough, he was also a member of a book group.

And yet all this felt like window dressing . . . the outer costume rather than the man himself. If I was going to write three books about him (and possibly more if he came to me with further investigations), I needed to know more. I was already quite sure that something must have happened to him, that he was in some way damaged, and I wanted to discover what it was if only to justify some of the extremes of his behaviour. You cannot have a central character who is simply, by his very nature, unpleasant, and although I wouldn't have used that word to describe Hawthorne there were moments – that 'limp-wristed' remark, for example – when he came close. In a way, I was trying to help him. He had chosen me as his biographer and I saw it as my job to picture him in the most sympathetic light. The trouble was, he was almost fanatical about keeping any personal or private details away from me. By inveigling myself into his flat for a second time, I hoped I might stumble on some clue that would explain what had turned him into the man he was and why, despite everything and against my better instincts, I was beginning to like him.

River Court is a low-rise block built in the seventies, a symphony of not terribly attractive beige-coloured balconies and rectangular windows that has somehow managed to find itself in the most wonderful position, right on the edge of the Thames. I'd walked past it dozens of times on the way to the National Theatre and the South Bank without even noticing it was there. That's one of the pleasures of living in London. It's so huge, so jammed with interesting buildings, that it's always taking you by surprise. Even now I can stroll down an alleyway and realise I'm seeing it for the first time even though it's only a few minutes from where I live.

I had turned up twenty minutes early. I knew that if I rang the bell, Hawthorne wouldn't let me in; he would

call down on the intercom system and keep me waiting
in the street. But I was smarter than that. I waited until
another resident emerged. At that moment, I reached
out with a set of keys that wouldn't actually have fitted
the lock and, with a smile, stopped the door from fully
closing and went in.

I was feeling quite pleased with myself as I took the
lift up to the twelfth floor but it was only as I stood
there, on my own, that I began to feel uneasy. Hawthorne would know perfectly well what I was up to
and although he had often been sarcastic or irritable,
I had never yet been a target of his anger. That might
be about to change. Well, it was too bad. I just had to
remember that he needed me. Despite his occasional
threats, I didn't think he would find it easy to get anyone else to write about him.

The lift door opened and at once I heard voices, one
of which was Hawthorne's. He was saying goodbye to
someone who had visited him in his flat, even though it
was still early – nine forty-five in the morning. I peeked
round the corner, doing my best to stay out of sight,
and saw a young man, about eighteen or nineteen years
old. It was hard to be sure of his age, partly because he
was some distance away but also because he was in a
motorised wheelchair. If that in itself wasn't surpris-

ing enough, he was also of Indian, perhaps Bengali, descent and, I could tell at a glance, he had some form of muscular dystrophy. One of his hands was holding an electric control, the other was resting on his lap. He was not on a ventilator but there was a plastic bottle attached to his chest with a drinking pipe reaching up to his lips. He had dark hair cut short and a wispy beard and moustache that spoiled what might otherwise have been film-star good looks: chiselled cheekbones, intense eyes, Valentino lips.

'All right then, I'll see you.' That was Hawthorne speaking.

'Thank you, Mr Hawthorne.'

'Thank *you*, Kevin, mate. I couldn't do it without you.'

Couldn't do what? Was this something to do with model-making? No. That was impossible. But what could Hawthorne possibly need a young man in a wheelchair to help him with? I'd come for clues but all I'd got for my pains was another mystery.

'I'll see you, then.'

'Yeah. Give my best to your mum.'

Hawthorne didn't go back into the flat. He stood there, watching Kevin as he made his way towards the lift.

I was lucky that this part of the corridor was in shadow or he would have spotted me for sure but even so I was still there, hiding inside the lift, and I realised that I'd put myself in a difficult position. If I stepped out and revealed myself, Hawthorne would see me and know I had been spying on him. At the same time, Kevin was rolling steadily towards me and would surely wonder what I was doing, lurking there, refusing to come out. I decided to stay where I was. As he manoeuvred himself into the lift, I studied the buttons as if I had just got in ahead of him and had forgotten where I wanted to go. I pressed Ground.

'Third floor, please.' Kevin was next to me, facing out. The doors slid shut and suddenly we were alone together in the confined space, he in a sitting position and so some distance below me. There were two leather pads holding his head in place. I pressed the button for him. Painfully slowly, the lift began to descend.

'I could have done it myself,' he said. 'It's only getting up to the twelfth that I find difficult.'

'Why is that?' I asked.

'The button's too high.'

It took me a moment to work out that this was a variation on an old joke. 'Do you live here?' I asked.

'I live on the third.'

'Nice place.'

'It's got nice views,' he agreed.

'The river,' I said.

He frowned. 'What river?'

Briefly, I froze. How could he not have noticed it? Was it something to do with his disability? Then I saw him grinning at me and realised he was joking again. We lapsed into silence until, with a slight jerk, we arrived and the doors opened. Kevin pushed the lever forward and rolled out.

'Have a nice day,' I said. It's an Americanism but one I find myself using more and more these days.

'You too.'

The lift continued on its journey, taking me down to the ground floor. There were two people, perhaps a husband and wife, waiting to go up, and they too were puzzled when I refused to get out. 'Wrong floor!' I muttered, weakly. They stepped in and took the lift up to the ninth floor, which must have been where they lived. The doors closed again and finally, after what seemed like a very long time, I arrived back where I wanted to be.

I went straight to Hawthorne's flat and rang the bell. The door opened almost at once and there he was, with his raincoat over his arm, ready to go out. He didn't seem surprised to see me. I had intended to arrive early but with all the fuss going up and down in the lift, I was more or less on time.

'You should have rung the bell outside,' he said, cheerfully. 'It would have saved you coming up.' He led me back down the corridor and called the lift. 'How was the Old Vic?'

'Interesting,' I said. 'There's a board meeting next week.'

'So long as you've got time to write our book . . .'

'My first thought exactly.' Sarcasm was wasted on Hawthorne. For someone who used it so often, it was remarkable that he never recognised it.

The lift arrived. I was beginning to get sick of the sight of it. We went back down and my heart sank when we stopped at the ninth floor and the husband and wife that I had just met got in again. They looked at me curiously but said nothing. They didn't seem to know Hawthorne.

I was glad, finally, to leave the building. 'Are they expecting us?' I asked.

'Masefield Pryce Turnbull? Yes. I spoke to Oliver Masefield. They're just across the river . . . off Chancery Lane.'

'Then we can walk.'

Kevin couldn't walk. A teenager, disabled, from a

different culture; what on earth had he been doing in Hawthorne's flat? The two of them sounded like old friends. I was desperate to ask him but of course I couldn't.

I thought about nothing else the entire way.

After walking all the way across Blackfriars Bridge to see Hawthorne, I now followed my steps back again. Masefield Pryce Turnbull had offices in Carey Street, behind the Central London County Court and just round the corner from where I live. This part of London is dedicated to the legal profession and wants you to know it. Even the newer, more modern buildings are carefully traditional, utterly discreet.

Masefield Pryce Turnbull occupied the top two floors of a handsome townhouse that they shared with two other boutique firms. It was a twenty-first-century law firm in a nineteenth-century building; sliding glass doors and open-plan offices behind the classical arches and sculpted pediments. A young, smiling secretary took us through to a corner office where Oliver Masefield was waiting for us, sitting behind a massive, highly polished desk. This was a practice that specialised in divorce – matrimonial law, as they called it – and perhaps he needed a solid barrier between himself and the grief and anger of his clients.

He rose to greet us, a very imposing black man in a sleek, tailored suit, about fifty years old with a high, domed forehead and dark hair which was going grey around the temples in a way that entirely suited his profession and status. He had an extraordinarily cheerful disposition which he seemed unable to hide, even though we were here to make enquiries about the violent death of his partner. When I say there was a twinkle in his eye, I mean it quite literally. Perhaps it was the overhead lighting. Even when he arranged his features to show the expected empathy and remorse, he still gave the impression that he wanted to burst out laughing, to sweep us into his embrace and take us out for a drink.

'Please! Please, come in,' he began, although we already had. He had a loud, booming voice, on the edge of theatrical. 'Take a seat. I spoke to the police yesterday evening . . . An absolutely terrible business. Poor Richard! We'd worked together for many years, you know, and I want to say straight away that anything I can do to help you, I will do! Will you have a coffee or tea? No? This weather is so very damp and unpleasant. Perhaps a glass of water?'

There was a bottle on a sideboard and he poured two glasses while we sat down. He handed them to us, then went back to his place on the other side of the desk. 'Where do you want to start?'

'When was the last time you spoke to Mr Pryce?' Hawthorne asked.

'That would have been on Sunday, the day that it happened. We spoke at about six o'clock in the evening.'

'He rang you.'

'Yes, that's right.' Oliver Masefield sighed loudly. Everything he did was just a little bit larger than life. 'I can't tell you how bad I feel. He was worried about something. He phoned me for advice. But I wasn't able to speak to him.' He grimaced. 'I was going out with my wife to a concert at the Albert Hall. Mozart's Requiem. He couldn't have chosen a worse time to ring me.'

'So what did he say?'

'Not very much. He had already mentioned to me on one or two occasions that he had concerns about a recent hearing.' Before Hawthorne could interrupt, he continued. 'The Lockwood divorce. You do under-stand, gentlemen, that I have a duty to protect client confidentiality, but many of the facts are on public rec-ord and anything I'm telling you now you can find out for yourselves.'

With this established, he began.

'In this instance, our client was Adrian Lockwood,

who was seeking a divorce from his wife, Akira Anno, on grounds of unreasonable behaviour. I don't need to go into details, the more salient of which appeared in the newspapers. We came to an agreement at the Central Family Court and I have to say that it was very much in our client's favour. This was on Wednesday the sixteenth. You'll be aware that Ms Anno was put out – to say the least – by the way things had proceeded and happened to see Richard in a restaurant four or five days later. It was The Delaunay in the Aldwych. What followed was a common assault and could have landed her in serious trouble if Richard had chosen to pursue the matter further.'

'She threw wine at him.'

'That's right.'

'She also threatened him.'

'She swore at him and said words to the effect that she would like to attack him with a bottle. It was a very foolish thing to do but I understand that she is a highly strung woman.'

'You say he had concerns. What were they?' Hawthorne asked.

'I never found out exactly because I wasn't directly involved. But I can tell you that Richard suspected there had been fraudulent disclosure and it concerned him to the extent that he was even prepared to consider a set-aside.'

'It would help if you could speak in English, Mr Masefield.'

The lawyer's eyes narrowed and some of his bonhomie departed the room. 'I think I was doing precisely that, Mr Hawthorne. But I will try to explain it to you in language that a police officer, retired or otherwise, might understand.'

I smiled at that, then looked away so that Hawthorne wouldn't see.

Masefield continued. 'In the case of a high-income divorce, both sides have to make a full account of their income, their pensions, savings, property . . . their entire net value. This is all laid out in what we call a Form E. It does sometimes happen that one side may try to conceal some aspect of his or her wealth and were that to be discovered, the agreement – whether it was made inside or outside the court – might well be over-turned and effectively both parties would have to begin again.' He coughed. 'We call that a set-aside. I know that Richard did have some concerns that Ms Anno might have an income stream which she had failed to declare and he had been in touch with Navigant—'

'Navigant?'

'They are a consultancy in London. They have a first-class team of forensic accountants and we use them quite frequently.'

'And they were investigating Akira Anno?'

'To begin with, yes. But in the end their services were no longer required as Ms Anno, presumably being advised by her own counsel, accepted Mr Lockwood's terms quite soon after the FDR.'

'What's an FDR?' This time I was the one who asked, saving Hawthorne any further confrontation.

'I'm sorry. It's the Financial Dispute Resolution. You have to understand that we do everything we can to dissuade our clients from proceeding all the way to the final hearing. If they can come to an agreement before that, it will save them many thousands, perhaps even hundreds of thousands, of pounds. That was the case here. Richard had persuaded Ms Anno's team that they might as well quit while they were ahead. He had made a reasonable offer and in the end they agreed.' Masefield clasped his hands together. 'Clearly she wasn't entirely happy about it – witness what happened a few days later. But although she might not have believed it, it was almost certainly in her best interests.'

'So this is what I don't get,' Hawthorne said. 'It's a done deal. Richard Pryce has got the agreement he wanted. His client's happy—'

'Mr Lockwood was delighted.'

'So what's he doing calling you on that Sunday when the whole thing's over?'

'I have no answer to that, I'm afraid.'

'He didn't say anything at all?'

I didn't think Masefield would answer. He clearly didn't want to, torn between client confidentiality, his own sense of responsibility and, I think, a mild dislike of Hawthorne. But in the end, it was his sense of guilt that persuaded him.

'I should have listened to him!' he exclaimed. 'I blame myself – but as I say, I was on my way to a concert and I didn't want to be late. We spoke briefly and I could tell Richard was upset. He talked about consulting the Law Society ethics hotline. The Law Society is, as it were, our governing body and that would have been a very serious step.'

'It might have led to a set-aside.'

'It might indeed. And what is the point of having a set-aside if your side has already won? I'm not even sure it would have made any difference to the settlement if Ms Anno had been sitting on a vast pile of money, unless of course she had somehow extorted it or defrauded it from her ex-husband, and even then it was no real concern of ours.'

'So what did you say to him?'

'Broadly, I said there was no point raking over the coals and that we would talk about it first thing Monday. I wished him a pleasant evening and rang off.'

Richard Pryce had not had a pleasant evening. And for him, Monday had never come.

'Why was he called the Blunt Razor?' I asked – as much to fill the silence that had suddenly descended as anything else.

It made Masefield smile. He nodded at me. 'That's a very good question,' he said. 'And one that may explain a great deal of what we've been discussing. We don't normally take notice of these epithets but Richard had been involved in one or two high-profile cases and he was described that way by some journalist or other and it stuck. The thing about him is that he was razor-sharp but he was also scrupulously honest. He would be very reluctant to take on a client if he thought they were in any way compromised and he always spoke his mind. That was what upset Ms Anno so much. He wrote to her, as was completely normal and proper in such proceedings, but his language was, I imagine, very blunt.'

'He called a spade a spade,' Hawthorne said.

'Those aren't the words I would choose. But yes. He was forthright. And it was completely in character for him to call me over a weekend if there was something that was worrying him.' He shook his head. 'I will never forgive myself for not giving him my full attention. Richard and I had worked together for almost twenty years. We met at Clifford Chance before we decided to set up together. Maurice was too upset even to come in today.'

'Maurice?'

'Maurice Turnbull. My other senior partner.'

For a moment nobody spoke and I was aware how quiet it was in this office. If there was any traffic in Carey Street, the sound was being effectively blocked by the double glazing and although I could see secretaries and paralegals in the area on the other side of the glass partition, they could have been actors in a film with the volume turned down. From my experience, law firms are always quiet places. Maybe it's because they make words so expensive that they tend to use them sparingly among themselves.

I thought we had finished and would leave but Hawthorne took me by surprise with his next question. 'One last thing, Mr Masefield. I don't suppose you could tell us anything about your colleague's will?'

His will. That had never occurred to me but of course Richard Pryce was a wealthy man. There was the house in Fitzroy Park with its expensive art on the walls, the second home in Clacton-on-Sea, two luxury cars and almost certainly a whole lot more.

'As a matter of fact, I was discussing it with Richard only a few weeks ago. I am his executor so I'm very well acquainted with his last wishes.'

Hawthorne waited. 'And what were they?'

Once again, Masefield was hesitant. He had taken against Hawthorne but at the same time he was smart enough to know that in the end he would have no choice. 'The bulk of his estate is left to his husband,' he said. 'That includes the property in north London and the house in Clacton-on-Sea. He named a number of charities. But the only other large bequest, and I'm referring to a sum of about £100,000, goes to a Mrs Davina Richardson. If you wish to speak to her, my secretary can give you her address.'

'I do wish to speak to her,' Hawthorne said. There was a gleam in his eyes that I knew well, the aware-ness of another door opening, another line of enquiry for him to pursue. 'But maybe you can tell me why he should have been so generous to her.'

'I really don't see that it's any of my business.' Oliver Masefield was much less jovial than he had been when we came in. I'm afraid Hawthorne did have this effect on people. You could say that he was the needle and every witness, every suspect, the balloon. 'Mrs Rich-ardson is an interior decorator. She and Richard were close friends. He was also godfather to her son. I'll give you her telephone number.' He brought it up on his computer screen, then scribbled it down on a sheet of paper and handed it across. 'Anything more than that, you'll have to get from her.'

As we left the office, Hawthorne's mobile rang. It was Detective Inspector Grunshaw. She was ringing to let him know that Akira Anno had turned up and was ready to talk.

6
Her Story

Akira Anno lived somewhere in Holland Park but we didn't meet her at her home. Presumably because she didn't want her privacy invaded, she had chosen to be interviewed at Notting Hill Gate police station, a rather handsome and imposing building that stood at the corner of Ladbroke Grove. It's been shut down now, part of a brilliant scheme to close half of London's police stations and reduce uniformed officers on the street that has seen a surge in knife crime and made it impossible to use a mobile phone without the risk of it being snatched by thieves on motorbikes.

I was puzzled why Detective Inspector Grunshaw had invited us over, given that she had made it clear she viewed the investigation as a competition which she was determined to win.

'She thinks the Anno woman did it,' Hawthorne explained.

'How does that work?'

'She makes the arrest. She makes me look bad. I was there – but she was one step ahead of me.'

'You don't like her.'

'Nobody does.'

We showed our IDs and were eventually allowed into the police station. Grunshaw had booked a grim, magnolia-painted interview room on the ground floor. The windows were frosted glass, blanking out any view. There was a table bolted into the floor. No Farrow & Ball here. A collection of health and safety posters on the walls were the only decoration.

Akira Anno was sitting uncomfortably, poised on the edge of a particularly brutal wooden chair. She was a small woman, quite boyish, not exactly short but somehow unreal, as if she were a scaled-down model of herself. Her eyes were very dark and intense and only partially concealed by her round, mauve-tinted glasses. These were perched on porcelain cheeks and a sharply contoured nose that might have seen the edge of a plastic surgeon's knife. Her hair was black and too straight, hanging down to her shoulders and framing a face that was old and young at the same time. She gave the impression that she was extremely wise and knowledgeable, partly because she never smiled. She was sulking now. It turned out that she had just driven back from Oxford. She showed no sign of remorse that her ex-husband's lawyer had been brutally murdered, but she was indignant that anyone should think she had anything to do with it.

I had already met Akira Anno twice before.

As I write this, I don't want to give the impression that I had any animosity towards her or her work. In fact, at the time of Richard Pryce's death I'd never actually read anything she'd written apart from a couple of poems that had been published in the *New Statesman* and they hadn't made a word of sense. The first time I had come across her had been at the Edinburgh Book Festival and then, six months later, I had seen her at a launch party in London. Afterwards, I looked her up on the Virago website. That was the impression she made on me.

She was born in Tokyo in 1963, an only child. Her father was a banker who was transferred to New York when she was nine and that was where she was brought up. In 1986, she graduated from Smith College in Massachusetts and shortly afterwards published her first novel, *A Multitude of Gods*, 'a story of female submission and religious patriarchy set during the Kamakura period in Japan'. It catapulted her to international acclaim and received rave reviews, although the feature film adaptation starring Meryl Streep did less well. Among her other books, the best known were: *The Temizu Basin*, *A Cool Breeze in Hiroshima* and *My Father Never Knew Me*, a semi-autobiographical memoir of her early days in America. She had also published two volumes of poetry, the most recent of which had come out earlier in the year. It was called *Two Hundred Haikus* and contained exactly that. She had famously said that it could take her several years to write a novel because she treated every word not just as a stitch in a tapestry but as a tapestry in itself. I'm not entirely sure what she meant by that either.

She married the English cinematographer Marcus Brandt, who had worked on her film, and this was what had brought her to London where she now lived. It was an abusive relationship – described over nine pages in the *Sunday Times Magazine* and later in a BBC *Imagine* documentary – and it had come to an end in 2008. There were no children. Two years later, in 2010, much to the surprise of many newspaper pundits, she had married the property developer Adrian Lockwood.

At some stage in her life she had embraced Shinto, the traditional religion of Japan, and this was reflected in much of her work, particularly her belief in animism, the idea that inanimate objects contain some sort of spirituality, although as far as I could tell she wasn't known to visit shrines or, for that matter, to indulge in ritual dance. She also explored the nature of otherness, her own dual ethnicity and the disconnection that came from living in a culture separated from that in which she had been born. I'm quoting here from the flap of one of her books.

I had been introduced to her in the yurt, the Mongolian-style writers' tent they put up every year at the Edinburgh Book Festival. It's not huge but it's a quiet place to hang out and they serve coffee and snacks all day, with malt whisky in the evening – if they haven't already packed you off home. I was in Edinburgh to talk about my children's books. She was doing a poetry recital. I was sitting on my own when she arrived as part of a melee that included her publisher, her agent, her publicist, two journalists, a photographer and the director of the festival. For some reason she was wearing a man's three-piece suit, complete with bowler hat. Apart from a silver brooch – possibly a letter from the Japanese alphabet – pinned to her shoulder, she could have stepped out of a painting by Magritte.

There was hardly anyone else in the tent and after Akira had accepted a cup of green tea and refused a rather tired egg and cress sandwich, somebody noticed I was there and introduced me as the author of the Alex Rider series.

'Oh yes?'

Those were her first two words to me and I will never forget them – nor the handshake that followed. It was utterly indifferent, over in an instant.

I muttered something about admiring her work, which wasn't true but was something I felt I ought to say.

'Thank you. It's very nice to meet you.' If each word was a tapestry, it had been spun out of razor wire.

She was already doing that awful thing of looking over my shoulder to see if there was anyone more interesting in the yurt. When she established that there wasn't, she turned her back on me to check something with her publicist and a moment later the entire group ebbed away.

I wasn't exactly put out although I did think it was strange. The atmosphere at book festivals is nearly always friendly and non-competitive and it's rare to meet an author who grandstands. I gave Akira the benefit of the doubt. Perhaps she was nervous about her session. I'm the same. No matter how often I speak in public, I'm uneasy before I go onstage and find it hard to make conversation. I'm sure there are plenty of people who think I'm just rude.

But when I met her a few months later at the book launch, she snubbed me again and this time I was sure it was quite deliberate. She seemed to have no memory of having met me before and the moment she was told (again) that I was a children's author, she switched off. It really was as if a light had gone out in her eyes. By now she had started affecting those Yoko Ono-style tinted glasses. I thought she was rather ridiculous.

And here she was again, expensively dressed in a black trouser suit with a pale grey pashmina draped over her shoulders and twisted round one arm. Cara Grunshaw was sitting opposite her and the man I knew only as Darren was standing to one side, either chewing gum or pretending to, still holding his totemic notebook.

Grunshaw introduced Hawthorne but said nothing about me, which was probably just as well. I wasn't sure what Akira would have thought of my being there and I very much doubted that she would enjoy ending up in one of my books. This was an informal interview. There was no solicitor, no caution.

'I want to thank you for coming in,' Grunshaw began, addressing Akira. 'As you know, Richard Pryce was found dead at his home yesterday morning and we're hoping you can help us with our enquiries.'

Akira shrugged. 'I don't see why I should be able to help you. I hardly knew Mr Pryce. He represented my ex-husband but we never spoke. I had nothing to say to him. He made his living from the death of love and from the unmaking of people's dreams. What else is there to say?'

She had a strange accent, largely American but with a slight Japanese inflexion. Her voice was soft and completely emotionless. She sounded bored.

'You threatened him.'

'No. I did not.'

'With respect, Ms Anno, we have several witnesses who were present at The Delaunay restaurant on the twenty-first of October. You had been having dinner there. As you left the restaurant, you saw Mr Pryce, who was sitting with his husband. You threw a glass of wine at him.'

'I poured it over his head. He deserved it.'

'You called him a pig and you threatened to hit him with a bottle.'

'It was a joke!' There was an extraordinary malevo-lence in the four words, as if Grunshaw was deliberately overlooking something that was painfully obvious to ev-eryone else. 'I poured maybe two, three inches of wine and I said he was lucky he hadn't ordered a bottle or I'd have used that. My meaning was quite clear. It was that I would have poured more of the wine over him. Not that I would have used the bottle to injure him.'

'Given the way he died, it was still an unfortunate choice of words.'

She considered. I could see her replaying and analysing the scene at the restaurant as if she was going to turn it into a short story. Or a haiku. It was all there in those deep black eyes. She arrived at a conclusion. 'I don't regret anything that I said. I told you. It was a joke.'

'Not a very funny one.'

'I don't think a joke has to be funny, Detective Inspector. In my books, I use humour only to subvert the status quo. If you've ever read the French philosopher Alain Badiou, you'll know that he defines jokes as a type of rupture that opens up truths. I actually met him at the Sorbonne, by the way. He was a remarkable man. By ridiculing my enemy, I defeat him. That was the insight that Alain gave me and although I see no need to justify myself, that was precisely the mechanism I was using at The Delaunay.'

I could imagine Akira Anno and Alain Badiou together, talking into the small hours. I'm sure it would have been a barrel of laughs.

'Who had you been having dinner with, Ms Anno?'

'A friend of mine.'

'It might be helpful if you gave us his name.'

'It might be preferable not to. Anyway, it wasn't a man. It was a woman.'

DI Grunshaw took a breath. Next to her, Darren was scribbling away, his pen scratching at the paper. They weren't used to being spoken to in this way. 'If your dinner companion overheard the comments you made and if they were intended as a joke, then we might ask her for a statement and that might actually be helpful to you.'

'All right.' Akira shrugged. 'It was a publisher. Dawn Adams.'

'Is she *your* publisher?'

'No. She's just a friend.'

Darren added the name to his notebook and underlined it. I wondered why Akira had been so reluctant to provide such an irrelevant piece of information.

'Where were you last weekend, Ms Anno?'

'I was in a cottage near Lyndhurst. It belongs to another friend of mine. My yoga teacher.'

'And he will confirm this?'

'If someone hasn't murdered him with a wine bottle, I expect so.'

There she was, subverting the status quo again.

'Was anyone with you in Lyndhurst?' Hawthorne cut in.

'*Near* Lyndhurst.' Akira underlined the word with

her voice. 'The cottage is actually very remote and I was alone.'

'What time did you leave?' Hawthorne again. I could tell that he didn't believe her story.

'I left on Monday morning at about half past seven. I stopped for a coffee near Fleet but after that I went straight home. I showered and changed and then I went out again. I was giving a lecture at Oxford University and I stayed there overnight. I came back to London this morning and was told that the police had been looking for me and wanted to see me.' She levelled her eyes at Grunshaw. 'In all truth, I don't think I was so difficult to find. I hope you have more success with whoever committed the crime.'

'Where did you have the coffee?' Darren asked.

She almost yawned. 'It was a Welcome Break service station and it was busy. I'm sure quite a few people will have seen me. You can ask.'

'We will.'

'What did you have against Richard Pryce?' Hawthorne cut in. Akira threw a contemptuous glance in his direction but before she could answer, he went on. 'You said just now that you hardly knew him and you never spoke. He represented your husband and from what I hear your husband came away from his divorce with a big smile on his face. Did you blame Pryce for that? He could have done you for assault in that restaurant. Why did you attack him?'

She rearranged the pashmina before she answered, wrapping it more tightly around herself. 'Richard Pryce was a liar,' she said. 'He represented my ex-husband and deliberately lied and intimidated me to protect him.'

'What do you mean by that?' Hawthorne looked genuinely sympathetic and sounded so interested that even Akira was taken by surprise. That was another of his tricks. He had a way of getting people to tell him perhaps more than they intended.

'I will tell you,' she said. 'I don't care if you know because it's behind me now. I look on my divorce as a cleansing process. The water runs foul only when you step *into* the shower.'

'I'm sure.'

She composed herself. 'I never married Adrian Lockwood. I married the image, the smiling Cheshire cat, that I made of him. That's the truth even if it took me three years to see it. My first marriage was a degradation. Marcus, my first husband, was a professional narcissist, and I never knew where I was with him, in every sense. Moving with him to London took me not just from my place of birth, Tokyo, but from my home, New York. It was like falling through concentric circles, disappearing down a spiral that increasingly alienated me. In the end, there was only Marcus and he knew it. It was what gave him his power over me. He made my life miserable and when I found the strength to leave him, I had nothing.'

'You had your books,' I suggested, surprising myself. I hadn't intended to speak.

'The writer is only the shadow on the page. Yes. My books were appreciated all over the world, translated into forty-seven languages. I received many awards. I am sure you are familiar with my work.'

'Well, actually—'

'But I was *nothing.*' She brought her fist crashing down on the table but it was so small, her fingers so slender, that it made almost no sound. 'I had no inner life in myself, no confidence.

'And then, at a party, I met Adrian. A property developer! It would be hard to imagine any occupation more alien to my sensibilities. I did not find him attractive and yet I will admit that I was attracted to him. He was so loud and cheerful. And rich. Yes. He had houses all over the world, beautiful cars, a yacht in the Camargue. He never read, of course. He had no interest in literature. He went to the theatre and to the opera when he was taken there by his corporate friends, but he didn't care what he was seeing. It meant nothing to him.

'He provided me with a safe space in which I was able to rebuild my confidence, to discover something of my inner self. I found his very ignorance a solace. He looked up to me, of course. He admired me. Perhaps, in his own way, he loved me. But his love was never more than skin-deep.' She swept a hand through her hair. 'I could live with that.'

'So what went wrong?' Hawthorne asked.

She shrugged. 'I got bored. I found it increasingly difficult to reconcile my life as a serious writer, critic and performance poet with my role as his wife. Also, he was having affairs. He had nothing interesting to say. All he ever talked about was his business! He was a brute.' She shuddered. 'He had a foul temper and he could be violent. He made demands of my body that made me feel sick.'

'But it wasn't your husband you attacked in a restaurant, Ms Anno,' Grunshaw reminded her. 'It was his solicitor.'

'I already told you. Richard Pryce lied.' She closed her eyes. Her hair was hanging loose, her hands palms up on the table. For that brief moment, she could have been in one of her yoga classes. 'First, there was the question of the settlement. I was not acquisitive. I was not unreasonable. I can live without money. My currency is invested in the words that I write. I asked only for enough to support my lifestyle, my two houses, my travel and other expenses. I was fully prepared to go to court to fight for what was rightfully mine.

'Mr Pryce characterised me in a way that made that impossible. He belittled me. He made it seem that I had brought nothing to the marriage but had used Adrian as some sort of emotional crutch. I was not the one who was disabled! Yes, I will admit that he had filled a need, but I brought much into his life that had not been there before and he drank deep from the fountainhead that I provided. I was not a parasite!' These last words were spoken with a blaze of anger. 'My lawyers were concerned that I was unlikely to be viewed sympathetically if I insisted on a hearing and I needed little persuasion. The law has always been fundamental in the suppression of women. Why should I think it would treat me any differently?'

She fell silent, but DI Grunshaw hadn't finished yet. 'Were you aware that Richard Pryce had investigated you?' she asked. I was surprised she knew that. She must have spoken to Oliver Masefield.

'No.'

'Are you quite sure?'

'I was advised that he might be interested in my royalties and other earnings, but I didn't care. I had nothing to hide.'

Grunshaw glanced at Hawthorne, who briefly shook his head. There was nothing more he wanted to ask. 'We may need to speak to you again, Ms Anno,' she said. 'Do you have any plans to leave London?'

'I'm at the Aldeburgh Poetry Festival next week.'

'But you're not leaving the country?'

'No.'

'Then we'll be in touch with you soon.'

It might have ended there but suddenly I noticed that Akira Anno was staring at me. I turned away, trying to make myself invisible, but it was already too late. I actually saw the moment when she remembered who I was.

'I know you!' she exclaimed. 'We've met before.'

I said nothing. I was extremely uncomfortable but neither Hawthorne nor Grunshaw chose to help me out.

'You're a writer!' She was not using the word as a compliment. She stood up, her hands resting on the table, balled into fists. 'What are you doing here?' she demanded. Her accent, which had been Japanese American, now veered further towards Japanese.

'Well . . .' I began, still hoping Hawthorne would step in.

'Why is he here?' She turned vengefully on DI Grunshaw.

Grunshaw shrugged. 'I didn't invite him. He's writing a book.'

'A book about me? He's putting me in his book? I don't want to be in his fucking book! I want my lawyer in this room. If he puts me in his book, I'll fucking sue him.'

'I think you'd better go,' Grunshaw said to me.

'This is a fucking outrage! I don't give him permission. Do you hear me? If he writes about me, I'll kill him!'

She was screaming, her voice not exactly loud but high-pitched, her entire body shaking as Hawthorne and I excused ourselves and hurried out as quickly as we could. I had never seen anyone so angry and at that moment it was easy to imagine her picking up the bottle of wine, smashing it over Richard Pryce's head and then using the jagged end to make mincemeat of his neck.

If there had been another bottle handy, I had no doubt at all she would have done the same to me.

7
His Story

'I should never have married her!' Adrian Lockwood threw his head back and roared with laughter. 'It was one of my biggest mistakes, and God knows, I've made plenty of those. Mind you, she was a very sexy little piece . . . bloody attractive and the toast of the town. Everyone was talking about her. It was only when we got back from the honeymoon that I discovered she was totally self-obsessed and boring! Actually, I think I may have spotted it on the plane out now I come to think of it. I was on my third G and T before we were at the end of the runway – and I needed it.

'I really should have seen her for what she was from the start, but, you see, she was an intellectual. I never went to university myself and I've always had a respect for people who are good with words. But with her . . . well, there was no stopping her. It was all words, words, words, and I'm not just talking about her writing habits, although God knows she would lock herself away for hours at a time even when she was writing those bloody poems of hers. They only had three lines but I'd hear her pounding away at the computer from dawn to dusk.'

'Did you take an interest in her work?' Hawthorne asked.

'I'm not sure "interest" is the word I'd use. I read one of her novels but I'm more of a John Grisham fan myself and I couldn't really see the point of it. She gave me a copy of that haiku book of hers but by then things were already going off the rails. She signed it for me so maybe I can get a couple of quid for it on eBay. I've certainly got no other use for the bloody thing.'

Adrian Lockwood was the sort of man who was hard to dislike although he was doing everything he could to help us on our way. Lying back on the sofa with one denim-covered leg crossed over the other, a shining, black leather Chelsea boot dangling in front of us and his arms spread over the cushions, he looked every inch the shark he undoubtedly was. He had mean eyes that lurked behind sunglasses similar to those of his ex-wife, although in his case they were Porsche or Jaguar: racing-car chic. His black hair was tied back in a ponytail that didn't suit him at all – he was well into his fifties – and he had a deep tan that must have come from his yacht in the Camargue. As well as designer jeans, he was wearing a dark blue velvet jacket that showed just a few flecks of dandruff on the shoulders, and a soft white shirt, open at the neck.

We had met him that same afternoon at his home in Edwardes Square, a twenty-minute walk from the police station through Holland Park. It was one of a terrace of houses that were not just similar but seemed to have been purposely designed to have no variations – the same proportions, the same arched doorways, the same black railings and, almost certainly, the same class of multimillionaire owners. We could tell which one was his from the car that was parked outside: a silver Lexus sedan with the registration number RJL 1.

Lockwood was on his own although the house showed signs of a cleaner and maybe even a housekeeper too, with expensive flower arrangements in vases, rigorously hoovered carpets and not a spot of dust to be seen. He had met us at the door, taking Hawthorne's coat and hanging it on an art deco coat stand with a skull-handled umbrella – Alexander McQueen no less – poking out beneath. From there we had gone past an office and a home cinema and up to the first floor, which consisted of a single large space stretching the entire length of the building and offering views onto the square with its communal garden at the front and the smaller, very ornate, private garden behind.

This was the main living area, with an open-plan kitchen attached. A burst of October sunlight had flooded in, illuminating a thick, oyster-pink carpet, solid, quite traditional furniture, heavy, drooping curtains and a scattering of books on shelves. These included *Two Hundred Haikus* by Akira Anno, the book he had mentioned. A marble counter separated the kitchen from the rest of the room. The units could have come from one of those companies that manage to put three zeros on even a pedal bin and looked as if they had never been used.

'This was your second marriage,' Hawthorne said. He wasn't impressed by the house or its owner. He was perched on the edge of the sofa, facing Lockwood, his hands clenched below his knees and his whole body tense, as if about to pounce.

'That's right.' He was sober for a moment. 'As I'm sure you know perfectly well, my first marriage came to a very unhappy end.'

Lockwood's first wife had been Stephanie Brook, a *Coronation Street* actress who had reached the finals of *Strictly Come Dancing*. She had died of a drug overdose while she was on his yacht in Barbados and the tabloid press had been full of gossip about suicide – something he had always denied. I had looked at the stories on my phone before I had got here. Stephanie had been, according to one headline, 'big, blonde and bubbly'. The opposite of Akira.

'How did you meet your second wife?' Hawthorne continued.

'At Ronnie Scott's. Someone introduced us.'

'And you were married . . . ?'

'On the eighteenth of February 2010, three days after my birthday, as it happened. That was the last happy birthday I was going to have for a while! Westminster registry office and then lunch at the Dorchester for two hundred people. It's lucky I stipulated no presents or I'd have to send them all back!' Again, he laughed at his own joke. 'I have to tell you that when the police told me they were investigating a murder, for one brief, joyous moment I assumed someone must have done her in.'

'Why is that?' Hawthorne asked.

'Because she's horrible, that's why! She reminds me of a cat I used to have . . . a Siamese. It looked beautiful curled up in front of the fire and it would purr when you reached out to stroke it. But then a minute later, for no reason at all, it could twist round and sink its teeth into your hand. You never knew what was on its bloody mind.'

I remembered the way Akira had turned on me. 'What happened to the cat?' I asked.

'Oh. I had it put down.'

'So you must have been surprised when you were told that the victim was your solicitor, Richard Pryce,' Hawthorne said.

'I'll say!' He held up a finger, contradicting himself. 'Well, he was a lawyer. And you know what they say about lawyers! What do you call a thousand lawyers chained together at the bottom of the ocean?'

'I don't know.'

'A good start!'

He roared. Hawthorne was blank-faced. 'So what you're saying is that you would consider the murder of a lawyer to be justifiable.'

'I'm not being serious!' Lockwood stared at Hawthorne, carefully adjusting his features. 'Look – you're not really suggesting that I had anything to do with it, are you? Why would I have done something like that? Richard was a bit of a fusspot. He had to dot all the *i*'s and cross all the *t*'s and he could certainly be a bit long-winded, but then, of course, the more they talk, the more they get paid. But he did a terrific job. The divorce went exactly the way I wanted.'

'You gave him a gift, is that right?'

'A bottle of wine, yes.' Lockwood seemed unaware

that this had been the murder weapon. 'It wasn't very much,' he went on. 'But it was the least I could do. By persuading Akira not to go for a final hearing, he'd saved me thousands of pounds.' Lockwood glanced briefly at his gold cufflink and adjusted it. 'Actually, it was a waste of money giving it to him as I learned afterwards that he didn't drink. But, as they say, it's the thought that counts!'

'I'd be interested to know the details of what you agreed . . . the settlement between you and your wife.'

'I'm sure you would, Mr Hawthorne. But I wouldn't say it was any of your business.'

Hawthorne shrugged. 'You know that Richard Pryce had hired a team of forensic accountants to investigate your wife.'

'My ex-wife. Yes, of course I know. Navigant! Who do you think was paying the bills?'

'What you may not know is that almost the last thing he did before he was killed was to ring his partner – Oliver Masefield – and tell him that he was concerned about something that related to the settlement. He was even thinking about referring the matter to the Law Society. It could well be that he was murdered to prevent this. So it is very much my business, Mr Lockwood. And the police's business. You'd be doing yourself a favour if you got your version of events out there first.'

Lockwood was flustered. Two red pinpricks had appeared in his cheeks, fighting against the suntan. 'Well, I've got nothing to hide. Everything is on record and I'm sure you'll get access to all the papers. It's just that having put the whole thing behind me, I'm not keen on stirring it all up again.'

'I can understand that.' Hawthorne was a little more emollient now. But then he knew he was going to get what he wanted.

'It was actually very straightforward. Ms Anno, if I may call her that, thought she could get her hooks into half of everything I had but Richard very quickly put her right. Let's start with the fact that she had brought absolutely nothing to the marriage. Quite the opposite. I had to prop her up with her therapies and her health club and her yoga sessions and all the rest of it. After the honeymoon, she hardly ever let me into her bed and even on the honeymoon I had to chase her round the bloody ecolodge that she'd chosen in the middle of Mexico.'

There was a bowl of fruit – bilberries – on the table beside him. Lockwood reached in and scooped out a handful, which he ate, one after another, as he continued.

'But it's simpler than that. All we're talking about, really, is money. It's certainly what was on her mind!

For someone who calls herself a poet, she certainly has an eye for the hard stuff! Well, Mr Hawthorne, here's the truth. As you probably know, I've made my living out of property. I won't say I've done badly. In fact I've had some pretty good years. But it's an up-and-down business and sad though it is to say it, there have recently been more downs than ups. There was the credit crunch – and we still haven't shaken off the after-effects. The slowdown in London. Banks not lending. I don't need to go into the details. But it's been pretty grisly, I can tell you, and dear old Akira joined the team at exactly the worst time.

'In the three years I was married to her, I made nothing. Not a bean! Absolute zip. And *that* was the point. Akira was entitled to fifty per cent of nothing at all and I was more than happy to give it to her.'

'Did she believe you?' Hawthorne asked.

'Of course she didn't! Listen. I had my accountants work on the papers that we presented to her lawyers. I set out all my finances, down to the last euro, everything fair and square. I had to. That's the law. But Akira wouldn't accept it. She questioned every last bloody detail and she had her own forensic accountants looking into all my business dealings over God knows how many years. I have no idea what they hoped to find but they came up with nothing.'

Lockwood was becoming more relaxed, warming to his subject. The smile was back on his face.

'And while we're on the subject, maybe we should be talking about her own income. She was always very cagey about how much money she was earning but I can tell you that she had plenty of spare cash stashed away under the mattress. You can't be married to someone for three years and hide that sort of thing, even if the marriage is as useless as ours. She was loaded but here's the funny thing. Wherever the money was coming from, it wasn't from her writing. I happened to catch sight of one of her royalty statements from Virago Books and I can tell you, it wouldn't have paid for a wet weekend in Torquay! For all her airs and graces, it seems there isn't much of an audience for clinically depressed call girls surviving Hiroshima or weird Japanese poems that don't make any sense.'

He plucked out another handful of the bilberries.

'As a matter of fact, I was the one who suggested to Richard that he should call in Navigant and it's just as well I did because the moment she knew we were on to her, she caved in. Suddenly she was all for coming to an agreement and forget Justice Cocklecarrot and the rest of it. That was pretty much the end of it. We settled everything outside the court. She got the house in Holland Park and I let her keep the Jag. But the actual settlement was a tenth of what she'd hoped for, and frankly, if it had meant seeing the back of her, I'd have happily paid twice as much.'

Another bark of laughter. Nobody enjoyed their own witticisms more than Adrian Lockwood.

But Hawthorne still wasn't smiling. 'Why do you think Richard Pryce made that call on the day he died?' he asked. 'There was obviously something that was worrying him.'

'Are you certain it related to my divorce?'

'Yes.'

'Then I have no idea. Presumably he'd found out something about Akira, about her income – where it was coming from. If she was breaking the law, I'm sure he'd have wanted to take the matter further. But for what it's worth, I wouldn't have cared if she was the top hitwoman for the Mafia. I would have told him to forget it. As far as I was concerned, she was over. We'd come to an agreement. I was a single man. I never wanted to hear her name again.'

Lockwood sank back into the sofa, a smug look on his face.

'Just out of interest, where were you when your lawyer was killed, Mr Lockwood?' Hawthorne asked.

'Why on earth do you want to know?'

'Why do you think?' Hawthorne's voice was bleak,

on the edge of rude. 'We need to know where everyone was on Sunday evening between eight and nine o'clock.'

'So you can eliminate them from your enquiries? That's how you put it in police speak, I believe.'

'That's right.'

'Well, let me think. Sunday evening . . . I had a drink with a friend of mine over in Highgate – Davina Richardson. I got to her house around six and left about eight fifteen. After that, I drove home. I got in about nine o'clock and watched television.'

'What did you watch?'

'*Downton Abbey.* Does that answer your question, Mr Hawthorne?'

I sat up when he mentioned the name Davina Richardson although it had taken me a moment to remember where I had heard it before. Of course. She was the woman who had been left £100,000 in Richard Pryce's will. So she was part of the triangle that included Pryce and Lockwood! That had to mean something.

Hawthorne had certainly picked up on it. 'Tell me about Mrs Richardson,' he said, almost casually, as if he just needed the information to complete his notes.

'There's not much to tell. She's an interior designer I happen to have met. Actually, it was Richard who introduced her to me. She worked on my place in Antibes. Did a bloody good job too.'

'How did she first meet Richard Pryce?'

'You should ask her.'

'I will. But right now I'm asking you.'

'Well, if you insist. I don't particularly like talking about my friends behind their backs but if you really want to know, the two of them go back a long way. Richard was at university with her husband and he's godfather to their child. He was also there when the accident happened.'

'What accident?'

'I would have thought you'd have known all about that before you came here, Mr Hawthorne.' Lockwood was pleased with himself, seeing that he had taken the upper hand. 'I'm talking about the caving accident that happened six or seven years ago now. Davina's husband, Charles Richardson, and Richard Pryce were at university together and there was a third man too. I forget his name. Anyway, Charles got lost in the cave system – it was somewhere up in Yorkshire – and never made it out.'

He waggled a finger. 'Don't think for a minute that it was Richard's fault. There was a full inquiry and it turned out that nobody was to blame. From what Davina told me, he behaved magnificently when it was all over. He supported her and Colin – that's her son – even paying all the fees to put him through private education. He had no children of his own, of course. I'm sure I don't need to tell you that! He helped her set up her business – interior design – and he always told her she'd be looked after in his will.'

'Did she know that?' I asked.

Lockwood frowned. He seemed to notice me for the first time. 'I'm sorry,' he said. 'Who are you again?'

'I'm helping him,' I said. Better to be vague.

'Well if you think that Davina killed Richard for his money, you're barking up the wrong tree. She had his money anyway! Anything she wanted, he gave her. He did everything for her and he would probably have slept with her too except that he was gay.'

'Do you think your ex-wife killed him?' Hawthorne asked, abruptly.

'I have no idea.'

'But you did know that she had threatened him?'

'Yes. I heard about that business in the restaurant. That was typical Akira! She liked to grandstand. And I can absolutely see her beating someone to death because she was annoyed with them. Mind you, she'd probably torture them first by reading them one of her poems.'

He stood up. He had decided it was time for us to leave.

'If you really want to know who killed Richard

Pryce, then maybe you should start with the man who broke into my office,' he added, almost as an after-thought.

'Really?' Hawthorne had also got to his feet.

'I actually reported it to the police . . . not that they took a blind bit of notice.' He paused as if he expected us to agree that, yes, the police were completely use-less and should have spent more time and resources investigating his complaint. 'It happened last Thurs-day. I have a small suite of offices in Mayfair which I use mainly for meetings. There's not much there – just a girl on reception, a secretary, a young man who helps with accounts.

'Anyway, Thursday lunchtime I was out with a cli-ent when this chap turns up. Tells the girl on reception that he's from our IT company and he's come to fix a glitch on my Mac. She's stupid enough to let him in – and the next half-hour he's on his own in my office. She should have known that there was absolutely nothing wrong with my Mac and we don't even have an IT com-pany! Fortunately, I keep all my private documents in a safe and there's nothing of particular interest on my hard drive, so whatever he was after, I doubt if he got it. Nothing seemed to be taken. I did call the police, but, as I say, they took no interest. You'd have thought they'd have changed their minds when, just three days later, Richard Pryce was killed. But nobody seems to think there's any connection.'

'Was your receptionist able to provide a description of the man?' Hawthorne asked.

'She said he was about forty, medium height, white.'

'That's not much of a description.'

'He was wearing glasses. She remembered that. They were heavy, plastic things and they were blue. He may have had some kind of skin problem on the side of his face. Thinning hair. He was dressed in a suit and he had a briefcase. He showed her a business card but she didn't even read the name of the so-called IT company he worked for. Stupid girl. I fired her, of course.'

'It goes without saying,' Hawthorne muttered. 'There were no CCTV cameras in your office? It might help if we had an image of this man.'

Lockwood shook his head. 'There's one on the main stairs but it's not working. I'm glad you agree there's something in it.'

'I'm not sure I said that,' Hawthorne replied. 'But if he turns up again, let me know.'

Adrian Lockwood showed us out of the house and as we went, I noticed a collection of pills and medicines on the kitchen counter. They seemed to be mainly homeopathic. Prominent among them was a large bottle of vitamin A. It was odd. Lockwood hadn't struck me as the sort of person who would be into alternative medicine and I wondered what condition he might be suffering from.

It was too late to ask him. He showed us down the stairs, handed Hawthorne back his coat and opened the front door. He said nothing to me. The door closed behind us and once again we were outside, back in the street.

8
Mother and Son

I spent the afternoon at my flat in Farringdon.

It was hard to believe that only the day before I'd been on the set of *Foyle's War* and that the unit was still out there, shooting somewhere in London. All of that felt like a world away. I had to remind myself that I still had a lot of work to do, starting with the rewrite of the next episode, 'Sunflower'. I'd had notes from ITV, notes from the director, notes from Michael Kitchen, notes from Jill. That's the difference between writing books and writing television. When you write TV, everyone has an opinion.

I couldn't concentrate. My head was filled with the events of the past two days: the crime scene at Heron's Wake, Hawthorne, the various witnesses and suspects I'd met. In the end, I slid the script to one side and plugged my iPhone into my computer. Stephen Spencer, the neighbour, Henry Fairchild, Oliver Masefield . . . I listened to their responses as they were interviewed by Hawthorne and Grunshaw, with my own voice making occasional contributions from the side. Next came Akira Anno and her ex-husband, Adrian Lockwood, each of them investigating the other, trying to find evidence of hidden wealth that might or might not exist.

If you really want to know who killed Richard Pryce, then maybe you should start with the man who broke into my office . . .

That had been Adrian Lockwood, talking about the man in blue spectacles. The Man in Blue Spectacles. That might make a good chapter heading – but was he really involved in all this? Did he even exist?

Hawthorne seemed to think so. As we walked through Edwardes Square, he had muttered, almost as much to himself as me: 'He knew what he was doing.'

'Who?'

'Blue spectacles. You put something like that on your face, it's the only thing anyone will notice. You can pull the same trick with an Elastoplast or a gold tooth. Give people something they'll remember, they forget the rest.'

The break-in had happened on a Thursday, three days before the murder. It had to be related. But how?

It took me about two hours to type up my notes and at the end of it I found myself wondering, had I sat in a room with the killer? Had I already met the person who had murdered Richard Pryce? At the same time, another thought occurred to me. I might not be gifted with quite the same professional skills as Hawthorne – I had never, after all, been trained as a detective – but I had written dozens of murder mysteries for TV. I knew how it worked. Surely I could work this out for myself.

Akira Anno. I drew a circle around her name. She still seemed the most likely suspect, so far anyway. She'd even threatened to murder me!

The telephone rang. It was Hawthorne.

'Tony! Can you meet me at Highgate Tube station at six?'

I looked at my watch. It was five twenty. 'Why?' I asked.

'We're seeing Davina Richardson.' He rang off without waiting for an answer.

It wouldn't take me long to get up to Highgate. I went through my usual ritual, loading my glasses, keys, wallet and Oyster card into the black leather shoulder bag I always carry and was just on my way out when the doorbell rang. I went over to the intercom and pressed it. We have no video system but I recognised the voice that asked for me. It was Detective Inspector Cara Grunshaw. 'I wonder if I could come in?' she asked.

'What – now?'

'Yes.'

'Actually, I'm just leaving.'

'It won't take a minute.'

My heart sank. I couldn't get rid of her. 'All right. I'll come down.'

I could have buzzed the doors open for her but I didn't want her inside the flat. She'd sounded friendly enough out on the doorstep but I wondered what she was doing here and I felt nervous seeing her on my own. I took the six flights of stairs down and opened the front door. She was standing on my doorstep with her leather-jacketed assistant, Darren, slouching behind her.

'Detective Inspector . . .' I began.

'Can I have a word?' She seemed completely pleasant, relaxed.

'What is this about?'

'What do you think?'

'I've got a meeting . . .'

'This will only take a moment.'

She looked past me, inviting herself in, and I realised that I couldn't really refuse. She was a police officer, after all, and we were involved in the same case. There might be some information she wanted to share. I moved aside and the two of them stepped past me into the hallway, a wide area with my sons' bicycles on one side and an exposed brick wall on the other. I allowed the doors to swing shut. They fastened with magnetic locks.

'I hope you don't mind—' I was about to make some excuse as to why I wasn't going to invite her upstairs when she suddenly grabbed hold of me by the lapels of my jacket and slammed me into the wall with such force that the breath was punched out of my lungs and my spine did the neural equivalent of a Mexican wave. Suddenly her face was close to mine; so close that I could smell the fried food she'd had for lunch. Her little eyes were flaring and her mouth was twisted in an ugly grimace.

'Now you listen to me, you little fuck,' Grunshaw said. Her voice was thick with contempt. 'I don't know who you think you are, some smarmy kids' author, walking into my murder scene and thinking you can treat it like a chapter out of Alec Rider—'

'Alex Rider,' I managed to gurgle.

'It's bad enough Hawthorne being called in but at least he's a fucking detective. Or was until they threw him out. But if you think that gives you the right to go poncing around in a police investigation, you've got another thing coming.'

'You should take this up with Hawthorne,' I gasped.

She was still holding me, pinning me to the wall with fists like cannonballs. I had thought she was a big woman but I hadn't realised how much of that was muscle. Being gripped by her was like having a double heart attack. Meanwhile, Darren was watching all this with complete disinterest.

'I'm not talking to Hawthorne. I'm talking to you.' She relaxed a little, allowing my shoulder blades to scrape a few inches down the wall. 'Now, you listen to me,' she said again. 'There's only one reason I'm going to let you hang around. There's only one reason I'm not arresting you for obstructing a police officer in the course of their duty. And that's because you're going to help me.'

'I can't help you,' I said. 'I don't know anything!'

'I'm aware of that. It's bloody obvious.' She examined me with distaste. 'But here's the thing. There's no way Hawthorne is going to rain on my parade. I'm not having it. He's not walking away with the credit for this, the same way he's done before. This is my case and I'm going to be the one who makes the arrest.'

'Fine. But I don't see—'

She leaned forward, once again pressing me into the brickwork. Her lips were inches from my face, her breath moist on my cheek. 'You're going to tell me everything he knows and everything he does. Anything he finds out, you're going to be straight on the phone. Am I making myself clear? And if you tell Hawthorne I was here, you give him even an inkling we've had this conversation, I'll make your life hell.'

'She can do it,' Darren said, with a smile. They were the first words he'd spoken to me and I believed him.

'Do we understand each other?'

'Yes!' What else could I say?

'I'm glad to hear it.' She let me go and straightened up. At the same time, she took out a business card and shoved it into my top pocket, almost tearing the material. 'This is my mobile number. Ring it any time. If I don't answer, leave a message.'

'Hawthorne never tells me anything,' I protested. 'If he does work out anything, I'll be the last to know.'

'Call me,' Grunshaw said. It was an order. It was a threat.

The two of them left.

I stood where I was, hardly believing what had just happened, watching their shadows disappear on the other side of the glazed front door.

I was still unsettled when I met Hawthorne a few minutes after six and of course he noticed it at once. 'What's wrong, Tony?'

'Nothing!' I had already worked out what I was

going to say while I was being carried through the tunnels on the Northern line. 'I've been working on the script.'

'Michael Kitchen still giving you problems?'

'Michael hasn't even seen it yet. It's ITV.'

'You should stick to books, mate.'

I didn't mention the visit. I hadn't decided yet if I was going to do what Detective Inspector Cara Grunshaw had ordered, but I didn't think it would help informing Hawthorne that she had come to my home and threatened me. What could he do? Would he even try to protect me? More to the point, what would *she* do if I defied her? Speeding tickets? Some sort of interruption to *Foyle's War*? It was impossible to shoot in London without the co-operation of the police and it might well occur to a malign, borderline psychotic detective (I'd seen her now in her true colours) to throw all sorts of problems in our way. I'd already caused the production enough difficulties. I was behind with my script revisions. If co-operating with her would help them, surely I had no choice.

Highgate Tube station is built into the side of a hill with a steep flight of stairs leading up to Archway Road. Hawthorne had been waiting for me opposite the newspaper kiosk at the top of the escalators and now we took the lower exit into Priory Gardens, the quiet residential street where Davina Richardson lived. I actually knew the area very well. I'd lived in Crouch End for fifteen years before I moved to Clerkenwell and had often walked down Priory Gardens, taking my children – when they were children – to school. Davina had a pretty Victorian house, tall and narrow, with a tiny front garden and a chessboard front path leading to a door with stained-glass windows. It was on the right side of the road, which is to say the side that backed on to the woodland around Crouch End Playing Fields.

Hawthorne rang the doorbell and after what felt like a long wait it was opened by a woman who gave every impression of being in a constant battle with life without necessarily being on the winning side. She was completely dishevelled, wearing clothes that were hopelessly mismatched: a loose-knit jersey, a long dress, sandals, a chunky bead necklace. She had chestnut hair that tumbled down to her shoulders with a life of its own and slightly desperate hazel eyes. She looked worn out but she was still smiling as she opened the door, as if she had been expecting good news – a man from the Lottery telling her she had the winning ticket, or the arrival of a long-lost brother from Australia perhaps. She was a little disappointed when she realised who we were but did her best to conceal it.

'Mr Hawthorne?' she said.

'Mrs Richardson . . .'

'Please, come in.'

The hallway was narrow and so filled with clutter that it was hard to pass through. There were coats, bags, umbrellas, junk mail, a bicycle, Rollerblades, a cricket bat, swathes of fabric, colour charts, brochures: the entire life story of an interior-designer mother and her teenaged son told in paraphernalia. A staircase, straight ahead of us, led up to the next floor but she led us through an archway and into the kitchen where a washing machine was churning quietly, spinning the clothes in a slow, sudsy circle. A smell of cigarettes and fish fingers hung in the air.

Davina Richardson might have sophisticated clients with expensive houses but her own tastes were decidedly eclectic. I had never seen so many vivid colours fighting for attention. The hall carpet was a deep mauve, the walls a strident blue. Now I was looking at a bright green Aga and a yellow Smeg fridge. The Murano glass chandelier was lovely . . . but in a kitchen? The shelves were crowded with knick-knacks and it made me wonder which had come first. Was she an inveterate traveller who loved picking up souvenirs and needed somewhere to house them or had she simply built too many shelves and gone around the place feverishly trying to fill them?

'Will you have a glass of wine?' she asked. 'I just opened a bottle of white. I know I shouldn't but by the time it gets to six o'clock I find I'm gasping. Sorry about the smell. Colin just finished tea. He's doing his homework but I'm sure he'll be down in a minute. He got very excited when he heard a policeman was coming.' She had already taken a bottle of Chablis out of the fridge and suddenly noticed me. 'I'm sorry,' she said. 'I haven't even asked you your name.'

I told her.

'Are you the writer?'

'Yes.'

She was puzzled as to why I should be there but at the same time she was delighted. 'Colin won't believe it!' she exclaimed. 'He's read all your books. He loves them.'

It's funny but I never quite know what to say when people tell me that they like my books. I almost feel embarrassed. 'That's great,' I muttered. 'Thank you.'

'He doesn't read them any more. He's into Sherlock Holmes now. And Dan Brown. Colin loves reading.' She had poured three glasses of wine. She gave one to each of us although I knew that Hawthorne wouldn't touch his. I'm not sure he actually drank alcohol. 'This is about Richard, isn't it?' she added.

'You must have been very upset,' Hawthorne said in

that probing way of his that suggested he didn't believe it for a minute and that actually all she cared about was the cash.

But she surprised him. 'I was devastated! When I heard the news I had to go into my bedroom and close the door. I was in floods of tears. He hasn't just been a friend. He's been everything to me . . . and to Colin. I don't know how we're going to manage without him.' She took a glug of wine, half emptying the glass. 'You probably know that he was Colin's godfather. God! Do you mind if I smoke? I've been trying to give up and Colin does go on at me, but I like them too much.' She pulled a packet of Marlboros and a lighter out of her jersey pocket and lit up. All her movements were nervous and jumbled together so that she seemed to be in a state of constant flux.

'Richard always looked after us. After Charles died, he helped me pay off the mortgage on this house and he's been a fantastic support for the business too. I wasn't working before. At least, I had a few friends I was helping with furniture and design and things like that. But it was Richard's idea that I should actually set up full-time. He introduced me to quite a few of my clients. And then there were Colin's school fees! It was going to be either Fortismere or Highgate Wood and I've got nothing against either of them but of course Highgate

School is in a completely different league. He's going to be really thrilled to meet you, Anthony. He loves your books. I would never have been able to put him through if it hadn't been for Richard. I can't imagine why anyone would want to kill him. He's the last person in the world who anyone would want to harm.'

'You were helping him with his redecoration?'

'That's right. Richard and Stephen bought Heron's Wake ages ago. It's in Fitzroy Park – only a ten- or fifteen-minute drive from here. Have you been there?' She corrected herself. 'Of course you have. I'm sorry. My head's all over the place.' She dragged on her cigarette then reached out and tapped off the ash. 'The house needed freshening up. The whole place was feeling tired and there was too much white. I always think that white walls are overrated. The trouble is, they don't have any . . .' She searched for the word.

'Colour?' I suggested.

'Emotion. Everything in modern life is white and glass and those awful vertical blinds. It's so hard! But if you go to Venice or the South of France or any of the Mediterranean countries, what do you get? Wonderful blues. Deep purple. Everything vibrant and alive. Just because we live in a cold country, it doesn't mean we can't import a little tropical warmth.'

'I understand that Adrian Lockwood was here the

evening Richard Pryce died,' Hawthorne said, abruptly cutting into this meditation.

'Who told you that?' she asked, and I noticed a little tropical red creeping into her cheeks.

'He did.'

For the first time she fell silent and in that moment it became obvious what sort of relationship the two of them had had. What else would Adrian Lockwood have been doing here on a Sunday evening?

'Yes, he was here,' she admitted, eventually. 'It was actually Richard who introduced us. He was representing Adrian, who was going through a very painful divorce . . .'

'It didn't sound too painful, the way he talked about it,' Hawthorne said with a faint smile.

She ignored this. 'The two of us became friends and after it was over, if Adrian was on his own and he needed someone to talk to, he would come round here.' She paused. 'I also know what it's like to be alone. Anyway, that was what happened last Sunday. The two of us shared a bottle of wine. Actually, I had most of it. He was driving.'

'Did he tell you where he was going?'

'I think he was going home. He didn't say.'

'But you can tell us when he left.'

'As a matter of fact, I can tell you to the minute. Bertha told me.' She pointed into the corner and I noticed an art deco grandfather clock looking slightly incongruous, wedged between the washing machine and the door where we'd come in. No – it was too slender to be a grandfather clock and apparently it was known as Bertha. A grandmother clock. 'She chimes the hour,' Davina went on. 'Adrian left here just after eight o'clock.'

When Adrian Lockwood had spoken to us, he had put the time at eight fifteen but his story more or less tallied with hers, meaning that neither of them could have killed Richard Pryce – unless they had planned it together. But what possible motive could they have had? OK, perhaps they were having an affair, but Pryce wasn't in their way. Quite the opposite. He had brought them together. And he had given them both what they needed. Adrian Lockwood had his low-cost divorce. She had her business, her school fees and all the rest.

Hawthorne was about to ask her something else when Davina looked up sharply and called out, 'Colin? Is that you?'

A moment later, a boy appeared in the doorway. He was about fifteen years old, dressed in the black trousers and white shirt that were part of the Highgate School uniform. The distinctive tie, with its red and blue stripes, had been pulled down loose so it hung about halfway down his chest and his collar was open. He looked nothing like his mother. He was thin and gangly, tall for his age, with curly hair and freckles. He was caught somewhere between the boy he had been and the man he might become, as if his body hadn't quite made up its mind which way to go. The beginnings of a moustache showed faintly on his upper lip; although he hadn't started shaving yet, he needed to. When he spoke, it was with a hard, sandpapery voice that had only recently broken. There was an acne spot on his chin.

'Mum?' he asked.

'Colin! Were you listening on the stairs?'

'No. I heard voices. I came down.'

'This is the policeman I was telling you about. He's asking questions about poor Richard.'

Colin took this as an invitation to slouch into the room and slump into a chair.

'Do you want an apple juice?' his mother asked. I noticed that she had quickly stubbed out her cigarette.

'No, thanks.'

Then she remembered. She told him my name, adding: 'He writes those books you used to like.'

'What books?'

'The Alan Rider series.'

'Alex Rider,' I said.

Colin's eyes widened when he heard that. 'They were great!' he said. 'I read them at prep school. I liked *Point Blanc* best.' He frowned. 'What are you doing here?'

I pointed at Hawthorne. 'I'm helping him.'

'Are you writing about him?'

'Yes.' For once, it seemed unnecessary to deny it.

'Cool! You could do a detective series like Alex Rider! Have you found out who killed him yet?' Colin didn't seem at all put out by the death of his godfather. To him it was just another page in an adventure story.

'We've only just started investigating,' I said. I quite liked that 'we'. I didn't often get a chance to use it.

'There were loads of people who didn't like Richard,' Colin said.

'Colin!'

'That's what he said, Mum. He often used to say that he made an enemy every time he did a divorce, because someone had to win and someone had to lose.' He thought for a moment. 'Did you tell them he was being followed?'

'I don't know what you're talking about.'

'It's true!' Colin turned to Hawthorne. 'He said he was being followed. He told me when he was here.'

'When was that?' Hawthorne asked.

'He came over the day before my birthday. My birthday's the thirteenth of October and he came over on the twelfth. He bought me a telescope. It's in my bedroom. You can see it if you like.'

'Colin is interested in astronomy,' his mother explained.

'He stayed for tea and that was when he talked about it.' He glared at her accusingly. 'You were here!'

'The two of you were talking for ages. And I didn't hear what he said.'

'Did he describe the man who was following him?' Hawthorne said.

'Not really. No. He said he looked ill. He said that was why he noticed him, because there was something wrong with his face. It was ghastly. He said he'd seen him two or three times.'

'Where?'

'He was sitting at the table. Right where you are now.'

'No. I mean, where had he seen him?'

Colin screwed up his face in concentration. 'Well, it was outside his house at least one of the times. He said he saw him out of one of the upper windows. And he may have been at the office too.'

'You're not making this up, are you, Colin?' Davina asked. 'I'm sure Richard would have said something to me.'

'You were there!' Colin insisted. 'Anyway, he didn't

make a big deal about it. He just said it had happened. That was all.'

'When was the last time you saw your godfather?' Hawthorne asked.

'When I just told you. That was the last time.'

'I saw him more recently than that,' Davina said. 'I was at Heron's Wake last week. I went over with some colour samples for him to choose.'

That reminded me. 'I don't suppose the number one eight two means anything to you?' I asked.

'No. Why?'

Hawthorne was glaring at me. He hated it when I took the initiative. But I plunged on anyway. 'It was written on the wall in green paint,' I explained. 'Where the body was found.'

'Why would anyone do that?' Davina exclaimed.

'Does it mean anything to you?' Hawthorne asked.

'The number? No! I can't imagine . . .' She searched randomly around her as if she might find an answer to the question among the pots and pans, then lit another cigarette.

'Why do you have to smoke so much?' Colin scolded her.

She glanced at him, suddenly angry. 'I'll smoke if I want to. It's after six o'clock. It's adult time.' She blew smoke defiantly. 'Have you finished your homework?'

'No.'

'Then you should be getting on with it. And then have a bath before bed.'

'Mum . . .' He spoke the word in the way that only an adolescent can.

'One hour on the computer. Then I'll come up and see you.' He didn't move so she glared at him. 'Colin! Do as you're told!'

'All right.' He had slumped into the seat and he somehow managed to slump out of it too. He didn't say goodbye to us. He just nodded and went.

'I know he's right about the cigarettes but I hate him going on at me,' Davina said, after he'd gone. She was more relaxed now. She helped herself to some more wine from the fridge, then stood, resting against the counter with the washing machine chugging away behind her. 'And it hasn't been easy for him this last week. He may not seem very upset but he was absolutely devastated when he heard the news.' She had used the same word about herself. 'He's not going to show his feelings in front of you but I don't want you to think he hasn't got any.' She drank and smoked. 'It was awful for him when his father died and I'm not sure how we'd have got through it if it hadn't been for Richard. He became a second father to him . . . and not just with expensive birthday presents. If Colin had problems – at school, for example – he'd sometimes go to Richard before he came to me. This term, for example, he was being bullied. You'd think he could look after himself, the size of him and all that, but he's actually a very gentle boy and some of the others were picking on him. Richard sorted it out.'

'Can you tell us what happened to his father?' Hawthorne asked. 'I understand there was an accident.'

'Yes. To be honest, I don't really like talking about it . . .'

'I'm sure.'

She stood there with the clothes now silent, her glass in one hand, the cigarette in the other. She could see that Hawthorne wasn't going to let go. 'They used to go caving together,' she said. 'They'd been doing it since they were at university. That was where they met. They were at Oxford together. Richard, Charles and Gregory . . .'

'Gregory?'

'Gregory Taylor. He's a finance manager. He lives in Yorkshire.'

That was the county where the accident had happened.

'What did your husband do?' Hawthorne asked.

'He was in marketing.' She didn't go into any more detail and I guessed she still found it painful talking about him. 'They went away for a week every year,' she continued. 'I didn't like it. The very thought of going into a hole in the ground makes me shudder and to be honest with you I'm surprised they were up for it. But it was a chance for the three of them to let their hair down. They didn't just do it in England. They went all over the world. They'd been to France, Switzerland . . . and one year they even went all the way to Belize. They never took wives or partners. Gregory's married and I know Susan doesn't approve. But it would have been foolish to try to stop them. I was just glad when Charlie came home safe.'

She stopped and reached for her wine. She needed it to help her go on.

'Except one year he didn't,' she continued, after she'd taken a big gulp. 'In 2007, they went to a cave system near Ribblehead. It's called the Long Way Hole. There was an investigation afterwards and everyone agreed that they took all the right precautions. They'd made contact with the local caving club and left behind a contact sheet saying where they were going and what time they were expected back. They had spare torches and a medical kit and all the right equipment. Gregory was the most experienced of the three and he was the leader but that was just a formality. All three of them knew what they were doing.'

'So what happened?'

'What happened was that it began to rain. Heavily. This was April. None of the weather forecasters had predicted it but suddenly there was a flood. They were already well into the cave system but the exit was only a quarter of a mile away. They decided they had to get out as quickly as possible and that's what they tried to do.'

She took a deep breath.

'Somehow, Charles got separated from the group. He'd been third in line and when they looked back, he wasn't there. They'd come to a section that the local cavers called Spaghetti Junction and there was a choice of different passageways. He'd taken the wrong one. You have to remember that the situation was very dangerous. The water was rushing towards them and the danger was that if they spent too much time looking for Charles, they'd all drown. Even so, Richard and Gregory turned round. They risked their lives going back to find Charles, calling out to him and trying to find him, even though the passage was completely flooded. In the end, they had to give up. They had no choice. They got out and called for help, which was the right thing to do. But it was much too late.' She took a breath. 'Charles had managed to get himself stuck in what's called a contortion. It's like a narrow tube that connects two passages, one above the other. He was still there when the water came pouring in.' Another pause. 'He drowned.'

'The body was recovered?' Hawthorne asked. He took out his own pack of cigarettes, removed one and lit it.

She nodded. 'Early the next day.'

'Did you talk to the others? Richard Pryce and Gregory Taylor?'

'Of course I talked to them . . . at the inquest. We didn't say much. We were all too devastated – but they were the main witnesses. In the end, the verdict was that nobody was responsible. It was just an accident.' She sighed. 'Gregory took some of the blame . . . which is to say, he blamed himself. After all, he was the team leader. But how could he have known it was going to rain so heavily? How could any of them?'

'What about you?' Hawthorne asked. 'Did you blame Gregory Taylor for what happened?' He paused. 'Or Richard Pryce?'

Davina fell silent. Behind her the machine had gone into full spin and when she finally spoke, her voice was so soft that I could barely hear it. 'I never blamed him,' she said. 'But I did resent him . . . for a time, anyway. After all, he was alive and Charlie was dead and actually the trip had been Richard's idea. He had been much keener on it than Charlie and so to that extent, I suppose he was to blame.' She gulped down some wine, then, lowering her glass, continued: 'I loved Charlie very much. He was a wonderful man, fun to be with, a great dad. We'd wanted to have more children together after we had Colin but somehow it never happened. After he died, I felt a terrible emptiness and it was only natural that I should have directed my feelings at Richard. It didn't matter how kind he was to me. I thought he was buying his way out of jail, if you know what I mean. The more he gave me, the angrier I got.

'In a way, it was Colin who persuaded me I was wrong. He never saw it that way and when he and Richard were together . . . I could actually see them bonding. Colin needed a dad. And that's exactly what Richard became.'

She glanced into the wine glass. It was empty.

'One night, Richard and I got very drunk together – this was before he stopped drinking – and he actually broke down and all the pain and the guilt and the unhappiness that he had been feeling came flooding out. I realised then that I'd been unfair to him and that in a way he had been as much a victim of what had happened as Colin and me . . . and even Charlie. After that, I sort of gave in. I let him help me. When he offered to take over Colin's school fees, I didn't argue. Charlie had left me a bit of money but not a lot. There wasn't any point being cynical about what Richard was doing and anyway, I gave him the benefit of the doubt. He really was acting for the best.'

'Were you aware that he'd left you money in his will?'

'Yes. I don't know how much. But he always said I'd be all right if anything happened to him. He was very rich and Stephen must make a fortune from his gallery. I'm going in to see Oliver Masefield tomorrow. He'll tell me what happens next.' She looked at her watch. 'I hope you don't mind but if you don't have any more questions, I really have to get on. I want to make sure Colin is doing his homework. And I have to do some mood boards for a client . . .'

'Of course.' Hawthorne got to his feet. The cigarette was still in his hand. 'We may need to talk to you again.'

'I'll do anything I can to help.'

She waited until we had left the kitchen, then followed us out. We said goodbye at the door, then stepped back out into the street. It was quite dark by now, although

Priory Gardens always did seem quite a shadowy place, tucked away beneath the hill. We walked back to the station. For a while, Hawthorne didn't speak.

'What's the matter?' I asked.

'Tony, mate, I've told you this before. I don't like you asking questions. That's not why you're there.'

'Oh for heaven's sake!' I replied. 'What possible harm could I have done?'

'I don't know yet. But let's not forget what happened last time. You asked one stupid question and you almost destroyed the whole bloody case!'

'You're not telling me you think Davina Richardson had anything to do with the death, are you?'

'I'm not telling you anything, mate. I just don't want you to interfere.'

We entered the station. I plucked an *Evening Standard* off the pile, which was my way of saying that I didn't expect there to be any conversation on the journey. It was a redundant gesture anyway as we took different Tubes. Hawthorne left first on his way to Waterloo. I took the King's Cross branch. I would change there for Farringdon.

But we did have one last exchange, standing together on the platform.

'Colin said that Richard Pryce was being followed

by someone,' I said. 'Do you think it could have been the same man that Adrian Lockwood told us about, the one who broke into his office?'

Hawthorne shrugged. 'The kid said there was something wrong with his face . . .'

'He said that was what Richard told him.'

'Well, if that was the case, you'd have thought the receptionist at Lockwood's office would have noticed.'

'She said he had a skin problem.' It wasn't quite the same thing but it was close enough. 'Maybe that was why he was wearing the blue glasses. You said it yourself. He could have worn them on purpose to distract attention.'

'It's possible, I suppose. But Colin actually said something much more interesting.'

'What was that?'

'He used to read your books.'

Was Hawthorne trying to tell me something or was he just being annoying? Or both? I wasn't going to find out because that was when the first Tube came exploding out of the tunnel and ground to a halt along the platform's edge.

'I'll see you tomorrow,' Hawthorne said.

The doors slid shut behind him.

My Tube came four minutes later. I found a seat and opened the newspaper I had picked up. I read the front cover and the first couple of pages. I'd just reached Kentish Town when a tiny article, buried in the corner, caught my eye.

DEAD MAN IDENTIFIED

Police have named the man who was killed at King's Cross station on Saturday 26 October when he fell in front of an oncoming train. Gregory Taylor, who worked as a finance manager, was from Ingleton in Yorkshire. He was married with two teenaged daughters. The inquiry continues.

9
PUT

I've always had a fascination with secret passage-ways and places you're not allowed to go. When I was a child, my parents used to take me to expensive hotels and I still remember sneaking into the service areas: I loved the way the plush carpets and chande-liers suddenly stopped and everything was grubby and utilitarian. In Stanmore, north London, my sister and I would crawl under the fence to sneak around the of-fice complex next door to our home and even today, in a museum, a department store, a theatre, a Tube sta-tion, I'll find myself wondering what goes on behind those locked doors. I sometimes think that it's actually a good definition of creative writing: to unlock doors and take readers through to the other side.

So I felt an almost childish excitement the next day

when Hawthorne and I turned up at the offices of the British Transport Police at Euston station. Here was a small, nondescript door that I must have passed dozens of times without noticing, tucked away in a distant corner just past the Left Luggage Office and opposite the entrance to platforms 16–18. Of course it was going to be disappointing on the other side but that wasn't the point. It was somewhere I had never been.

The door opened into a reception area where we were greeted by a tired-looking woman in uniform, sitting behind a wire-mesh screen. Hawthorne gave her the name of our contact, Detective Constable James McCoy, and almost immediately he appeared, a thickset, square-jawed man with a military haircut and – jeans, sweatshirt, anorak – civilian clothes.

'Mr Hawthorne?'

'Yes.'

'Come on through . . .'

We filled in a form and another door buzzed open, taking us into a maze of narrow corridors and tiny offices that extended much further than I would have thought possible. Everything was remarkably shabby. We followed a blue carpet covered in all manner of stains past a softly vibrating drinks dispenser and on round another corner. Some of the rooms were hardly bigger than cupboards. A criminal being interviewed there would

be able to touch knees with the officer who had arrested him. We passed an incident room and I glimpsed
half a dozen men and women examining printouts and
transferring the contents to the whiteboards that surrounded them. Forget modern technology. This might
be the front line against crime and terrorism but it was
all resolutely old-fashioned, with chunky Hewlett Packard computers on Formica-covered desks and a whole
crowd of cheap swivel chairs. There were no windows.
This really was a world apart.

Hawthorne had arranged the meeting. I hadn't
needed to tell him about the newspaper article. He'd
seen it himself and had called me that same evening. I
hadn't spoken to Cara Grunshaw either. I hadn't forgotten the way she had threatened me but I'd decided to
leave any further contact for at least a week, by which
time, hopefully, Hawthorne would have solved the case
anyway. Or maybe I would. I was still quite attracted to
the idea that I would be the one who made sense of it all
and that when the suspects were gathered together in
one room in the final chapter, I'd be the one doing the
talking.

There was a second man waiting for us in the statement room. This was a uniformed officer, barely out of
his twenties, who had been brought across to talk to us.
His name was Ahmed Salim and he had been the first

to deal with the body. I was puzzled to find myself in Euston, incidentally, when the death had happened in King's Cross, but apparently there was no CID division there. As McCoy explained, he was responsible for all incidents north of the Central line, travelling as far as Stratford East and Chelmsford. He had now been put in charge of the inquiry into Gregory Taylor's death.

This, according to the two men, was what had happened.

Gregory Taylor had come to London on the morning of Saturday 26 October, one day before Richard Pryce had died. He had taken an early train from Horton-in-Ribblesdale – there is no station in Ingleton – and was now on his way back home. The station was unusually crowded for a Saturday. There had been a football match that day – Leeds vs Arsenal – and the platform was jammed with supporters. Normally, Virgin won't allow passengers through the ticket barrier until the train has pulled in, but they change the rules when there's a major disruption and as it happened there had been a signal failure at Peterborough and the service was running late. So there were up to four hundred people waiting as the train drew in.

Taylor reached the platform at twelve minutes past six. He was in no hurry. He had bought himself a coffee at Starbucks and a thick doorstop of a book at W. H.

Smith. This was *Prisoners of Blood*, the third volume in the Doomworld series by the bestselling author Mark Belladonna. By coincidence, I knew the series because I'd recently been approached by Sky to adapt it for TV. Doomworld had been compared (unfavourably) to *Game of Thrones*, which was then in its third season. It was a fantasy version of England in the time of King Arthur, weaving magic and mystery with really quite extreme levels of violence and pornography. The *Daily Mail* had branded the books 'pure porn poison', which the publishers had cheekily reprinted on the cover. I'd read about half of the first volume but I hadn't really enjoyed it and it had been an easy decision to turn the show down.

The third volume had just arrived in the shops and it was on special offer. Taylor bought it and received a free Kit Kat and a bottle of water.

He went through the ticket barrier and started walking up the platform, staying behind the yellow line but still fairly close to the edge. At the same time, the delayed train appeared in the distance, moving towards him. Police Constable Salim told us what happened next.

'I'd just arrived at the station for the evening shift when it all kicked off. I knew we had a PUT before I got the call over my radio . . .'

'What's a PUT?' I asked.

'Person Under a Train.'

'We also call them "one unders",' McCoy added.

'I could hear screaming,' Salim went on. 'And the driver had sounded his horn, which is standard practice. So I knew something was up and I went straight to the platform, which is how I came to be the first on the scene.

'My immediate thought was that it must be a suicide. But King's Cross is an end-of-line station so we don't get that many of those. Anyway, there's the Harry Potter experience on the main concourse and that cheers people up. So maybe it was an accidental – but that doesn't happen very often either. I don't know. I just wanted to get there and see what I could do to help.

'Well, it turned out that the poor guy had made it about two-thirds of the way up the platform before he'd slipped over the side, straight into the path of the oncoming train. He might have been lucky. He might just have been injured – badly. But I'm afraid it wasn't like that. He'd fallen across both rails and he'd lost both his legs and he'd been decapitated, so he wasn't going anywhere in a hurry.'

My iPhone was on low battery and I was writing all this down. He waited for me to catch up. Both McCoy and Salim knew I was a writer and they were enjoying talking to me. It's funny how many people are keen to have their work described in books.

'My first job was to clear the area. There were a lot of people screaming. A couple of them had been sick. There was one woman in shock. And of course there were the usual perverts filming the whole thing on their mobile phones. Most of them were wearing football kit – scarves, hoodies, beanies . . . that sort of thing. It was hard to tell who was who. I started to move people back and I told them not to leave the immediate area. We'd need to take names and addresses, witness statements and all the rest of it. By now, quite a few more officers had arrived and I knew BT Central Control were on to it. The London Ambulance Service and the Air Ambulance Service would be on the way. My biggest worry was that someone was going to have a heart attack. It's happened before and it just makes everything twice as complicated.

'We managed to get a cordon up and we had the environment under control, but now we had to get the deceased out from under the train. And we only had forty-five minutes.'

'Why was that?' I asked. I was fascinated by the whole procedure.

'It's the cost,' Salim explained. 'When this sort of thing happens, we have to clear the platforms and keep the trains running. We can't afford to hang around.'

'Was it you who got the body out?' Hawthorne asked.

Salim nodded. 'Yeah. You get a fifty-quid bonus if you're up for that and I'm saving up for a holiday with my mum. It could have been worse. The train hadn't been moving very fast so there were no body parts flying into the air or anything like that. And there was no need for a specialist unit to lift up the train. The driver was pretty shaken up but I got him to shunt the train back and it was fairly easy after that. We got the body out and I bagged up the hands and all the rest of it. After that, DC McCoy arrived and he took over.'

McCoy did the same now.

'There wasn't a lot left for me to do,' he said. 'I got the dead man's ID from his wallet and I got the North Yorkshire police to send round a couple of PCs to inform the widow. She was at home with two young daughters and I didn't want her to hear it over the phone. She left for London straight away and I actually saw her the day after. Susan Taylor. Totally shocked. Couldn't believe it had happened. Her husband hadn't been well and the two of them had financial difficulties, which is to say they were skint like everyone else, but there was no history of depression. In fact, she said his trip had been a big success. The two of them had booked a restaurant, planning a celebration on Sunday night.' He drew a breath. 'Well, that didn't happen.'

'What was he doing in London?' Hawthorne asked.

'Seeing a friend.'

Hawthorne waited for more information, then saw that McCoy had nothing more to add.

'That's all she told me,' he explained. 'I interviewed her: she was staying at the Holiday Inn off the Euston Road. But I couldn't get much sense out of her. The poor woman was in pieces. Her husband under a train! The two of them had been married twenty years. She had to ID the body and that was horrible for her. I'd already decided it was an unexplained. I didn't think there was anything much she could add.'

'An unexplained?' I jotted down the word.

'We have three classifications. Unexplained, explained and suspicious. There was certainly nothing suspicious as far as I could see, but even with the CCTV images there was no obvious reason why Mr Taylor had taken that fall.'

'There was that witness statement,' Salim reminded him.

'What was that?' Hawthorne asked.

McCoy glanced at Salim, perhaps a little annoyed

that he'd been contradicted by a junior officer. 'Just before he fell, Taylor cried out. It was only two words. "Look out!" But quite a few people heard him.'

'Someone had bumped into him?'

'They'd have had to bump into him pretty hard to project him out like that. He was almost horizontal when he hit the tracks. At the same time, quite a few of the people waiting for that train had had their fair share of booze. You know what it's like after a football game.'

'Could he have been deliberately pushed?'

'Nobody saw anything. They just heard him shout and then it was over. But we've got the CCTV images. You can look for yourself.' McCoy had a laptop computer. He swung it round so we could see the screen. At the same time, he explained: 'The first thing I did when I got to the station was to call up Alpha Victor in Victoria. They had the images downloaded to me in no time. Thanks to them, we were able to follow him back to the Starbucks and the newsagent. We saw him arrive at the station.'

'How did he get there?'

'He took the Tube down from Highgate.'

Highgate. It couldn't be a coincidence.

'Here . . .' McCoy hit the button.

The images we manufacture on television and the big screen are nothing like the real thing. The pictures recorded at King's Cross Station were indistinct and grainy, as if a layer of dust had deposited itself on the lens. The camera was in the wrong position, too high up and at an oblique angle. The colours were muted, slightly off-kilter. The navy and gold of the Leeds United football strip, for example, were more nightfall and French mustard. Gregory Taylor's death was seen at its most mundane, stripped of any art or excitement. Here one minute, gone the next.

At first, I couldn't see the train, just a large crowd, many of them football supporters, milling around.

'That's Taylor there,' McCoy said.

Sure enough, a blurry figure was making its way along the outside of the platform, close to the edge but not so close as to put himself in danger. He wasn't in a hurry. There was no sound with the image and he was very small and far away but I got the impression that he was politely asking people to allow him to pass. Then three things happened almost simultaneously. Gregory Taylor disappeared from sight, swallowed up by the crowd just as the bright red Virgin train appeared. It had been moving quite slowly in real life but it seemed to take no time at all to reach the edge of the screen. Then Gregory fell in front of it. His back was to the camera but even if we'd been able to see it, it would have been impossible to make out any expression on his face. He was little more than a paint stroke, brushed across the canvas. He plunged down and disappeared a second time. The train continued implacably, crushing him. There was a few seconds' delay before people realised what had just happened. Then the crowd recoiled, forming a pattern like an exploding sun. I could easily imagine the screams.

'These are from the camera on the front of the train,' McCoy said.

The same sequence but seen this time from the driver's point of view. The tracks stretched out ahead. The waiting passengers were over to the right. Then something – it could have been anything – scythed through the image. That was Gregory Taylor in the last second of his life. The driver might have hit the brakes but the train didn't seem to slow down.

I had just watched a man die.

McCoy closed his laptop, folding the lid down. 'The coroner at King's Cross gave us permission to move the body and he was taken off to the nearest mortuary. I've handed the file to the Fatality Investigation Team and of course there'll be an inquest. But in all honesty, I can't see any evidence of foul play. I'm ninety per cent sure it was an accident. Just one of those things.'

'Did he have enemies?' Salim asked. 'Is that why you're investigating?'

'He may have been involved in a murder that took place in Hampstead the next day,' Hawthorne said.

'Well at least he's one suspect you can cross off your list,' Salim muttered, reflectively. 'He wouldn't have been up for anything.'

We left the offices and walked out to the area in front of the concourse. As soon as we were in the fresh air, Hawthorne lit a cigarette. I could see him turning over everything he had just heard. There were times where he reminded me of a scientist on the threshold of a great discovery or an archaeologist about to open a tomb. He showed almost no emotion but I could feel his energy and excitement.

'What do you think?' I asked.

'He was in Highgate.'

'Maybe he'd come to London to see Davina Richardson.'

'Or Richard Pryce. You could walk to either of their places from the same station.'

'Well, it can't be a coincidence. He died almost exactly twenty-four hours before the murder.'

'You're right there, Tony. It's not a coincidence.'

He smoked his cigarette in silence. Euston is one of the ugliest stations in London and I felt grubby even standing there, surrounded by fast-food restaurants and concrete. Finally, Hawthorne spoke. 'Ingleton.' The way he spoke that single word, I got the impression he'd been there before. And that he hadn't liked it.

'What about it?'

'Are you busy at the moment?'

'You know I am.'

'We're going to have to go there.' Again, he wasn't enthusiastic.

He finished his cigarette and we went into the ticket office and bought the tickets, leaving the next day.

10
Ingleton, Yorkshire

Hawthorne wasn't in a good mood when we met at King's Cross station the next day – but then, of course, there was nothing unusual about that. When we were together his manner ranged from distant and off-putting to downright rude and I often thought that he had spent so long investigating murderers that some of their sociopathy had rubbed off on him. There were times when I wondered if he wasn't simply playing the role of the hard-bitten detective . . . that he slipped into it just as he did his collection of white shirts and dark suits. Why was he so reluctant to tell me anything about himself? Why did he never talk about the films he had seen, the people he'd met, what he'd done at the weekend or anything outside the business that had brought us together? What was he afraid of?

Even so, I had been hoping that this trip to York-shire would give him a chance to unwind. After all, we would be spending at least four hours in close proximity and surely we might bond over a Virgin coffee and a bacon sandwich? Some chance. As the train pulled out, he sat hunched up, gazing morosely out of the window. There was something in his manner, in those searching brown eyes of his and the tiny, old-fashioned suitcase that he had brought with him, that made me think of a child being evacuated in the war. When I asked him if he wanted something to eat, he just shook his head. I had bought us first-class tickets, by the way. I needed to work and I thought Hawthorne would appreciate the extra space. He hadn't even noticed.

It was clear that he didn't want to leave London. Ten minutes later, when we had picked up speed and were rattling through the northern suburbs, he was still staring at the flats and offices that were already thinning out. The green spaces in between seemed to alarm him and it occurred to me that apart from one day in Kent, we had never left the city. I had never seen him wearing jeans or trainers. Did he even take exercise? I wondered.

A ticket collector came along, and I used the interruption to tackle Hawthorne, albeit gently. 'You're very quiet,' I said. 'Is something wrong?'

'No.'

'I'm looking forward to a couple of days in the countryside. It's nice to get out.'

'You know Yorkshire?'

'I was at university in York.'

He knew that perfectly well. He knew everything about me. He must have meant something else by the question and, running it back, I picked up the dread in his voice and understood what he was implying. 'You don't like Yorkshire,' I said.

'Not really.'

'Why is that?'

He hesitated. 'I spent a bit of time there.'

'When?'

'It doesn't matter.'

He pulled a paperback book out of his pocket and slapped it down on the table, signalling that the conversation was at an end. I looked down and saw that he had chosen *A Study in Scarlet* by Sir Arthur Conan Doyle. 'Is that for your book club?' I asked.

'That's right.' There was something else he wanted to tell me but we were another ten miles up the track before he forced it out. 'They want you to come to the next session.'

'Who?'

'The book club.' I looked blank so he added, 'You've

written about Sherlock Holmes. That last novel of yours. They want to know what you think.'

'Of course,' I said. 'I was just wondering how they knew about me . . . I mean, the fact that you know me.'

'Well, I didn't tell them.'

'I'm sure.'

Hawthorne drew a breath. I could tell that he wanted a cigarette. 'Someone saw you when you came into the building,' he explained.

'River Court?'

'Yes. When you came up in the lift.'

I remembered the young man in the wheelchair and there had also been the married couple I had met on the ground floor. I've occasionally been on TV and my photograph is on my book jackets. It's possible they would have recognised me.

'They asked me to ask you to come,' Hawthorne said.

'Is that what's worrying you? I'll be happy to.'

'I was worried that was what you were going to say.'

Hawthorne opened his book and began to read while at the same time I took out a pen and started working on my script. In 'Sunflower', Foyle was asked to protect an ex-Nazi living in London at the end of the war and this led to his discovery of a massacre that had taken place in France. As usual, there were production problems. I had written a climax, a bloody execution in a field of brilliant yellow sunflowers, but this being October there were none growing anywhere in the UK. Plastic flowers wouldn't work. CGI would be too expensive. So far, I had resisted attempts to change the title to 'Parsnip'.

We changed trains at Leeds and from that point I found myself entranced by the increasingly beautiful countryside. The stations became smaller and more isolated and the landscape more unspoiled until by the time we reached Gargrave and Hellifield it was as if we'd arrived in another world, one perhaps imagined by Tolkien. An autumn sun was shining and the hills, as green and as rolling as I'd ever seen, were stitched out with drystone walls, hedgerows and sheep. It made me wonder why I spent ten hours a day, every day, in a room in the middle of a city when there was all of this only a few hours away.

None of it had any impact on Hawthorne. He continued to read his book and when he did look out of the window it was with a grim acquiescence, as if his very worst fears were being realised. My guess was that he had been here or somewhere nearby for part of his childhood. He'd said he'd spent 'a bit of time' in Yorkshire and since he had lived in London for at least the past twelve years – he had an eleven-year-old son

in Gants Hill – it must have been a while ago. He definitely didn't want to be here now. It was fascinating to
see him so out of sorts.

We reached Ribblehead, a tiny station that seemed
to have no reason to be there as, apart from the station
house itself and a single pub/hotel, there were virtually
no other buildings for as far as the eye could see. This
was where we would be staying the night. We were the
only people to get off the train, which chuffed off, leaving us on a long, empty platform with a single figure
waiting for us at the far end. Hawthorne had made all
the arrangements from London and I knew that he had
been in contact with the local cave rescue team. The
man waiting for us was called Dave Gallivan. He was
the duty controller who had been called out when Charlie Richardson had gone missing in Long Way Hole and
it had been he who had found the body.

We walked towards each other. The landscape was
so huge and the station so deserted that I was reminded
of cowboys in a Wild West film squaring up for a
shoot-out. As we drew closer he revealed himself to be
a pleasant-looking man in his fifties. He was tough and
muscular, with thick, white hair and the ruddy com-
plexion that comes from living life outdoors, particularly in the Yorkshire Dales with all their extremes of
weather.

'You Hawthorne?' he demanded when he reached us.

'That's me.' Hawthorne nodded.

'You want to check into your room? You need the toilet or anything like that?'

'No. We're all right.'

'Let's go then.'

Nobody had asked me but I wasn't surprised. Why would I have expected otherwise?

Ingleton was an attractive village that had managed to wrap itself into a rather less attractive town. It was built on the edge of what might have been a quarry with steps and ornamental gardens leading steeply down so that as we drove along the high street we were actually far above the tiled roofs and chimneys of many of the houses below. A huge viaduct, now disused, extended over to one side; looking at it, I wondered if the navvies who had sweated and sworn over its construction had had any idea that one day it would be considered beautiful. We continued past a café, two shops specialising in potholing books and equipment, and then, quite oddly, a disproportionately large nursing home that might have owed something to Sherlock Holmes. It reminded me that Doyle's mother had once lived nearby and that the writer himself had come here often.

Susan Taylor lived about two minutes up the hill in

a 1920s end-of-terrace house that had been vandalised with a modern front door, double-glazed windows and, projecting out of the back, a really nasty conservatory, but then driving through Ingleton it was clear that very few of the residents had any time for architectural nice-ties. There was something very masculine about the building – its solid walls, its very squareness – and yet it was now occupied by a widow and her two young daughters. Charlotte Brontë might well have used it as a setting for a novel. But she'd have had to turn a blind eye to the conservatory.

Dave Gallivan knocked on the door and without waiting for an answer opened it and went in. We fol-lowed him into a bright, airy home, simply furnished with sisal mats on the floor, dried bulrushes in vases, photographs of caves and crevices on the walls. On one side, a door opened into a living room with an upright piano and a fireplace with more dried flowers in the hearth. A cat was lying asleep on a rug. We turned the other way and went into the kitchen, where Susan was standing, waiting for us with an enormous knife in her hand.

For that reason, her first appearance struck me as quite menacing although in fact we had simply caught her preparing vegetables for dinner. There were chunks of carrot and potato spread out in front of her and as we came in she used the blade to sweep them off the chopping board and into a casserole.

It had been five days since she had heard that she had lost not just her husband but her entire world and she was still in shock. She wasn't just unsmiling. She barely seemed to notice that we had come into the room. She had a square face with skin the colour and texture of damp clay. Her hair was drab and lifeless. She was wearing a dress that was either too long or too short but looked just wrong, cut off at her calves, which were stout and beefy. She didn't speak as Gallivan ushered us in but I could tell at once that she wished we weren't there.

'Sue – this is Mr Hawthorne,' Gallivan announced.

'Oh yes. I suppose you'll be having some tea, will you?'

I wasn't sure if this was an invitation to make us some or a weary prediction as to what might be about to happen but it was uttered with an almost startling lack of enthusiasm.

To my surprise, Hawthorne replied with alacrity. 'A cup of tea. That would be lovely, Mrs Taylor.'

'I'll make it.' Gallivan made his way over to the kettle. He clearly knew his way around the kitchen.

Susan put down the knife and sat at the kitchen table. She was in her forties but looked a lot older, a punchbag of a woman whose every movement told us she'd had more than enough. We sat opposite her and she examined us for the first time.

'I hope this won't take too long,' she said. She had a solid Yorkshire accent. 'I've got to finish the supper and the girls will be home from school. The week's been difficult enough already. I don't want them to find you here.'

'I'm very sorry for your loss, Mrs Taylor,' Hawthorne said.

'Did you ever meet my Greg?'

'No.'

'And you've never met me, so don't bother me with your condolences. I've got no use for them.'

'We need to know what happened to him.'

'You know what happened to him. He fell under a train.'

Hawthorne looked apologetic. 'That may not be the case . . .'

'What are you saying?' Her eyes flared briefly.

Hawthorne examined her for a moment before continuing. 'I don't want to upset you, Mrs Taylor, but we haven't discounted the possibility that he was pushed.'

I was surprised that he had put it as baldly as that and I wondered what her reaction would be. She hadn't had the time to come to terms with the fact that he was dead, let alone that he might have been murdered. It seemed insensitive even by his standards.

In fact, she seemed remarkably unconcerned. 'Who would want to do a thing like that?' she said. 'I can't think of anyone who would want to hurt Greg. And nobody knew he was going to London except me. He didn't even tell the girls.'

'Why was he in London?'

The kettle had boiled. Susan didn't answer until Gallivan had made the tea and brought it over to the table. He had left the bags in the mugs with the little label attached by a thread hanging over the sides.

'He was ill,' she said. 'He needed money.'

'How ill?' Again, Hawthorne wasn't giving her any leeway.

'Seriously ill. But don't you be getting any wrong ideas. He was going to be all right. That was the reason he was there.'

'So who did he go to see?'

'Let me explain to you, Mr Hawthorne. I'll tell it to you my way, if you don't mind. It'll make it easier for you and less painful for me if I don't have to answer every one of your damn questions.'

Hawthorne took out his cigarettes. 'Do you mind if I smoke?' he asked.

'You can smoke all you like. But not in my house.'

She stared moodily at her tea, then picked up her cup and sipped without removing the bag. I did the same. Gallivan had added a couple of spoonfuls of sugar without asking. He was hovering over the kettle, leaving the three of us grouped at the table.

'When I first met him, Greg was an accountant,' she began. 'He did all right for himself. He was working in a big firm in Leeds and he was climbing the ladder, if you know what I mean. I had bar work and that's how the two of us met. We went out. We got married. We had kids. But he was never happy in the city. He loved being out on the Dales – hiking, birding, sleeping out under the stars. And not just on the Dales. Underneath them. He was a caver through and through. He was coming here every other weekend and to hell with what I had to say about the matter, so in the end it made sense to sell up and move here. He took a job at Atkinsons, even though it was less well paid.'

'They're a builders' merchant,' Gallivan muttered from the side.

'That's right. He was their finance manager.'

'Do you have a photograph of your husband?' I asked. I had no idea what he looked like and I thought it would be useful to know, if she was going to talk about him.

She glanced at me as if I had offended her, then

nodded very briefly. Gallivan came over to the table, carrying a photograph in a plastic frame. It showed a large, smiling man with a rugby player's face, complete with broken nose. He was wearing a brightly coloured anorak. At least half the picture was taken up by his beard, which seemed to be exploding out of his face. He was grinning and making a thumbs up to the camera: one of life's celebrants.

'We scraped by, Greg and I. We weren't rich, but you don't need money in a place like this. I'm not complaining. We had our friends. June and Maisie – our two girls. And of course the Dales. I work three days a week at the nursing home. Ingleton's not a bad place once you get used to it. Too many tourists in the summer and you can't move in the high street, but that's the same all over the Dales. We liked it best in the winter. You should see this place in the snow. It's beautiful.

'Then Greg got ill. It started about six months ago and of course we didn't think anything of it at first. He was having difficulty walking, particularly up and down stairs. I persuaded him to go to the doctor but she just said he had a touch of arthritis in his knees and packed him off with anti-inflammatory pills . . . silly cow. But then it was in his arms and his neck. Greg tried not to say too much about it but it just got worse and worse. His neck was the worst part of it. He started getting bruises on his skin. He had trouble breathing. We went back to the doctor and this time she sent us down to Leeds, but it was still a while before they were able to diagnose what he had.'

She paused. Her eyes looked into the middle-distance.

'It's called Ehlers-Danlos syndrome. The first time I heard it, it sounded like double Dutch but that's its name. EDS for short. He always referred to it as Ed. "Ed's here." That's what he'd say. Greg always tried to make a joke about everything.'

'He did that,' Gallivan agreed.

'But this was nothing to laugh about. There wasn't anything funny at all. Ed was going to kill him. It was as simple as that. His neck was dislocating, which meant that his brainstem couldn't function. Another few months and he'd have been bedridden. He'd have seizures. He'd become paralysed. And then he'd die.'

She had a way of turning experiences into sound bites. She had compartmentalised her husband's slow death in exactly the same way as her courtship and marriage. This followed by this and then that.

'EDS had a cure,' she went on. 'There was some support group that got in touch with us and they told us about it . . . an operation. It would fuse all the vertebrae together so that his neck would be stabilised. It would save his life. The trouble was, you couldn't get it on the NHS. It was too expensive and too complicated. Greg would have to go to Spain. The doctors out there had had a lot of success but it wasn't going to be cheap. With the flights and the treatment and the hospital and everything else, it would cost him £200,000.

'We didn't have anything like that. We've got this house but there's a mortgage on it and Greg was never any good at saving money, which is strange because money was what his work was all about. He did have a life insurance policy worth a quarter of a million pounds: he'd taken it out when he was in Leeds. But that was no bloody good at all because he'd have to die first to claim it. So what was the point in that?'

'But he had a rich friend in London,' Hawthorne said.

'That's right. You've got there ahead of me. He'd been to Oxford University when he was nineteen and he made two good friends there . . . Richard Pryce and Charlie Richardson. Dicky and Tricky, he used to call them. They used to go caving together – that was how they met – and it became a sort of ritual, all the boys together. My Greg used to look forward to seeing them. It was the high point of the year. Most often they stayed in England but there were times they went to Europe and even to South America. And here's the thing. They knew he couldn't afford exotic holidays. But when they went long haul, they'd put their hands in their pockets just to help him out a little. None of them ever said as much and Greg didn't like to talk about it – he was a Yorkshireman and he had his pride – but he would never have been able to do it without them.

'That all came to an end when Charlie died at the Long Way Hole back in 2007. Richard was here for the inquest but he and Greg never saw each other after that. Maybe it was that they both felt guilty about what had happened and couldn't look each other in the eye, although there was no reason for that as they were both exonerated. Dave here was a witness and he was the first person to tell them that no one had done anything wrong. It was just one of those things. An accident.'

Gallivan had been watching her intently as she spoke, but, hearing his name, he turned away. It was as if he didn't want to be involved.

'It was me who persuaded Greg to go down to London and talk to Richard,' she went on. 'Richard had done all right for himself as a high-class lawyer. He had houses in London and in the country. Maybe he wouldn't be able to give all the money but if he put his

hand in his pocket he could get us started and somehow the two of us would find a way to raise the rest.
Crowdfunding or something like that. Greg didn't like
the idea. He thought it was over as far as he and Richard
were concerned. They hadn't spoken for six years.'

'He went down on the Saturday,' Hawthorne said.

'That's right. I drove him to the station myself. I'd
told Greg in no uncertain terms – I'd divorce him if he
didn't get on that train. And I'd get Richard Pryce to
represent me in court. He laughed at that even though
it was hurting him to laugh by then. That was the last
time I saw him, first thing in the morning, on the platform at Ribblehead. He was only going to be in London
a few hours. I expected him home for tea.'

'Richard Pryce refused to help,' I said.

I was quite sure that was what she would tell us. It
was the only way this made any sense. Richard hadn't
wanted to provide the money. Greg had thrown himself under a train. And Susan had been in London the
following day. Maybe she was the one who had killed
Richard.

'That's what you'd expect – but you couldn't be more
wrong,' Susan replied, tartly. 'He was a good man,
Richard Pryce. Maybe he blamed himself for what had
happened at Long Way Hole. Like I told you, my Greg

blamed himself too. But they had never blamed each other. They made the decision to get out of there together and everyone agreed it was the right decision.'

She looked to Dave Gallivan for confirmation but he was still looking away.

'Greg had arranged to see him at his home up in Hampstead,' she continued. 'That would have been about lunchtime. Richard had said he'd be on his own. Well, I don't know the long and the short of it, but he took Greg in like the six years had never happened and they were the best of friends again. He listened to what Greg had to say and he agreed not just to pay £20,000 or £50,000 but to put his hand in his pocket for the whole lot. That was the sort of man he was. He was a saint.'

'How do you know this, Mrs Taylor?' Hawthorne asked.

'Greg telephoned me.' She looked him straight in the eye, at the same time rummaging in her pocket. Finally, she took out a mobile phone and laid it on the table. 'I was driving when he called. I take June to her dance class on Saturday afternoons. He should have remembered that. So he left a message.'

She reached out and touched a couple of buttons. We had seen the dead man's picture. Now we heard his voice.

'Hello, love. I've just left. Richard was fantastic. I can't believe it. He took me into his house – you should have seen it, by the way – and we had a cup of tea and . . . anyway, he says he may be able to pay for the whole thing. All of it. Can you believe it? It's like he wants to make up for what happened all those years ago. I told him how much it was going to cost but he says his company has a fund for just this sort of thing and—' The voice broke off. 'I'm heading back to King's Cross now. I'll call you when I'm on the train or you try me. Let's go out Sunday night. Over to the Marton Arms. We've actually got something to celebrate. I'll talk to you later. All right? I love you.'

There was a faint click and silence.

'The police took a recording of that,' Susan said. 'I never want to lose it. We spoke again when he arrived at the station but that's the last memory I have of his voice. And he sent me this . . .'

She spun the phone round to show us a photograph that Gregory Taylor had taken – a selfie. He was standing on a road that I immediately recognised. It was Hornsey Lane in Highgate. The Hornsey Lane Bridge, which runs high above the Archway Road, was just behind him. He was smiling.

'That's the one thing that consoles me in all this,' Susan went on. 'When he died, he couldn't have been happier. He was on top of the world. He thought he was going to be all right.'

Those words set off another thought in my head. Gregory Taylor wasn't going to be all right. The operation would never happen. Could that be why Pryce was killed? Could it actually have been to prevent the payment being made?

Hawthorne seemed to be thinking along the same lines. 'Your husband was in a good mood when he was on his way home,' he said. 'So what do you think happened at King's Cross?'

'That's your job to find out,' Susan replied. 'I have no idea and the police won't show me the CCTV. But they say there were a lot of Leeds supporters on the platform. They'd been drinking.' She clutched her telephone as if it was a sacred relic containing the ashes of the man she had loved. For the first time I saw tears in her eyes. 'I don't even want to think about it. And now I've told you everything that happened, so if you don't mind . . .'

Gallivan stepped forward as if to show us out but Hawthorne wasn't moving. 'You had to go down to London,' he said.

'I went there on Sunday morning. I met a police officer, a man called McCoy. Dave here looked after the girls.'

'You identified the body.'

'They showed me photographs, yes.'

'When did you get back?' There could only be one reason why Hawthorne was asking her this. Susan Taylor had been in London when Richard Pryce was killed! But there was no possible way she could have had anything to do with it. That made no sense at all.

'I stayed over until Monday. They put me up in a hotel near the station. A horrible place – but it was too late to catch the train.'

'What did you do on Sunday night?'

'I went dancing and then out to dinner.' She scowled. 'What do you think I did? I sat on my own and counted the hours until I could leave.'

She would have seen us out then and there but Hawthorne still hadn't finished with her. 'There is one more thing, Mrs Taylor,' he said. He was completely unapologetic. 'I need to ask you about Long Way Hole.'

'I can tell you about that,' Gallivan said.

'I'd like to hear it from Mrs Taylor.'

'It was six years ago.'

'You said that Richard Pryce and your husband never blamed each other. But maybe someone else did.'

Her eyes started. 'Why do you say that?'

'Because like it or not, both of them have died in unusual circumstances almost within twenty-four hours of one another, Mrs Taylor. And Long Way Hole seems to be the one thing that connects them.'

Susan Taylor glanced at her watch, then signalled to Gallivan. She wasn't happy about it but she would give us a little more time.

'I can only tell you what Greg told me but I suppose that's what you want to know. It was a weekend in April. The two of them – Richard Pryce and Charlie Richardson – had come up from London. They all stayed at the Station Inn over at Ribblehead. Greg took a room there too. It was a waste of money really. It's only twenty minutes from here. But it meant the three of them could drink together and they did quite a bit of that, I'm sure. All boys together. Reliving the old days. All that nonsense.'

'Did you meet Richard Pryce?'

'Of course I met him, a few times. I didn't warm to him if you want the truth. Too much of a smooth-talker for my taste. Greg never brought him here. I think he was ashamed of the house, which is just rubbish, but we'd go out for dinner at the Marton Arms or wherever. I saw him at the inquest too. But we didn't speak – not then. I wasn't speaking to anyone.

'Anyway, what came out at the inquest was exactly what Greg had already said to me. It was April and it had been warm. There had been two weeks of sunshine but that day the forecast was for rain. There'd even been talk of a storm but Greg looked at the clouds and he figured it was going to be localised, a long way off Old Ing Lane, which was where they started. Greg knew the weather. He wasn't ever wrong. They went in before midday and should have been out by late afternoon. It's a grade-four pot, if that means anything to you. Two miles long. A lot of pitches to navigate. Quite tricky in parts.

'Well, when the storm broke, it broke right above them and the trouble was that the ground was hard-baked, which meant that the water came in all the faster. They knew they were in trouble pretty much straight away and they had a choice. They could climb up to higher ground or they could move as fast as they could and make it to the exit. The three of them decided to do that. There was one contortion they had to manage but after that it was fairly easy-going . . . a bit of crawling, a bit of stooping. But as long as they kept ahead of the water, they'd be all right.

'So that's what they did. They all agreed on it. But somehow, in the hurry to get out, Charlie Richardson got separated and left behind. The other two only noticed he wasn't there when they reached the final passage with the exit just in front of them. So what are they to do? They can see daylight right in front of them. It would be madness to go back with the water rushing towards them. They shout for him but that's a waste of time. He could be five metres away, but with the noise of the water and all the rest of it, he won't hear them. So they decide to go back in. The path they've just taken has become a fast-flowing river with the water coming out towards them but it's what they call a vertical crack . . .'

'It's very high but it's narrow,' Gallivan explained. 'They can move above the flow, using their hips and their elbows, pinning themselves between the walls.'

'It's still dangerous,' Susan Taylor added. 'Because if they slip they're going to get swept away. But the two of them fight their way back in and there's still no sign of Charlie.'

She stopped herself as if there was no point telling any more.

'They decided he must have missed the contortion altogether and continued straight into a tangle of different passageways. It's like an underground maze.'

'Spaghetti Junction,' Gallivan said. That was the name that Davina Richardson had told us.

'There was no way they could get back there so they made a second decision, which was to get back out and call for help.'

'They went up to Ing Lane Farm.' Gallivan picked

up the story. 'The farmer there is Chris Jackson and they knew that if he wasn't in his wife would be. They went there and rang the police. They contacted me directly. I logged the call at five past five and called out the team. We were down Long Way Hole by seven.'

'The police called me too.' Susan lifted her cup of tea but it had gone cold. She grimaced and put it down again. 'That's when I knew there was something wrong. But it wasn't until the next day that they found him . . .'

'That's enough,' Gallivan growled. 'You should read the inquest if you want to know more. It's all out in the open. I think you should leave now.'

'The girls will be back soon,' Susan said. She reached for a tissue and I saw that her hand was trembling. Looking up, I realised she had begun to cry.

'Wait for me outside.' Gallivan went over to her.

Hawthorne stood up. 'Thank you for seeing us, Mrs Taylor,' he said. 'We'll find out what happened at King's Cross station. I promise you that.'

She glanced up at him almost balefully, as if she actually blamed him. She had a point. His visit had only opened the wounds, forcing her to relive what had happened all over again. I nodded but said nothing. We left the room.

But we didn't leave the house straight away. Making sure he wasn't being seen, Hawthorne crossed the front hall and went into the living room. I followed him. The room was empty to the point of being austere. Apart from the fireplace and the piano there was a television, two sofas, a coffee table with a cactus in a pot and a few photographs of the family in happier times. A pair of French windows opened into the conservatory. The cat had curled up on one of the chairs. That was everything. There was nothing else.

'What exactly are you looking for?' I whispered.

'You don't see it?' Hawthorne replied.

I waited for him to continue. He didn't.

'No,' I said.

Hawthorne shook his head. 'It's right in front of your eyes, mate.'

Whenever Hawthorne saw anything or worked something out, he deliberately kept it from me as if the whole thing was some sort of game. This is often the case in detective stories and I always find it infuriating, but I knew only too well that there was nothing I could do. We left the living room and tiptoed back out into the street. As soon as we were outside, he lit a cigarette.

'Did you really have to be so hard on her?' I said.

Hawthorne looked genuinely surprised. 'Was I?'

'She was upset.'

'She was nervous.'

Had she been nervous? I didn't think so. I certainly

hadn't seen it. And what did she have to be nervous of? As I turned these thoughts over in my head, I remembered the one thing I knew that Hawthorne probably didn't. It came from having lived in Crouch End for sixteen years and although it almost certainly wasn't relevant, I decided to share it. At least it allowed me to contribute something to the day.

'You know that photograph she showed us,' I said.

'The one he sent his wife?'

'I happen to know where it was taken.' I paused for effect. 'That's Hornsey Lane in Highgate. It's about a minute away from Suicide Bridge.'

'Suicide Bridge?'

'It's what everyone calls it. Hornsey Lane Bridge. If he wanted to commit suicide, he could have jumped off – but what's really interesting is that it's only a five-minute walk from Davina Richardson's house.'

Hawthorne took this in. 'That is interesting,' he agreed. 'But I'll tell you something that interests me even more.'

'What's that?'

'King's Cross station. W. H. Smith. Why did he buy that book?'

11

At the Station Inn

I thought we might go back to the hotel after Ingleton but first of all Hawthorne wanted to visit the entrance to Long Way Hole. I didn't see how it could help but I was just grateful he wasn't suggesting we kit up and drop into the cave system ourselves. Dave Gallivan drove us in his Land Rover, which was so beaten-up that I was nervous the whole thing would collapse when we drove over the next bump or a cattle grid. Hawthorne sat in the front. I was in the back, hemmed in between plastic barrels, ropes and backpacks, looking out through windows streaked and splattered with mud.

The railway line had slashed through the countryside but the roads allowed us to weave our way across it more gently. Everything – the cottages and farmhouses, streams and bridges, woodland and hills – looked even lovelier at close quarters. Gallivan gave us an occasional commentary but his observations seemed almost deliberately prosaic, as if he felt uncomfortable having a writer with him in the car.

'That's Whernside. It's the tallest of the three peaks. And that's Ingleborough. If you look up there, that ridge is carboniferous limestone. Those are Swaledale.' (He was pointing at a flock of sheep.) 'They've been grazing here two hundred year or more.'

Sitting next to him, Hawthorne had the best view, but again he showed no interest, sinking into his seat, saying nothing.

A rough lane forked off from the road and we followed it into the glorious green emptiness of the Dales, finally stopping at a gate built into a drystone wall. Apart from the crunch of our feet on the gravel, there was barely a sound as we walked away from the car, through the gate and up another track. It had been sunny when we were in Ingleton but now the weather was closing in and it occurred to me that this must have been what it looked like when Richard Pryce, Charles Richardson and Gregory Taylor had set out on their last trip. There was still plenty of blue sky but far away the clouds were rubbing up against each other, throwing dark shadows across the fields, broken only by the light slanting down in godlike shafts.

We came to a stream that bubbled cheerfully along until it reached a stone ledge where it suddenly spilled over and became a waterfall. It was impossible to see how deep it was but it seemed to continue into the very bowels of the earth. A hill rose up ahead with the dark mouth of a cave, surrounded by ivy and moss, looking very much like something out of a story designed to frighten children. This was where the three men had begun their descent, allowing themselves to be swallowed up by the dark.

'Where's the exit?' Hawthorne asked.

Gallivan pointed. 'Two miles east. Round the back of Drear Hill. You want to go there?'

Hawthorne shook his head. Scanning the horizon, he picked out a white-painted farmhouse, isolated, surrounded by grass. 'Who lives there?'

'That's the man I told you about. Chris Jackson. That's Ing Lane Farm.'

'Will he be in?'

'He might be. You want to talk to him?'

'If you don't mind.'

'Suit yourself.'

We didn't walk. We went back to the car and drove

through the gate and on along an even rougher track, the tyres spitting out stones and dust. I wondered if we were on the roof of Long Way Hole. This whole expedition seemed a little pointless to me. Did Hawthorne think that something suspicious had happened when the three men had gone caving together? It would be a good place to commit murder, far underground. At least there would be no need to bury the body. Suppose Richard and Gregory had murdered Charles Richardson. Someone had found out and had taken revenge, bludgeoning one of the killers and pushing the other under a train. It was a reasonable enough supposition. But why now? And why would three old university friends who only saw each other occasionally for adventure holidays have suddenly come to blows?

We reached the farm, which was about a mile away to the north, resting against the side of the hill like an old man, with discarded pieces of farm machinery and plastic sacks of animal feed piled up all round. Once again it was Dave Gallivan who knocked on the door but this time he waited until it was opened by a wiry, whip-thin man with grey hair and a straggling moustache, wearing a T-shirt and jeans. He was ex-army. I could see it before he spoke a word. It was in the way he stood, the tattoos on his arms, the hardness of his eyes.

''Ey up?' I won't try to replicate the Yorkshire dialect – it will look ridiculous on the page – but those were his first two words as he carefully examined us.

Gallivan explained who we were and why we'd come.

'You'd best come inside then.'

The front door led straight into the kitchen, which had a stone floor and nothing of comfort. We sat at the table. He didn't offer us tea.

'I knew there were going to be trouble that day,' he told us. 'The rain came bucketing down that afternoon and I feared the worst. I took a look out of the window at the stream that runs out the back. It's bone dry half the year round, but, four o'clock, there was water gushing along. That stream's a marker if ever there was one.'

'A conditions marker,' Gallivan added. 'There are plenty of them around here. You know not to go caving if there's so much as a trickle.'

'That's what I said to Barbara.' He glanced upwards, which was presumably where his wife was to be found. 'I just hoped there was no one stupid enough to be underground. But then, an hour later, there's a knock at the door and two men come in – in a terrible state, soaking wet, one of them with a bloody nose. It took me a minute or two to recognise Greg Taylor. I didn't know the chap who was with him. Anyway, they told me what had happened down at Long Way Hole. They'd been trying to fight their way back in to find their friend and they were beside themselves with worry. I got Barbara to make them a drink while I called the police.'

'Did the two of them say anything more while they were here?' Hawthorne asked.

'They said a lot of things but not a lot of it made much sense. The rain was still coming down and we were waiting for cave rescue to arrive. I'll tell you something, though. Greg was the worse of the two of them. The other chap was silent. He was sitting there like he was haunted or something. But Greg? "This is my fault." That's what he said. "This is my fault. This is my fault." He said it over and over. There was no stopping him.'

'What happened then?'

'A police car came and took them away. By that time, Dave and his team were doing what they could, although it was already too late. The last I saw, Greg was staring out of the window like a dead man. But he weren't the one that died that day.'

'He's dead now,' Gallivan muttered.

'Aye. So I hear. Maybe it was his reckoning. Who can say? It catches up with us all in the end.'

We had dinner at the Station Inn that evening in a cosy room with low ceilings and varnished beams. A single railway line had been set along the floor next to the bar, acting as a footrest. I could imagine the place heaving in the summer but it was very quiet that evening. In one corner there was a massive fruit machine that sat there like an alien invader, blinking and flickering, but nobody played it. A plump Labrador dog slumbered in its basket.

Hawthorne had asked Gallivan to join us and the three of us sat at a table by the window with views across to another viaduct, a sister to the one I had seen at Ingleton. We had been served gigantic portions of steak and kidney pudding which Hawthorne ate warily, as if he was suspicious of the contents. Gallivan and I had pints of Yorkshire bitter. As usual, Hawthorne had water.

We talked generally for a while – tourism, caving, local gossip – but there was only one reason Hawthorne would have invited Gallivan along and that was because there was something he wanted to know, and sure enough it wasn't long before he pounced.

'So maybe you can tell me what it is you're hiding, Dave?' he asked.

'I don't know what you mean.' Gallivan stopped, his fork halfway to his mouth.

'When we were with Susan Taylor, she mentioned you were at the inquest.'

'I was.'

'You told them there was nothing suspicious, nobody to blame.'

'That was the truth.'

'Are you sure about that?' Gallivan said nothing, so Hawthorne went on. 'You were uncomfortable with her and you're uncomfortable now. I didn't spend twenty years in the police not to notice when someone's lying to me. What is it you're not telling us?'

'There's nothing . . .'

'Two people are dead, Dave. Your mate Greg went under a train. The last person he saw got bludgeoned to death twenty-four hours later. It may be connected to what happened here and I need to know.'

'All right!' Gallivan put his fork down. His eyes flared. 'I didn't want to talk about it in front of her and I'm not sure I want to tell you now. There's no proof. Nothing. It's just a feeling.'

'Go on.'

'Well, Charlie Richardson may not have been a professional but he was an experienced caver. He knew what he was doing. So I never understood how he could have been so bloody stupid. The simple fact of the matter is that there was no reason for him to die.'

Now that he had started, the food was forgotten. It

was as if he had been waiting to tell his side of the story ever since the accident had occurred. His eyes were bleak as he went back. 'Gregory Taylor leads them into the cave. Richard Pryce is next. Charlie Richardson brings up the rear. Of course, they don't know it yet, but the rain has been pouring down above ground. By the time they realise what's happening, it's too late. A flood pulse has formed and it's heading their way.'

'How would they know if they can't see it?' I asked.

'They can hear it. It's a sort of booming and a mumbling . . . the worst sound in the world and it's all around them, getting louder and louder. And very soon they can feel it. The rain has made its way through, coming off the cracks and the stalactites.' He dismissed me angrily, turning back to Hawthorne. 'They have to make a decision fast. They've got maybe ten minutes. A quarter of an hour at most. So they decide to keep going and, as you know, Richardson misses Drake's Passage – that's the name of the contortion – and continues into Spaghetti Junction. It's easily enough done, particularly if you're in a hurry. But here's what I don't understand.' He tapped his finger on the table for emphasis. 'Once he was there, why didn't he just stay where he was? He could have found higher ground and sat it out until all the water had passed through. The worst that would have happened was that he'd have been left on his own in the dark and might have had to wait for us to come and find him.'

'Maybe he panicked,' I suggested.

Gallivan shook his head. 'An experienced caver doesn't panic. He had plenty of battery power. More than that, he was carrying a safety bag.' He explained what it was before we could ask. 'It's made of water-proof fabric. You pull it over your head and sit inside. It keeps you warm while you wait to be rescued. But Charlie allowed it to kill him.'

'How was that?' Hawthorne asked.

'That was how he got stuck. The safety bag was at-tached to his caving harness by a short rope and it got caught in the contortion as he dropped down. Do you understand what I'm saying?' He made a shape with his hands, a narrow tube running vertically. 'He leaves Spaghetti Junction and finds his way back to Drake's Passage. He drops down, trying to catch up with the others, but the bag gets stuck. He's got his full weight on the cord and there's nothing he can do. He's got no purchase to climb up again without his mates there to assist him. The silly bugger isn't carrying a knife, so he can't cut the rope and he's left dangling. When the pulse hits, he drowns.' He paused. 'That was how I found him. Maybe he'd been knocked out first. That would have been a mercy.'

'Did you ever talk about any of this with Gregory Taylor?' Hawthorne asked.

'Of course I talked to him. Apart from the fact that we were mates, it was my job as duty controller. But he wasn't there when the other man died. He and Pryce had already gone on ahead. What was going on in Richardson's head right then? Your guess is as good as mine.'

'Why didn't all three of them wait in Spaghetti Junction? If you say it was safer there.'

'Maybe they should have done. But Greg told me he was afraid that once they went in, they'd never find their way out. And he had a point. I've been in there and it's a bloody nightmare.' Gallivan sighed. 'Anyway, it's easy enough to be wise after the event. They heard the water coming and they wanted out. I might have made the same decision if I'd been with them.'

There was a long silence. I became aware that I was the only one who was still eating. I put down my knife and fork.

'There is one other thing you might want to know,' Gallivan added. 'Greg rang me from London, the day he died.'

'The Saturday?' Hawthorne said.

'That's right. Saturday afternoon. He was on his way to the station. He said he wanted to talk to me about Long Way Hole – about what really happened.'

'Is that what he said? Were those his exact words?'

'That's right. He said he'd been thinking about it and there was something he wanted to get off his chest. We arranged to meet here, at this very pub, on Monday night. Seven o'clock.'

'But he never got home.'

'He went under that train and that was it.'

There was a moment of clarity that came to me in much the same way as water must have come rushing through Long Way Hole. It was suddenly obvious. Gregory Taylor knew something that nobody else did. Something had happened just before the fatal accident. He had wanted to tell Dave Gallivan. But he had been killed before he could get home.

He had been murdered. And that was the reason.

I said as much to Hawthorne later that evening after Gallivan had left but, annoyingly, he didn't seem quite so sure. 'It doesn't quite stack up, mate. If he made the call on the way to the station and someone overheard him, they'd have had to be with him, and according to his wife he was on his own.'

'He could have met someone in London.' I thought about the time frame. 'It could have been Davina Richardson. We know he was near her home.'

'What? And you think she followed him to King's Cross station and pushed him under a train?'

'Why not? If she blamed Richard Pryce and Gregory Taylor for the death of her husband, she could have killed both of them.'

'But she didn't blame them. She'd forgiven Pryce and she hadn't seen Taylor for six years. We don't even know if she saw him the day he died.'

'Presumably you're going to ask her.'

Hawthorne gave me his most reasonable smile. 'Of course we'll ask her. You liked her, didn't you?'

'She seemed nice enough.'

'And she had a son who read your books!'

'Unlike your son. Yes!'

There was one other odd development that evening. We'd finished early as we had a seven o'clock start the next morning and we were about to go up to our rooms when a man came into the pub. I noticed him standing by the door, looking at us, puzzled. He was late thirties, fair-haired, short and quite slender, wearing a hoody and jeans. He hesitated, then came over to us and I assumed that he had recognised me and was going to say something about my books.

But actually it was Hawthorne he thought he knew. 'Billy!' The single word was somewhere between a statement and a question. Hawthorne looked up at him but showed no recognition at all and now the man doubted himself. 'It's Mike,' he said. 'Mike Carlyle.'

'I'm sorry, mate.' Hawthorne shook his head. 'My name's not Billy. And I don't know any Mike Carlyle.'

The man was completely thrown. He had recognised the face and he thought he knew the voice too. 'You weren't in Reeth?'

'No. I don't know what you're talking about. I'm just up from London. I've never been to anywhere called Reeth.'

'But . . .' He wanted to continue but Hawthorne hadn't just been definitive. He'd been almost hostile. 'I'm sorry,' the man stammered. He was still staring at Hawthorne. He couldn't bring himself to leave.

Hawthorne picked up his glass of water. 'No problem.' I could hear the steel in his voice. It was also there in his eyes.

'Sorry.' The man got the message. He didn't just back away. If he'd come here for a pint, he'd changed his mind. He left the way he had come.

'I'm going to bed,' Hawthorne said.

I wanted to ask him what had just happened. Had he once been known as William or Billy or had it simply been a case of mistaken identity? These things happen. But somehow I was sure there was more to it than that and that somehow Mike Carlyle was connected to the strange mood Hawthorne had been in all day.

Hawthorne left without saying another word and he didn't mention it again when we met for breakfast the next morning, or on the train all the way back to London.

12
The Haiku

I could tell things were still going wrong as soon as I walked into the *Foyle's War* production base later that same day. Jangling phones, printers churning out fresh paperwork, accountants staring desperately into computer screens, runners chasing around as if being chased themselves, a sense of tightly controlled panic . . . All that was normal. It was the silence that worried me, the way everyone avoided my eye as I made my way into Jill's office.

'What's happened?' I asked.

She was standing at her desk (she never sits), just ending a phone call, checking her emails and dictating a note to her assistant, all at the same time. As she has often told me, only women know how to multitask. 'Nothing you need to worry about,' she said.

'No. Tell me!'

'We've lost a location,' she said.

'Which one?'

'The chase. All of it.' It was a rare moment of action in the series, with Foyle and Sam being tracked through London streets by an armed Russian assassin. 'The police have withdrawn permission,' she went on. 'They won't even give us a sensible reason.'

'What did they say?' I asked. There was an unpleasant feeling in the pit of my stomach.

'I don't know. It was something about a murder inquiry. It sounds completely unlikely. They say someone's been killed and they've had to cordon off a whole load of streets. There's nothing we can do. They won't let us shoot there.'

Cara Grunshaw. It had to be. That mention of a murder inquiry was a direct shot across my bows. I didn't dare say anything to Jill but crept back to my desk, which was tucked away in a corner. The business card that Cara had given me was still in my pocket. I took it out and stared at it for a long time, then picked up the phone and dialled. It rang twice before she answered. I had hoped it would go straight to voicemail.

'Yes?' Her voice was curt, almost brutal.

'This is Anthony—'

'I know who it is. What do you want?'

'Have you stopped our production team filming in Hackney?'

There was a brief pause, an intake of breath, then . . . 'Are you phoning me to ask me that? Who the fuck do you think you are?'

'I'm phoning you to give you information!' I cut in quickly. I didn't want her to go on shouting at me.

'What information?' The voice was utterly disembodied. It wasn't just the phone line. It didn't seem to be connected to a human being.

'We've just been to Yorkshire . . . Hawthorne and me. It may be that Pryce's murder is connected to a caving accident that happened there six years ago.'

I felt horrible betraying Hawthorne, but if it was a choice between him and Jill what else could I do? The production had to come first. But even as I spoke, I was choosing my words carefully, determined not to give too much away.

'We know about the accident.' Now she sounded flat, bored, but I wondered if she was telling the truth. She certainly hadn't been to Ingleton ahead of us. Susan Taylor would have said.

'A man called Gregory Taylor fell under a train at King's Cross station on Saturday, the day before Richard Pryce was murdered,' I went on. 'Hawthorne thinks that he knew something about what happened and that maybe he was pushed. Someone didn't want him to talk.'

This wasn't true. It was actually my own theory and although Hawthorne hadn't completely dismissed it, he most certainly hadn't accepted it either. It seemed a reasonable bone to throw Grunshaw's way. If she did decide to check up on it, she might discover that we had arranged to see Davina Richardson again that very afternoon.

'Gregory Taylor's got nothing to do with the fucking case,' Grunshaw said. I hated the way she swore all the time. Hawthorne was almost as bad but somehow she made it uglier and more personal.

'What makes you say that?'

'You don't ask the questions! And if you do ask them, don't think I'm going to fucking answer them. Hawthorne's in Yorkshire?'

'We were there yesterday.'

'He's wasting his time. What else can you tell me?'

I tried to think of everything that had happened, searching for something innocuous. 'Someone broke into Adrian Lockwood's office the week before the murder,' I said. 'There may be a connection.'

'We know about that too.' I didn't need to see the contempt on her face. I could hear it in her voice. 'Don't ring me again until you've got something I actually want to hear.'

'Someone has stopped us filming—' I tried again.

She wasn't having any of it. The phone went dead.

For a while I sat there, doing very little. I couldn't focus on my work, not after that conversation with Grunshaw. But slowly I came to a resolution. Thinking about her and the way she was treating me, I was more determined than ever to solve the case myself. In fact, Hawthorne was almost as bad as her and it occurred to me how much it would satisfy me to put a finger up to both of them and find the killer on my own. That would certainly be one way to get them both off my back.

Ignoring all the activity around me, I opened my laptop and quietly set about typing up all my notes from the meetings in Yorkshire. I produced hard copies on the office printer, then laid the pages out – chapter by chapter – so that I could read everything that had happened in sequence, up to the point where I was now. My hope was that I could work out where I might be heading next.

The first question. Was this one murder or two? Had Gregory Taylor been pushed under a train, had he fallen – or had he jumped?

If he had been killed, then the two deaths had to be related. Hawthorne had said as much when he was interviewing Susan Taylor: *Because like it or not, both of them have died in unusual circumstances almost within twenty-four hours of one another, Mrs Taylor. And Long Way Hole seems to be the one thing that connects them.* I had written it down, word for word, in my notebook. He had said much the same thing to me outside Euston station: *It's not a coincidence.* So if Richard Pryce and Gregory Taylor had been targeted for the same reason, then everything went back to the accident and the killer surely had to be one of the two widows: Davina Richardson or Susan Taylor. Both of them had been in London on the day, although Davina had an alibi. She had been with Adrian Lockwood around the time the murder had taken place.

And then there was Dave Gallivan's extraordinary revelation: *He said he wanted to talk to me about Long Way Hole – about what really happened.* But if Taylor had been killed to stop him from talking, surely that ruled out Davina and Susan? Might there be someone else – perhaps Chris Jackson, the farmer we'd met in Yorkshire, or someone involved in what had happened – who urgently wanted to keep him silent?

But then again, the entire scenario, the accident at Long Way Hole, could be completely irrelevant. That was a worrying thought. Was I going to end up writing two or three chapters – the visit to Ribblehead, the Station Inn and all the rest of it – when actually it was a giant red herring and a complete waste of time? Hawthorne had almost suggested as much before we'd got on the train back to London. *It doesn't quite stack up, mate.* Suppose I took the entire Yorkshire sequence out of consideration. Where did that leave me?

Richard Pryce, a wealthy divorce lawyer, had been murdered in his own house. Just a few days before, Akira Anno, a woman he had deliberately set out to humiliate, had threatened to smash a bottle over his head and that was exactly how he had died. *Then she killed him!* Those were my words. I had spoken them to Hawthorne when he had first outlined the case and at the time the conclusion had seemed inescapable. Had she really been in a remote cottage near Lyndhurst on the Sunday evening? Hawthorne seemed to doubt it. And what about the secret income stream that Oliver Masefield had mentioned and which Richard had been investigating?

And then there was her ex-husband, Adrian Lockwood. As far as I could see, he had no motive to kill his lawyer: Pryce had managed to get him exactly the divorce he wanted; indeed, he had rewarded him with that very expensive bottle of wine. It was also impossible for Lockwood to have committed the murder, at least on his own. He had been with Davina until just after eight o'clock in the evening. Pryce's neighbour, the unpleasant Mr Fairchild, had seen someone approaching the house (*holding a torch*) around five to eight and there had been the timing of the telephone call too. There was no way he could have got there in time.

Ignoring him, I turned to Stephen Spencer, Richard's husband. He had almost certainly been lying when he said he was in Frinton with his sick mother and it did make me wonder. Why does nobody ever tell the truth when a murder has been committed? You'd have thought people would have fallen over themselves to co-operate – but no, not a bit of it. It was almost as if they were all queuing up to be suspects. So where was he? With another man . . . or with a woman? Richard Pryce had been talking about his will quite recently. Could Stephen have discovered he was about to be cut out?

I thought about Davina Richardson. She had told us that she had forgiven Richard Pryce for his part in her husband's death and I believed her. She had taken money from him and allowed him to become a second father to her son. She seemed to get many of her clients from him and she had even been redecorating his house. Was it possible that she was harbouring some secret hatred for him and if so, why? No one had ever suggested that he had been responsible for what happened at Long Way Hole. Quite the contrary. *This is my fault.* That was what Gregory Taylor had said – repeatedly – when he reached Ing Lane Farm. If she had any argument, it was with him.

Finally, there was the man with the blue glasses and the rash or whatever it was on his face who had broken into Adrian Lockwood's office. I still had no idea who he was but it seemed probable that he was the same man whom Richard Pryce had mentioned to Colin Richardson, Davina's son. *There was something wrong with his face.* According to Colin, Pryce had been worried about the mystery man for some time. Suppose the man worked for Akira Anno? She knew that both Adrian and Richard Pryce were investigating her. She could have hired him to find out what they knew.

When I next looked at my watch, a couple of hours had passed and I was still no nearer the truth. There were notes and scribbles everywhere: it's funny how the surface of my desk always reflects the state of my mind. Right now, it was a mess. I snatched hold of a page and read: *What are you doing here? It's a bit late.*

Richard Pryce's last words, overheard on the telephone by his husband, Stephen Spencer. But it had only been eight o'clock. So whoever had come to the door had arrived too late in another sense.

I took out a red pen and underlined the words that had been spoken. I knew they were important. I just couldn't figure out why.

Hawthorne wasn't there when I reached Davina Richardson's house but it was only ten to five: I had arrived a few minutes early. I was standing in the street looking out for him when the front door opened and Davina appeared on the doorstep, calling me in.

'I saw you out of the window,' she explained. 'Are you waiting for your friend?'

'He's not exactly my friend,' I said.

'You said you were writing a book about him. Does that mean I'm going to be one of the characters?'

'Not if you don't want to be.'

She smiled. 'It doesn't bother me at all. Why don't you come in?'

It was drizzling again – this horrible autumn weather. There seemed no point hanging around in the street so I followed her through the cluttered hallway and back into the kitchen. The smell of cigarette smoke was everywhere. I gave up cigarettes thirty years ago but even when I smoked it was never inside the house and I wondered how she lived with it. I sat down at the kitchen table, at the same time noticing that she had been reading *Two Hundred Haikus* by Akira Anno. There was a brand-new copy that had been left face down, with the pages fanning out.

'Will you have some tea?'

'Not for me, thank you.'

'The kettle's just boiled.' She brought a plate of chocolate digestives to the table. 'I shouldn't really be eating these but Colin loves them and you know how it is once you've opened the packet . . .'

'Where is Colin?' I asked.

'He's doing his homework with a friend.' She bit into a biscuit. By the time I left, she would have eaten four or five. She was wearing a baggy mohair jersey but I didn't think she had chosen it to hide her shape. For all her apologies, she didn't strike me as a woman who was particularly self-conscious. She was completely comfortable with who and what she was. I still didn't know for certain that she had been having an affair with Adrian Lockwood, but if she had, I was sure she would have been better suited to him than Akira Anno. She would have looked after him like she looked after Colin – nagging him, cajoling him, but at the end of the day doing everything she could to make him happy.

'How well do you know Adrian Lockwood?' I asked.

She stopped mid-bite. 'I thought I told you that the last time you were here. He was introduced to me as a client but he's become a sort of friend. Why do you ask?'

'No particular reason.'

'I miss having a man in the house.' She looked genuinely wistful. 'I know I shouldn't say it in this day and age but I'm absolutely useless without a man. There isn't a moment I don't miss Charlie. I never get anything right. I can't work out the buttons on the TV remote control. Parking the car is a nightmare even though it's only a Toyota Prius and it isn't that big. I forget to put the clocks back and I wake up an hour early or an hour late or whatever it is. I hate taking the rubbish out, and you try putting on a duvet cover by yourself!' She sighed. 'Adrian was never happy with Akira. He never said as much to me, not in so many words, but I could tell. Women can, you know. We always know when something's not right.'

While she was talking, I was nervously listening out for Hawthorne. He probably wouldn't be too happy, me being here without him. He hated me asking questions even when he was in the room and I certainly didn't want to say anything that might undermine his investigation, not after what had happened before. So

I glanced at the book on the table and asked conversationally, 'Have you been reading these?'

'Oh yes. Someone gave them to me because they knew I was friends with Adrian.' She gestured at it vaguely. 'I don't really understand them, to be honest with you. She's far too clever for me.'

I picked it up. Like many books of poetry, *Two Hundred Haikus* was a fairly slim volume – only about forty pages long – and at £15 it wasn't cheap either. But I suppose that's fair enough. Poetry has limited sales and it's rare that you're going to find any poet's work with a half-price sticker on the front table at Waterstones. It was a hardback with a tiny detail taken from a woodblock, I think by Hokusai, on the front cover. The haikus were arranged in groups of four or five on high-quality paper. There was a black and white photograph of Akira Anno on the back. She wasn't smiling.

I was introduced to haikus when I was at school. I wasn't a particularly bright child and I remember liking them because they were so short. It was Matsuo Bashō in the seventeenth century who made them famous. *An ancient pond / A frog jumps in / The splash of water.* It's one of the few poems I can still quote in its entirety, although in the original Japanese it has five syllables in the first line, seven in the second and then another five in the third. That's the whole point.

I cast my eye over Akira's efforts, which were in English, though printed in curving black letters that imitated Japanese calligraphy. The book had been left open on haikus 174–181 (each one was numbered, with no title). On an impulse, I turned the page and my eye was immediately drawn to haiku 182 at the top of the page.

You breathe in my ear
Your every word a trial
The sentence is death

182.

The number painted on the wall next to the dead body of Richard Pryce.

My head was spinning. I couldn't believe what I was looking at. Akira Anno hadn't just threatened Pryce with murder, she had written about it in a book of poetry. No. That wasn't fair. She had written a poem about the nature of murder . . . if that was what the haiku meant. I wasn't completely sure. Even so, the words had to relate to what had happened in the room. The number couldn't be a clearer signpost.

But if she had killed Richard Pryce, would she have left a clue that incriminated herself so obviously? And if she hadn't painted the number, who had and why? I wanted to ask Davina if she had read the haiku but she was looking at me completely innocently, wondering why I was so flabbergasted.

It was at that precise moment that the doorbell rang and I realised Hawthorne had arrived. I was relieved. This was one of those few moments when I actually wanted to see him. He could deal with Davina and ask the questions that needed to be asked, and when we left he could make sense of what I had just discovered.

'That's your friend!'

'Yes.' The doorbell rang a second time. 'You'd better let him in,' I said.

Davina seemed unwilling to leave me on my own but got up and drifted out of the room.

I read the haiku three more times, turning all sorts of possibilities over in my mind. At the same time, I heard Davina's voice out in the hall, explaining that I was already here, and I wasn't surprised a few moments later to see Hawthorne glowering at me from the doorway.

'You're early,' he said. Not a statement. An accusation.

'I was waiting outside—' I began.

'I saw him and I invited him in.' Davina came to my rescue.

'We've just been chatting.' I was trying to reassure him. 'Mrs Richardson was showing me some poetry.'

Hawthorne still looked suspicious. He sat down, folding his ever-present raincoat over the arm of the sofa. Davina offered him tea, which he refused, plunging straight in as if to make up for lost time. 'Did you by any chance see Gregory Taylor last weekend? Possibly sometime late afternoon?'

'Who?' She looked perplexed.

'The man who went caving with your husband.'

'I know who he is. Of course I know who you mean. Why are you asking me about him?'

'I don't want to upset you, Mrs Richardson, but he died last Saturday . . . one day before the murder of Richard Pryce.'

She wasn't upset. She was shocked. 'Gregory's dead?'

'He fell under a train,' I said and immediately wished I hadn't as it drew another baleful glance from Hawthorne.

'You didn't see it in the newspapers?'

'I don't really read the newspapers. It's all so gloomy. I sometimes watch the news on the TV but I didn't see anything. Well, they probably wouldn't report it, would they? If a man falls under a train . . .'

'I'm not entirely sure he fell.' Hawthorne was sitting

very straight, his legs apart, gazing at her with what might have been a sympathetic smile. With his hair cut so close around the ears and his black suit and tie, he managed to look both innocent and aggressive.

'What? I don't understand . . .'

'He didn't come here?'

'No. I've just told you. I wasn't here anyway. I went out at half past four. No. I mean half past three. I don't know what I mean . . . I keep getting confused! It was half past three and I went over to Brent Cross. I took Colin with me. He's growing so fast, he needed new football kit. What makes you think Gregory was here?'

'One of the last things he did before he died was to send his wife a selfie he took on Hornsey Lane.'

She thought about that. 'That's quite near here,' she admitted. 'I can't imagine what he'd be doing there. He was still living in Yorkshire as far as I knew.' She shook her head. 'I hadn't seen or heard from him for six years. He sent me a letter after the inquest, offering his condolences, but otherwise we'd had no contact and to be honest with you I'm not sure I would have wanted him to come into my home. I already told you. Richard wasn't to blame for what happened that day, when Charlie died. But Gregory Taylor was supposed to be in charge. He was the one who decided they should go ahead even though the forecast predicted rain. I don't think I'd have had anything to say to him.'

'So what was he doing on Hornsey Lane?'

'I have no idea. I'm sorry you've wasted your time coming over here today. I could have told you over the phone. I didn't see him.'

It hadn't been a waste of time. I couldn't wait to tell Hawthorne about the haiku.

Hawthorne picked up his raincoat and got to his feet. 'Thank you for seeing us,' he said. Then, almost as an afterthought: 'I'm sorry to have to ask this, Mrs Richardson, but I need you to tell me. What exactly is your relationship with Adrian Lockwood?'

She blushed, just as she had when we were first with her, but this time it was more anger than embarrassment. 'I really don't see what business it is of yours, Mr Hawthorne. Adrian is a client but he's become a friend. A good friend. I tried to support him. He found the divorce proceedings very stressful and he was so angry with Richard. He came here to unwind. That's all, really. He thought of me as someone he could trust.'

'Why was he angry with Richard Pryce?'

'Did I say that? I didn't mean it. He was angry about the whole thing . . . the amount of time it took . . . Akira. He knew he'd made a mistake marrying her and— You really will have to ask him about it. Not me.

I don't think it's right for me to talk about him behind his back.'

That was the end of it. She showed us to the door and a few moments later we were back in the street, walking towards Highgate Tube. As soon as I was alone with Hawthorne, I told him what had happened. It seemed inescapable to me that the number 182, painted on the wall at Heron's Wake, related to the poem. I recited it, emphasising the third line.

'*The sentence is death.* She's saying she has to kill him because she can't bear living with him. I know it's crazy but she wanted the whole world to know what she intended to do.'

Hawthorne looked doubtful. 'When was the book published?'

'I don't know. Earlier this year.'

'So she could have written that poem a long time ago.'

'She was still married to Lockwood. She still hated him.'

'But she didn't kill Lockwood. She killed Richard Pryce. At least, that's what you're suggesting.'

'She wrote a poem about death. And look at that second line! Maybe the trial she's talking about is her divorce.'

'Well, I'll tell you one thing.' The rain was getting

heavier. Hawthorne drew on his coat. 'On the night of the murder, Akira wasn't in Lyndhurst or anywhere near it. She lied to us.'

'How do you know?'

'CCTV footage from the Welcome Break service station at Fleet. She was never there. And ANPR records on the M27 and the A31.'

'What's ANPR?'

'Automatic number-plate recognition. Ms Anno drives a Jaguar F-Type convertible. There are cameras on both roads and unless she drove the entire journey cross-country, there's no trace of her.'

'Did DI Grunshaw tell you that?'

'That's right.'

I found that surprising. Grunshaw loathed Hawthorne. She'd allowed him to be present at a couple of interviews – probably because she'd been forced to – but would she share ANPR data with him? I doubted it. On the other hand, what other way could he have got the information?

'Anyway, Grunshaw spoke to the yoga teacher,' Hawthorne continued. 'The man who owns the cottage. At first he said that he'd lent it to Akira but under the first bit of pressure he broke down and said he didn't know if she'd gone there or not.'

So what did that mean? Suddenly it looked as if the case had nothing to do with Long Way Hole in Yorkshire. We were back to the divorce, the husband and wife at each other's throats. And the lawyer who had come between them.

'What about the haiku?' I asked.

'How exactly did you come across it?' He raised a hand, silencing me before I could answer. 'Do me a favour, Tony. Write the chapter. That's the easiest way. Describe what happened when you visited Mrs Richardson – without me – and maybe I can work out what actually happened.'

'I don't like writing out of sequence.'

'Don't worry. I'll never read the rest of it.'

We had reached the escalators. There were a few people coming up but we were alone as we descended into what felt like the bowels of the earth.

'Don't forget the book club,' Hawthorne said.

'When is it?'

'Monday night.'

'I'm sorry. I'm at the theatre Monday night.'

'But you said you'd come. What were you seeing?' In his mind, it had already slipped into the past tense.

'*Ghosts.*' It was a hot ticket. Richard Eyre directing Henrik Ibsen at the Almeida.

He shook his head regretfully. 'Well, I've promised them now. You'll have to miss it.'

I stood there, a few steps behind him. I wasn't moving but I was being carried further and further down into the shadows and I remember thinking that I'd put that into Hawthorne's chapter, right at the end.

It was exactly how I felt.

13
Bury Street

Who was Mike Carlyle?

I spent an hour searching the internet but couldn't find anything that related to the man who had come into the Station Inn in Ribblehead. He had been about the same age as Hawthorne – maybe a couple of years younger – and unless he had been on holiday, which seemed unlikely in late October, I guessed he must live in the Yorkshire Dales. What would that make him? A farmer? Something connected to tourism? Of course, it could have been Carlisle. I tried that spelling too. Michael Carlyle. Mike Carlisle. I was directed to LinkedIn, Facebook and Twitter, to an office stationery supply company in Manchester and the Director of Missions at a Baptist church in Victoria,

Australia. There were dozens of photographs to choose from but none resembled the man I had met.

I couldn't get the encounter out of my head. It seemed to tie in with Hawthorne's strange mood, his nervousness as we left London. Carlyle had been quite sure it was Hawthorne even if he had referred to him as 'Billy'. He had known him from somewhere called Reeth – a village in nearby Swaledale and 'a well-known centre for hand-knitting and the local lead industry', as Wikipedia helpfully informed me. Hawthorne's behaviour hadn't just been defensive, it had been borderline rude. I couldn't be certain but it seemed quite possible to me that 'Billy' had lied to 'Mike'. They had known each other once.

I was thinking this over when the telephone rang. It was Hawthorne arranging to meet me at the Bury Street Gallery in Mayfair – which was where Stephen Spencer worked.

'We can go on to Marylebone afterwards,' he said.

'What's in Marylebone?'

'Akira Anno is giving a talk in a bookshop.' I heard the rustle of paper as he turned a page. '"Women of mass destruction: sexual objectification and gender coding in modern warfare".'

'That sounds fun,' I said.

'We can talk to her and if you're lucky you can get her book of haikus signed.'

He rang off.

I spent the next couple of hours working. I went for a walk. I wrote a quick draft of the chapter Hawthorne wanted. I know it all sounds a bit dull laid out like that but I'm afraid I'm describing very much my life as a writer. I spend at least half the day on my own and in silence. I flit from one project to another, channelling thousands of words – first with a pen and then with a computer – onto the page. That's why I enjoy writing Alex Rider. Even if I'm not having adventures, I can at least imagine them.

It was less satisfying writing about Hawthorne. I had become a prisoner of circumstance. For example, I would have loved to have opened a chapter with something surprising: Davina Richardson in bed with Adrian Lockwood, perhaps. Or Susan Taylor, dressed in black, being driven to her husband's funeral in the Yorkshire Dales, the cortège slowly winding its way through those twisting country lanes. It would have been a real challenge to imagine myself inside Long Way Hole, describing the last moments of Charlie Richardson as he drowned, or I could have turned myself into a fly on the wall inside the room when Richard Pryce's killer had struck. Sadly, none of these possibilities was available to me. I was stuck with the facts. My job was to follow Hawthorne's investigation, setting down his questions and occasionally trying, without much success, to make sense of the answers. It was really quite frustrating. It wasn't so much writing as recording.

I was still glad to get out of the house. I took the Tube over to Green Park and walked into Mayfair. This time Hawthorne had arrived ahead of me. He was waiting outside an art gallery contained in a small, elegant building, the sort of place that warned you to stay away unless you were well heeled. The name was spelled out in discreet lettering and there were just three works in the window, with no prices. I recognised a Wadsworth and a Paul Nash – a nice watercolour of a shingle beach. The glass door was locked but there was an assistant on the other side and he buzzed us in.

'Can I help you?' he asked. He was from the Middle East with very dark skin and a jet-black beard. He was in his late twenties, wearing an expensive, tailored suit that made Hawthorne's look resolutely off the peg, but no tie. He had a gold chain around his neck and a gold band on the third finger of his left hand.

Needless to say, Hawthorne had taken an immediate dislike to him. 'Who are you?' he demanded.

'I'm sorry?' The assistant was quick to take offence.

'I'd like to talk to Stephen Spencer.'

'Mr Spencer's busy.'

'It's all right, Faraz. I know these people.'

Spencer had appeared from a back office, making his way across the thick-pile carpet that swallowed up any sound. He was also in a suit and looked much recovered from when I had last seen him. His fair hair was carefully groomed and he had the pink, clean-shaven looks of someone who has just stepped out of the bath.

'How can I help you?' he asked. 'I take it you're not here to buy art.' He was being starchy with us and I could understand why. The last time we had seen him, he had been at his most vulnerable, in tears, and Hawthorne hadn't exactly been sympathetic. There was a simmering hostility between them even now. Hawthorne was homophobic. It was his least endearing trait. I'm sure Spencer had picked up on it.

'I want to know where you were last weekend,' Hawthorne said. His voice and manner were unsparing.

Spencer turned to his assistant. 'Why don't you go back into the office, Faraz?'

'Stephen—'

'It's all right.' Spencer waited until the other man had gone, then answered: 'I already told you.'

'You lied to us. I've spoken to your mother at the

St Osyth Care Home in Frinton. She has no memory of you visiting her.'

Spencer bristled. 'My mother is in the fairly advanced stages of Alzheimer's. There are times when she doesn't even remember who I am.'

'And have all the nurses got Alzheimer's too? None of them remember seeing you either.'

I thought Spencer would deny it but he was cleverer than that. He considered for a moment, then shrugged. 'All right. I was lying.'

'You were with your boyfriend, Faraz. Where is he from, by the way? Iran?'

'Yes. He is. But what makes you think—'

'Please don't treat me like an idiot, Mr Spencer. This is a murder investigation and right now you could be done for obstructing a police officer.'

'You're not a police officer.'

'You lied to DI Grunshaw and you certainly don't want to get on the wrong side of her!' That was true, as I knew only too well. 'That's a very distinctive aftershave your Iranian friend wears and your car stank of it.' Hawthorne sniffed. 'I can smell it on you now. You didn't wait very long for your husband to pass on, did you? Has he moved into your place in Hampstead?'

'No!'

'But Richard Pryce had found out about the two of

you, hadn't he? The marriage, the civil contract, whatever you want to call it, was all over as far as he was concerned. He wanted you to move out.'

'That's not true! Who told you that?' Spencer's eyes narrowed. 'Was it Oliver Masefield?'

'As a matter of fact, it was.' Hawthorne continued before Spencer could interrupt: 'Your late husband's law partner is also the executor of his will. He was actually very discreet but he did mention that the two of them had discussed the contents just a few weeks ago. Now there's only one reason you talk about a will and that's if you're going to change it. And given the fact that you and Davina Richardson are the main beneficiaries and she hasn't done anything to piss him off, while you've been gallivanting around at the weekends with Ali Baba out there' – he jerked a thumb in the direction of the office and I closed my eyes, quietly adding casual racism to the charge sheet against Hawthorne – 'it was a fair bet that he'd rumbled you and that he was about to do something about it.

'The telephone call that you made to Richard at eight o'clock on Sunday evening originated in Chiswick, which is, by coincidence, where your mate Faraz Delijani lives. Cara Grunshaw already knows that and I'm surprised she hasn't been round here already. So before that happens you might as well tell me what you were really up to – you can spare me the graphic details, if you don't mind – and with a bit of luck it'll persuade me that you didn't creep home and commit murder.'

'I didn't kill anyone!' There was a bottle of mineral water on a shelf. Spencer went over and twisted it open. I heard the rush of escaping gas. He poured himself a glass. 'Richard and I had been having difficulties. Yes. We'd talked about spending time apart. And yes – I spent the weekend with Faraz in his flat in Chiswick. Lots of people saw us. On Sunday night we had dinner at a place called L'Auberge on the Upper Richmond Road.' He took out his wallet and produced a slip of paper that he offered to Hawthorne. 'Here's the receipt, but you can ask them if you like. We had a table in the window.'

'I will ask them.' Hawthorne took the receipt.

'This may surprise you, Mr Hawthorne, but I loved Richard very much and I wouldn't have done anything to hurt him.'

'Except for sleeping around behind his back.'

'We had an open marriage. We tolerated each other's indiscretions. And if Richard was going to change his will, it could just as easily have been to do with Davina as me.'

'Why would he have done that?'

'Forget it.' It was clear that Spencer had decided he'd said too much and was regretting it.

'I think you'd better tell me, Mr Spencer.'

'All right.' He frowned. 'If you really must know, she was wearing him out . . . all her demands. He set up her business. He put her son through private education. He was always round there, listening to her problems. But it was never enough. She was bleeding him dry to get more clients who wanted interior decorating and for what it's worth, he didn't even much like her taste. It was all reds and yellows and that horrible shade of green. "Gangreen", he called it! He was desperate to get her out of his life but he couldn't do it because of what had happened in Yorkshire. I never understood it, personally. It wasn't as if it had been his fault. I told him to tell her to fuck off – and maybe he did. Maybe he finally got her out of his system.'

'Do you think she killed him?' Hawthorne asked, a little more gently.

Spencer shook his head. 'No. I've already told you. It was Akira. I was there in the restaurant when she threatened him and I heard it with my own ears. And there was something else . . .'

He paused for effect and for the first time I glanced around the gallery, at the oil paintings and watercolours displayed on the walls, each one carefully isolated in its private pool of light. It would have made a perfect setting if anyone had chosen to film this.

'Richard was on to her,' Spencer continued. 'He told me that he'd had her investigated. You need to talk to Graham Hain at Navigant business management. He's a forensic accountant who worked with Richard and he'd discovered that Akira had a limited company and an income stream that she didn't want anyone to know about. Richard thought she was doing something illegal.'

'Like what?' In fact we already knew this. Oliver Masefield had told us as much, although he had put it less baldly.

'He didn't say. But she'd done everything she could to keep it hidden and it might have had an impact on the divorce. Both sides have to say how much they're worth and he knew she was lying.'

Hawthorne made a mental note of it. He never wrote down anything. He had a prodigious memory – and of course he had me. 'Why didn't you tell me this before?' he asked.

'I was upset when you saw me in Hampstead and I wasn't thinking straight. That's also why I lied to you about Faraz. I didn't want to drag him into this, but the truth is that I really don't have anything to hide. Now, if you don't mind, I have work to do.'

Spencer padded off towards the office. Hawthorne didn't try to stop him.

Back out in the street, I turned on him.

'You can't behave that way!' I exclaimed. 'What happened in there . . . that Ali Baba joke, your whole attitude. You can't talk like that!'

'I did what I had to.' For once, I'd taken Hawthorne by surprise. 'I had to get under his skin, Tony. Don't you see it? He's standing in his smart gallery, surrounded by a million quid's worth of art. And he's lying to us! He thinks he can get away with it. I had to break him down and that's what I did.'

'But I can't put that sort of stuff in the book,' I said.

'Why not?'

'People won't like it.' I paused. 'They won't like you.'

That jolted him. Just for a second I saw the vulnerability, the child he had once been, spark in his eyes and before he could stop himself he asked: 'Do you like me?'

I wasn't sure how to answer. 'I don't know,' I stammered eventually.

He looked at me.

'I don't need you to fucking like me. I just need you to write the fucking book.'

We stood there, staring at each other. There was nothing more to say.

14
Daunt's Bookshop

Daunt's is one of my favourite bookshops in London. It's halfway down Marylebone High Street, which itself has a pleasant, old-fashioned feel; more a neighbourhood than a shopping precinct. Every time I go in – and it's not that far from where I live – I get a sense that I'm stepping back into a more civilised city. (Charing Cross Road used to be the same until high rents drove most of the second-hand bookshops away.) It actually occupies two shops, 83 and 84, knocked together with two doorways and two corridors, one on either side of a sales desk that forms a sort of island in between. The interior has the feel of a Methodist chapel, complete with the reticulated window at the end. The books are stacked on old wooden shelves and as an added quirk they are listed not by author or by subject but by country. Everything feels very narrow. About halfway in, a staircase disappears down to a basement, leaving a rectangular space on the other side where authors are invited to give talks. I have given one or two there myself.

This was where Akira Anno was speaking at half past six that evening. Hawthorne and I arrived in time to get a couple of seats at the back. It was interesting to see how relaxed he was inside the bookshop; certainly more than he had been in Yorkshire. He was completely cheerful as we sat down and it reminded me that he was a member of a book club, one which I would be joining on Monday night. I hadn't read *A Study in Scarlet* for some time. I'd have to spend a few hours with it on Sunday.

About a hundred people had turned up for Akira's event and every seat was taken. There were more people standing at the back. When she finally appeared, making her way down the side, the applause was loud and enthusiastic. I was quite surprised. She didn't have a new book out so there was actually no reason for her – or her audience – to be there. And the title of the talk certainly wouldn't have dragged me out on a miserable November evening.

She was interviewed by a slim man with a tangle of

black hair, black glasses, a black jacket and a black polo neck, a lecturer at the School of Oriental and African Studies whose name I didn't catch. He spent much of the hour discussing her earlier work, *A Cool Breeze in Hiroshima*. The main character, a Korean comfort woman called Jung-soon, finds redemption in the days after the atom bomb is dropped, only to die a few chapters later of leukaemia. I knew the book from the blurb on the back cover and drifted in and out during the next forty minutes, but I did manage to jot down some of what she said.

'The sexualisation of the nuclear arsenal, as a trope, is of course self-evident. It is no coincidence that the first two bombs were Fat *Man* and Little *Boy*, while both the cities have inherently feminine-sounding names, particularly with the unvoiced phoneme at the start of "Hiroshima". As I've explained, I use the rape of Jung-soon that opens the book to some extent to pre-figure what history informs us will come. History or, in this case, her story. But I think we have to be careful. For too long we have allowed such issues as missile pro-liferation, cyberwarfare and nuclear strategy to be seen from a state-centric and male-dominated perspective. If we accept the masculinised identity of the discussion, then it becomes more difficult to challenge it. We cannot allow politics to become gender hierarchical and I think that language can all too easily affect the very way we think.'

All of this may be true but I'm afraid it went right over my head. It wasn't just the sense of what Akira was saying that lost me, it was the manner of her delivery. She spoke very softly and with almost no emotion so that if her talk had been translated into one of those wavelengths you see in medical dramas, it would have appeared as an almost flat line.

The audience loved it. That line about the unvoiced phoneme even got a laugh and the university man was nodding so much his glasses almost fell off. There's no lonelier place than an audience where you're the only person having a bad time – I've often felt this in the theatre – and I was glad when the first part of the talk came to an end and Akira took questions from the floor. At the same time, Hawthorne (who had been blank-faced throughout) nudged me and pointed to a pair of seats about five rows in front of us.

I felt my stomach shrink as I recognised Detective Inspector Cara Grunshaw and her leather-jacketed assistant. They had come to the talk as well, presumably planning to interview Akira a second time when it was over. My worry was that I hadn't informed them we would be there and the moment they saw me they would know I wasn't living up to my side of the agreement that had been forced on me. Worse still, what would I do if she referred to our recent telephone conversation in front of Hawthorne?

I sweated out the question-and-answer session and didn't hear very much of it. I've admired the work of feminist writers from Virginia Woolf to Doris Lessing and Angela Carter, but Akira's brand of humourless introspection – along with her audience's appreciation of it – left me cold. At long last there was a round of applause, an announcement that Akira would be signing books, including her recent collection of haikus, and everyone got to their feet. Hawthorne and I stayed where we were, watching as a short line formed. For all their enthusiasm, not many people stayed to buy books, but presumably they had them already. Grunshaw and her friend Darren were sitting with their backs to us. I wondered if they knew we were there.

We waited until everyone had gone, then moved forward, all four of us descending on Akira in a pincer movement, coming at her from both sides. She was clearly alarmed to see us, giving the lecturer a quick peck on each cheek and sending him hastily on his way. Grunshaw noticed Hawthorne and turned to him first.

'I didn't expect to see you here.' She glanced at me and I couldn't escape the glint in her eye which under-

lined what she had just said with a streak of malevo-
lence.

'You don't mind if we join you, do you?' Hawthorne
asked, indifferently.

'Not at all.' Now she focused on Akira. 'We need to
have a few more words, Ms Anno. Do you mind?'

'Does my opinion really matter?'

'Not really. Is there somewhere we can go?'

One of the managers showed us downstairs. It
wasn't completely private but there was a wicker table
and some chairs tucked away in an alcove and it was at
least a little quieter. Grunshaw had come on her own,
leaving Darren upstairs. Hawthorne took the chair
next to her, facing Akira, who sat with her legs crossed,
glowering behind her mauve spectacles. I stood leaning against West Africa with South Africa in front of
me and Italy just across the corridor. There was little
natural light down here. Glass tiles in the ceiling gave
a blurry view of the area where Akira had just been
speaking.

Once we were settled, Grunshaw weighed in with
the obvious question that had brought her here. 'So
where were you on Sunday night, Miss Anno?'

'I told you . . .' Akira began.

'We know that you weren't at Glasshayes Cottage

in Lyndhurst. Did you really think we wouldn't check what you'd said?'

Akira shrugged as if to suggest that was exactly what she'd expected.

'You realise that lying to a police officer involved in a murder investigation is a very serious offence?'

'I didn't lie to you, Detective Inspector. My life is a very busy one. I sometimes have difficulty remembering.'

It wasn't true. She didn't even try to make it sound so.

'So where were you?'

She blinked a couple of times, then pointed at me. 'I'm not talking in front of him. He is a commercial writer. He has no business here.'

I had never heard anyone make the word 'commercial' sound so dirty.

'He's staying,' Hawthorne said. I was surprised he had taken my side, but then of course he would want me to write what happened.

'Where were you?' Grunshaw repeated the question. I was quite surprised she didn't try to get rid of me.

Akira, too, had seen that she wasn't going to get her way. She shrugged a second time. 'With a friend. In London.'

'And the name of your friend?'

Still Akira hesitated and I wondered what she was so desperate to hide. But she had no choice. 'Dawn Adams.'

That was the publisher she had been having dinner with the night she threw a glass of wine over Richard Pryce.

'You were with her for the whole weekend?'

'No. On Sunday. She lives in Wimbledon.'

This last piece of information was offered grudgingly, as if it would get Grunshaw off her back. But the detective inspector had only just started. 'What time did you arrive? What time did you leave?'

Akira sighed in an ill-natured way. She would rather have been answering questions about unvoiced phonemes. I wondered if she and Dawn Adams had been having an affair, although I'd have thought she would have volunteered such information willingly. Still, there was definitely something she didn't want us to know. 'I arrived maybe six o'clock. I left the next day.'

'You stayed overnight?'

'We talked. We had too much to drink. I didn't want to drive. So she put me up.'

'You do realise we'll ask Ms Adams for a statement.'

'I'm not lying to you!' Akira scowled. 'I don't like

telling you about my private life. Certainly not in front of him.' Again the finger with its long, pointed nail jabbed in my direction. 'She's a friend of mine. That's all. She got divorced last year and now she's on her own.'

'She went to court?'

'Yes.'

'Who represented her?'

'I don't know.'

'Who represented her ex-husband?'

There was a long pause. Akira really didn't want to tell us. 'It was Richard Pryce.'

I didn't like to admit it, but DI Grunshaw had certainly hit the nail on the head. Two women, one a writer, the other a publisher, had both come up against the same lawyer. At least one of them had been trashed by him and had threatened to kill him. And now the other one was providing an alibi for her.

I managed to catch Hawthorne's eye and silently urged him to ask the one thing I wanted to know. For once, he obliged. 'I've been reading your poetry,' he said brightly, addressing Akira.

Akira might have been flattered but she said nothing.

'I was interested in one of your haikus . . .'

'Are you taking the piss?' Grunshaw demanded.

'It was haiku number one eight two.'

That surprised her. She waited for Hawthorne to continue but in fact I was the one who recited it.

'*Your breath in my ear / Your every word a trial / The sentence is death.*'

'What does that mean?' Hawthorne asked.

'What do you think it means?' Akira returned.

Hawthorne shrugged, unfazed. 'It could mean all sorts of things. If it was about Richard Pryce, it could be that you didn't like what he said about you. He was going to lie about you in court. That's what you told us. So you decided to kill him.'

There was a brief silence. Then Akira laughed. It was strange because there was absolutely no humour in it at all. If she had grabbed hold of a stinging nettle and gasped in pain, it would have sounded much the same.

'You have not understood a single word I wrote,' she said. She turned to me. 'And the first line is *You breathe in my ear*. If you're going to quote my work, you could at least get it right!' She was pleased with herself, scoring a point. 'Do I really have to explain it to you?' she continued. 'The haiku was not about Richard Pryce. I wrote it before I knew of his existence. It's about my marriage. It was written for Adrian Lockwood. I read it to him! He was the one who demeaned me, who humiliated me with his self-regard and his indifference to my needs. The imagery is obvious.' Her nostrils flared. 'The first line is sexual. It is Claudius with Gertrude. He is lying next to me in bed, close enough for me to feel his breath. It is not just what he says. It is what he is. I have come to realise that by marrying a second time, I have placed myself in the condemned cell. I use the word "trial" in two senses. It refers to my day-to-day suffering but also to the fact that I am legally his wife, that this is my status in a court of law. And I am not sentencing him to death. In fact, it is exactly the other way round. I am the one who is dying, although the last line is of course a paraprosdokian, with the double entendre in "sentence" – which gives rise to the suggestion that, despite all the evidence, I will survive.'

All of this had come out in a flat sort of whisper but she raised her voice for the last three words, adding a touch of Gloria Gaynor. Grunshaw was uninterested but Hawthorne ploughed on anyway.

'Were you aware that Richard Pryce was investigating you?'

'He was fascinated by me. He wanted to understand me.'

'That's not what I mean. He had employed a forensic accountant called Graham Hain to look into your finances. He thought you were fiddling him.'

'That's ridiculous.'

'But it's true.'

'He would have found nothing. I have nothing to hide.' But both her eyes and her lips had narrowed and her body language was defensive.

'I'd like a contact number for Dawn Adams,' Grunshaw said, taking over the interview once again.

'You can reach her at Kingston Press.'

Kingston Press was an independent publishing house. I'd vaguely heard of them.

'She works there?'

'She owns it.'

'Thank you, Ms Anno.' That was Grunshaw talking. I got the feeling that she had come to her own conclusions about Akira and the verdict was 'Not guilty'.

We stood up and made our way back to street level. Akira went first, with Hawthorne next to her and then Cara Grunshaw a few steps behind. I was last and so I was isolated, with nowhere to go, when Grunshaw suddenly stopped and turned on me, halfway up the stairs.

'You didn't tell me you were coming here,' she said. Her body seemed massive, blocking the stairwell, and her eyes behind those chunky black spectacles were extraordinarily aggressive.

I looked for Hawthorne but he had disappeared ahead. 'I was going to call you this evening,' I said. 'It's a complete waste of time trying to get information out of me. Hawthorne never tells me anything.'

'You've got ears. You've got eyes. Use them.' She glared at me. 'This is your last warning.'

'You blocked *Foyle's War*—'

'If you find out who killed Pryce before me, you'll never shoot a frame of your fucking television series again, I promise you.'

She swivelled round and with her black-clad thighs and buttocks waddling in front of me, continued up to the entrance.

I thought my adventures at Daunt Books were over but there was still one more twist to come. Darren was waiting for us and as I reached the ground floor and hurried over to Hawthorne, he bumped into me, almost knocking me off my feet. 'Sorry,' he said, making it quite clear that he had done it deliberately.

Akira Anno was standing at the door. Hawthorne was in front of the sales desk with one of the managers behind. The door to the street was open and it was raining yet again, the rain tapping at the windows. I hadn't brought an umbrella. I thought we'd have to call a taxi.

I took a step towards the exit and it was then that Cara Grunshaw called out to me, her voice rising in indignation. 'Excuse me!'

I turned round. 'I'm sorry?'

'Aren't you going to pay for that book?' She said it so loudly that everyone in the shop must have heard.

My head swam. 'I don't know what you're talking about.'

'I saw you pick up a book just now. You put it in your case.'

It was true that I was carrying my black shoulder bag. Jill had given it to me as a birthday present and I nearly always have it with me. Was it heavier than it had been when I came in? My hand dropped to my side and felt the leather. There was something in the outer compartment and, I noticed, the straps had come loose.

'I didn't—' I began.

'Can I help?' The manager had come out from behind the sales desk. I had met her before when I had come to give talks at the shop and she had always been very friendly, a bit like a schoolteacher with her closely cropped grey hair and bright, blue eyes.

'Do you run this place?' Grunshaw asked.

'Yes. I'm Rebecca LeFevre. Who are you?'

'Detective Inspector Cara Grunshaw.' She gestured at her partner, giving me his full name for the first time. 'DC Darren Mills.'

LeFevre looked at me with astonishment. 'Do you mind if we look in your bag?' she asked.

I glanced at Hawthorne but he wasn't in any hurry to help. If anything, he was amused. I already knew what had happened. Darren Mills had done this when he bumped into me at the top of the stairs. He had slipped a book into my case to embarrass me, to punish me, perhaps even to have me arrested, and if I had been sensible I would have left it there and simply walked out or at least tried to explain. Instead I opened the case and took out a thick paperback, a book called *Excalibur Rising*, the second volume in the Doomworld series by Mark Belladonna. This was the same series that Gregory Taylor had bought on the day he died. The book had actually been on display on a table at the front of the shop and there it was, resting in my hand.

Akira Anno was staring at the book with a look of queasy horror on her face. It took her a moment to find the words. 'He's a thief!' she exclaimed.

'I'm not a thief . . .' I began. 'This is a set-up!' I pointed at Mills. 'He put it in my case. He barged into me when I came upstairs.'

Mills raised his hands in a show of surrender. 'Why would I do a thing like that?' he demanded.

Grunshaw looked at me thunderously. 'Are you accusing a police officer of planting evidence?'

'Yes! I am!'

'You realise I could arrest you?' She turned to LeFevre. 'Do you want me to arrest him?'

'Wait a minute.' LeFevre was looking at me in dismay. If she had reminded me of a teacher before, she was now more like a headmistress with a child who had once been her favourite. 'You've let the bookshop down. You've let your readers down. You've let yourself down.' I could almost hear her saying it. 'Could I have it back?' That was what she actually said.

I handed the book to her. I could feel my cheeks burning.

'The policy at Daunt's is to refer all shoplifters to the police,' she went on. 'I have to say, I'm surprised and very disappointed, but it's up to the police to decide if they want to take any further action.'

'I didn't do it!' I knew I sounded pathetic. I couldn't help myself.

'I will say, though, that you're not welcome back in this shop, Anthony. I'm very sorry. And I don't think we'll be stocking you after this.'

I'd had enough. I really couldn't take any more. I pushed past Hawthorne and Akira and, with their eyes burning into me, hurried out into the rain.

15

Rum and Coke

I didn't see Hawthorne again until Monday evening, when, instead of going to see *Ghosts* at the Almeida, I rang the doorbell at River Court to join him at his book club. At least this time I was expected. Normally, which is to say on the last two occasions, I had to resort to subterfuge to get anywhere near the flat where he lived. We'd arranged to meet at seven o'clock and the idea was that we would go together to wherever the group met.

He was standing in the corridor when the lift doors opened and I was afraid he was going to step in and take me straight back down. But his own front door was open and he seemed quite genial as he led me back towards the flat.

'How are you, Tony?'

'I'm all right.' But I wasn't, not after what had happened at Daunt's and I wanted him to know it.

'You sound like you got out of bed on the wrong side. Come in and have a rum and Coke. That'll cheer you up.'

I hardly ever drink Coca-Cola and I don't much like rum, but the invitation intrigued me on all sorts of levels. I followed him in.

Hawthorne's flat would have told me more about him if it had actually belonged to him but it was exactly as I remembered from the one time I'd been there, bare to the point of depressing with windows that were too narrow for the wonderful view they could have provided: the River Thames flowing darkly through the evening gloom. There were still no pictures, no flowers, no clutter . . . nothing that would suggest he did anything but sleep here.

Except, of course, for the models. I had discovered Hawthorne's liking for Airfix kits on my first visit and although he had been sheepish at first, he had allowed his enthusiasm to take over and this had led to one of our very few conversations that wasn't about crime. The surfaces were crowded with tanks, jeeps, ambulances, anti-aircraft guns, battleships, aircraft carriers and so on, while dozens of different aircraft dangled from the ceiling on wires. I noticed the Chieftain Mark 10 that he had been working on the last time I came. It had been perfectly assembled, with not a smear of glue nor a paint stroke out of place. The collection must have taken up thousands of hours of his time. I could imagine Hawthorne, hunched over the table, working into the night. They would also be hours when he could completely cut himself off from the world outside.

I had asked him when he had started model-making. *It was a hobby when I was a kid.* The more time I spent with Hawthorne, the more I suspected that something traumatic must have happened to him when he was young and it had created the adult he had become. I don't just mean the casual homophobia, the moodiness, his attitude to me. Becoming a detective, marrying, separating, living alone in an empty flat, making models . . . all of it seemed to be driven by the same catastrophe, which might have happened in Yorkshire and which might have led him to change his name.

'You've started a new model,' I said.

It was spread out on the table, a helicopter with RAF RESCUE printed on the side.

'Westland Sea King,' he said. 'WS-61. Used in the Falklands, the Gulf War, Iraq, Afghanistan . . . Search and Rescue. You want that drink?'

'Do you have any wine?'

'No. I've got some rum.'

'That's fine.'

Hawthorne didn't drink. He had never told me that but nor had I ever seen him with anything alcoholic. Even at the Station Inn in Ribblehead he'd stuck to water. I followed him into the kitchen, which connected to the living area through a wide doorway. You can learn a lot about someone from their kitchen – but this one was useless. Everything was high-end, brand new and looked as clean as the day it had been fitted. It doesn't matter how many times I clean my own flat, I'm always embarrassed by the oven, which greets visitors with the carbonised memories of a hundred meals. Hawthorne's oven had pristine glass doors and silver gas rings that I doubted had ever been switched on.

And there, standing on a marble counter, was the bottle of rum he had offered me. Had he gone out and bought it? I thought it was more likely that he had been given it by someone as a gift, like Richard Pryce and his £2,000 bottle of wine. Either way, the plastic around the cap was unbroken. Along with the single glass that had been placed next to it, it was somehow totemic. I knew at once that this was the only alcohol in the house and that it had been placed there deliberately for me.

Hawthorne went to the fridge and opened the door. Casually, trying not to look too nosy, I turned my head to examine the contents. I wasn't surprised to see that the interior was as clinical as the rest of the kitchen. In my house, we either have too much food or none at all and there are times when I find myself furiously ransacking the fridge to find the single ingredient I need. Hawthorne's fridge was monastic by comparison. He mainly seemed to eat ready meals. There were about half a dozen of them in plastic trays, stacked so neatly and with so much space around them that they had become quite unappetising, like an artwork by Damien Hirst. The vegetable trays were half empty, although I could see what looked like a bunch of carrots through the frosted plastic. It was the fridge of a man who had no particular interest in food. He would take out a packet and microwave it and he might not even examine the lid to see what he was going to eat. Now, he plucked a can of Coke out of the door, took some ice from the freezer and brought them over to the table.

'You're not going to join me,' I said.

'I've got some coffee.' There was a single white mug beside the sink. I hadn't noticed it before.

Two lumps of ice, about an inch of rum, half the can, a slice of lemon that he produced from somewhere . . . he made the drink mechanically, but slid it towards me with a certain pride. Again, as so often with Hawthorne, I got a sense of a child playing at being an adult.

He took his coffee, then sat down at the table. I produced four folded sheets of paper out of my pocket and slid them across. 'These are the pages you wanted,' I said, still keeping my distance.

'What pages?'

'From the book. When I met Davina Richardson without you. You said you wanted to see them.'

'Oh. Right.' He placed them to one side. He didn't even open them.

'You could at least say thank you.'

He looked at me carefully, puzzled as to why I should be so annoyed. Could he really have forgotten what I had been through at Daunt's? 'All right,' he admitted, finally. 'So you rubbed Cara up the wrong way.'

'Nice of you to notice.' I took the first sip of my drink, wishing he could have found it in himself to get me a glass of wine or a gin and tonic.

'I assumed it was her who slipped that book into your bag. I somehow don't see you enjoying the Doom-world series.'

'What? And if it had been Charles Dickens or Sarah Waters, you think I might have been tempted to go on a shoplifting spree?'

'No, mate. That's not what I meant.' His voice was apologetic now but it struck me that he still looked quite amused.

'You don't seem to understand. What happened at

that bookshop was terrible! It could be the end of my career. If it gets into the papers, I'll be destroyed.' I was almost trembling with anger and indignation. 'Anyway, it wasn't her. It was her assistant. Mills.'

'He's a nasty piece of work too. They suit each other. So what have you done to piss them off?'

I had no choice. I had to explain what had happened, how DI Grunshaw had visited my home and assaulted me. 'She wants to solve the case before you do,' I said. 'She wants me to contact her and tell her everything I know.'

'That's ridiculous!' Hawthorne exclaimed. 'You don't know anything!'

'Wait a minute . . . !' I found my hand tightening around my glass. 'I may not know who killed Richard Pryce – but for that matter, nor do you.'

'I've narrowed it down to one of two suspects.' Hawthorne blinked at me over his coffee.

'Which two suspects?'

'That's my point. You don't know. So you can't say.'

'As a matter of fact, I called her.' Even in my anger, I felt guilty having to admit it. 'I didn't have any choice. She blocked the filming of *Foyle's War*. At least, I think she did. I told her that we'd been to Yorkshire and that Gregory Taylor had been killed. I also told her about the break-in at Adrian Lockwood's office.' I waited for Hawthorne to respond and when he said nothing, I added: 'I had to tell her something. And she said she knew all that anyway.'

'She was lying.' I had thought Hawthorne would be more annoyed with me, but he was unconcerned. 'Cara Grunshaw and Darren Mills are both thick as shit. I've met police dogs with more intelligence than those two. You could tell them everything we've done, down to the last word, and they'd still end up running round in a circle, sniffing each other's arses.'

'Do you have to be quite so picturesque?'

'You can call them every day if it'll keep them off your back. You should have told me about this sooner. Honestly, mate. We're streets ahead of them. You'll have your book finished and in the Oxfam shops before they work out who did it. That's why I was called in. The police know they're going nowhere with this one. They need all the help they can get.'

There was a long pause. I drank some more. He had used real Coke and it was horribly sweet. Sugar with sugar.

'Do you really know who killed Richard Pryce?' I asked.

He nodded. 'One of two.'

'Well, at least give me a little help! I've been everywhere you've been. I've seen everything you've seen. And yet I haven't got the faintest idea who killed him. Just tell me one clue that I've missed – one clue that makes it all make sense.'

'It's not like that, Tony.' I could tell that Hawthorne wanted a cigarette but he couldn't smoke, not when he was surrounded by someone else's fittings and furniture. 'I've told you before. You've got to find the shape. That's all.'

I frowned, not following him.

'I'd have thought it's the same when you write a book. Isn't that how you start . . . looking for the shape?'

I was thrown by what Hawthorne had said because he was absolutely right. At the very start of the process, when I'm creating a story, I do think of it as having a particular, geometrical shape. For example, I was about to start work on *Moriarty*, my Sherlock Holmes sequel, and it had occurred to me that the twisting narrative, which would turn in on itself at the end, was rather like a Möbius strip. *The House of Silk* had the appearance of a letter Y. A novel is a container for 80,000 to 90,000 words and you might see it as a jelly mould. You pour them all in and hope they'll set. But it had never occurred to me that a detective might see his world in the same way.

'OK,' I said. 'So exactly what shape does the murder of Richard Pryce have?'

'It wasn't just Richard Pryce who died. You've got to remember Gregory Taylor went under that train and there are three explanations for that.'

'It was an accident. It was suicide. Someone deliberately killed him.'

'That's right. And each one of those possibilities changes the shape of the whole thing.'

My head was spinning: Hawthorne wasn't making a great deal of sense. Or perhaps it was the rum. 'Did you always want to be a detective?' I asked him.

The question took him by surprise. 'Yes.'

'Since you were a child?'

At once he was on the defensive. 'Why are you asking me that? Why do you want to know?'

'I've told you. Because I'm writing about you.' I wasn't sure if I dared ask the next question but this seemed the right moment. I plunged in. 'Did you know that man in Yorkshire?'

'Which man?'

'Mike Carlyle. He called you Billy. Is that really your name?'

Hawthorne said nothing. Briefly, he lowered his head as if wondering what to do. When he looked up at me again, there was something in his eyes that I had never seen before and it took me a few seconds to realise what it was. He was in pain.

'I told you, I'd never seen him before. He was just someone who was making a mistake.'

'I'm not sure I believe you.'

And then the shutters came down. That was the thing about Hawthorne. He had a way of cutting off anyone who got too close – he might have been doing it all his life – and when he spoke again it was very softly and with no emotion at all. 'I'll tell you something, mate. Suppose I'm having second thoughts about you and me? Suppose I've decided this was a bad idea?'

I couldn't believe what I was hearing. I was the one who had been dragged into this. I was the one that didn't want to be here.

'This wasn't my idea,' I reminded him. 'It was yours.'

'We could stop right now. Who gives a toss about another book. There are plenty of books.' He pointed. 'You could walk out that door.'

'It's a bit late for that. I've signed a three-book contract . . . remember? *We've* signed a three-book contract.'

'You don't need me. You can make up the next one.'

'Believe me, I'd love to. It would be an awful lot easier. But I've already spent a week on this one and I'm not going to stop until I work out your shape or your pattern, or whatever you want to call it, and find out who killed Richard Pryce.'

We sat there, glaring at each other. Then Hawthorne looked at his watch. 'We should go downstairs. They'll be waiting for us.'

'I'm not your enemy, Hawthorne,' I said. 'I'm trying to help you.'

'Yeah. Well, you've been a lot of help so far.'

He walked away. I had drunk less than half of the rum and Coke. I left the rest behind.

16
The Book Group

We took the lift down together and it was very strange because by the time we arrived, Hawthorne was quite back to his old self. It was as if the sliding door had acted like a wipe in one of those old-fashioned feature films, cutting off all the animosity between us and taking us to a new scene where we were friends again. Certainly, as we stepped out on the third floor, the argument had been forgotten. Hawthorne was jaunty, wired up, a little nervous. I knew how protective he was of his private life. He hadn't really wanted me to come to his book group – presumably he had been cajoled by the other members. At the same time, though, these weren't close friends I was about to meet. He had once told me that they'd all come together from the local library. Was that true? At least one of them had a flat in the same block as him. Perhaps they all did.

I smelled Indian cooking as we walked down the corridor. There was an open door about halfway along and we stopped outside. Hawthorne undid the single button of his jacket; his one concession to informality.

'Who lives here?' I asked.

'Her name is Lisa Chakraborty.'

'The last time I came to this building, I met a young man in a wheelchair . . .'

Hawthorne cast a doleful glance in my direction. It was already more than he wanted me to know. 'That's her son.'

Kevin Chakraborty. The boy with muscular dystrophy who had made a joke about reaching the top button in the lift.

We went in.

It was surprising how two flats in the same building, both about the same shape and size, could be so very different. Lisa Chakraborty lived in a space that was the opposite of open-plan. An enclosed, L-shaped corridor led almost reluctantly into a living room that was darker and more cluttered, with heavy furniture, wallpaper, chandeliers. The sofas were fat, smothered in cushions, facing each other like old enemies across the low, ornate coffee table that kept them apart. The carpet actually had a swirly pattern, something I hadn't seen for some time. There were ornaments everywhere: porcelain figures, vases, glass paperweights, Tiffany lamps, different pieces of silverware. The room was as crowded, and as random, as an antique shop.

I noticed something odd about the layout although it took me a moment to work out what it was. Despite the clutter, a single wide space had been left, leading into the room from the entrance. The doors and corridors were perhaps one-third wider than average. I realised it had been designed that way for Kevin, who would have to manoeuvre his way round in his wheelchair.

He was not there, but an assortment of people stood clutching drinks, looking awkward in the way guests always do when they choose to stand together even though they're surrounded by places to sit. My first impression, possibly unfair, was that they seemed to be quite freakish – mainly because they were all so very different. A very tall woman with a very short man. A pair of identical twins. A plump lady in a sari. A silver-haired, distinguished-looking man, perhaps South American. An extravagantly bearded man in a kilt, another small and shrimpy man with round glasses, in tweed. There were about a dozen of them in all. If I hadn't known they were connected by books it would have been difficult to find a reason for them being in the same room.

The woman in the sari stepped forward, beaming. She had black hair streaked with grey and wide, searching eyes. I had never seen anyone with so much silver jewellery: three necklaces, rings on every finger and one in her nose, a sari brooch shaped like a peacock and earrings that brushed against her shoulders. She was about fifty years old but her skin was unlined and she positively radiated warmth and good humour.

'Mr Hawthorne!' she exclaimed. 'You're very naughty! We were beginning to think you weren't going to come. And this is your friend?'

I introduced myself.

'We are so delighted you could join us. Come in, come in. I'm Lisa Chakraborty but you must call me Lisa, please, and I shall call you Tony.'

'Well, actually—'

'I'm afraid I'm on my own tonight. My husband never takes part in our little gatherings. He has actually no interest at all in books. He's gone to the cinema.' She spoke as if she was in a hurry, the words falling over each other in their enthusiasm to leave her mouth. 'We're starting with a little glass of wine and some food and then we'll get down to business. Sherlock Holmes, no less! And to have a real investigator and an author who has written about the great detective himself – it's a very special treat! Mr Brannigan! Have you a glass of wine for our guest?'

Mr Brannigan was the short husband with the tall wife. He had been smiling as I came in and the smile was still there, fixed into place and giving him a slightly manic quality. He was almost completely bald, with a round, eager-to-please face and a moustache that trembled on his upper lip. 'Hello there!' he barked, thrusting a glass of lukewarm white wine into my hand. 'Kenneth Brannigan. Very nice to meet you, Tony. Very good of you to come. Let me introduce you to my better half. This is Angela.'

His wife – gaunt and imperious-looking – had joined him. 'How nice to meet you,' she said. She had a cut-glass voice and didn't smile. 'You write the Eric Rider books?'

'Alex Rider, yes.'

She gave me a sad look. 'I don't think our children ever read them, I'm afraid.'

'Hammy did!' Kenneth contradicted her. He blinked at me. 'Hammy read quite a few of them when he was twelve. *Artemis Fowl.* That was his favourite.'

'Actually, that was Eoin Colfer,' I said.

'I'll be interested to hear what you think about Sherlock Holmes,' Angela said, going on quickly before I could tell her. 'I find him very difficult, personally. I don't know why he was chosen.'

'Not our cup of Horlicks at all,' Kenneth agreed. 'But we've all been watching Benedict Cumberbatch in *Sherlock* on the telly. I suppose it might be interesting to see where it all began.'

Gradually, I made my way around the room. I met a veterinary surgeon, a psychiatrist and a retired concert pianist. Hawthorne hadn't joined me. He was standing on his own, watching me warily from the side. But if he was afraid I was going to find out more about his private life, he needn't have worried. I did try to dig a little, asking some of the people I met about him, but nobody seemed to know anything very much, or perhaps it was just that they were reluctant to tell me. He was simply Hawthorne, the man who lived on his own upstairs, who used to be a detective. I got the sense that he was as much a mystery to everyone else as he was to me. Only the man in the kilt (a meat trader, working at Smithfield Market, as it turned out) added a little more. Lowering his voice, he complained that Hawthorne was the only member of the group who didn't allow them to meet in his flat. 'I don't know what he's hiding,' he muttered in clipped tones. 'But I don't think it's right.'

Meanwhile, Lisa Chakraborty was bustling around

with plates of food that included samosas, croquettes and other Indian snacks that were actually more pastry than anything else. Brannigan dutifully followed her with the wine. I didn't feel like eating or drinking and I was relieved when Lisa announced that the discussion would begin in five minutes. As various members of the group took their seats, I picked up a couple of dirty plates and followed her into the kitchen.

'You're very kind, Tony. Thank you. Please put them by the dishwasher.'

'How did the book group begin?' I asked her as I carried them across.

'It was my idea. I put an advertisement in the local library. We've been going now for almost five years.'

'Has Hawthorne always been a member?'

'Oh yes. Absolutely! From the very beginning. I met him in the lift, you know. He lives on his own upstairs.'

We were interrupted by a soft whirring sound and, looking around, I saw Kevin appear at the doorway, wheeling himself in. He seemed pleased rather than surprised to see me standing there with his mother, but then of course it was he who had been responsible for my invitation. He had not only recognised me in the lift, he had also known who I was visiting – which meant that Hawthorne must have told him about me. I wondered what he must have thought of my going all the way back down to the ground floor like that. He quickly let me know.

'Hello,' he said. He had quickly recognised me and smiled knowingly. 'Have you been up and down and up and down in any more lifts?'

'It's nice to meet you again, Kevin,' I said. 'How are you?'

'Fairly terrible. Mustn't complain.'

Lisa cut in. 'The book group is about to begin, my dear. Is there something that you want?'

'Are there any samosas left?'

'Of course.'

'And can I have a Coke?'

She went to the fridge, took out a can and opened it for him. She added a straw, then placed it in a holder on the side of his wheelchair. She arranged three samosas on a plate and rested it on his lap.

Kevin looked up at me cheerfully. 'I flick them into my mouth,' he said, answering a question I hadn't asked. 'Like tiddlywinks.'

'You know that's not true,' his mother scolded him. 'And you shouldn't tell jokes like that! Kevin has Duchenne muscular dystrophy,' she explained to me, barely taking a breath. 'But he still has some movement in both his arms. Enough to eat.' She waggled a finger. 'And he eats too much.'

'It's your fault. You shouldn't be such a good cook.'

'You're going to be too heavy for that wheelchair and then where shall we be?'

'Bye, Anthony!' Kevin grinned and spun round. The kitchen was designed, like the rest of the house, so that there was plenty of space for him. We both watched him as he wheeled himself back down the corridor, the electric motor humming. There was a door open at the end but I couldn't see anything of his room. He disappeared inside.

'His arms are getting weaker,' Lisa said, more quietly. 'And there will come a time when he won't be able to eat either. After that it will just be liquid food. We both know that but we try not to talk about it. That's the trouble with Duchenne. It's one thing after another, really.'

'I'm very sorry,' I muttered. I was embarrassed. I wasn't quite sure what to say.

'You don't need to be. He's a lovely boy. Handsome, like his father. I'm very lucky to have him.' She was beaming at me. 'Of course, he gets depressed sometimes and we ask ourselves how we're going to cope. We have our up days and our down days. But your friend Mr Hawthorne has been an absolute godsend. He's a remarkable man. From the moment he entered our lives, it's hard to explain the difference he's made. He and Kevin are best friends. They spend hours together.' She lowered her voice. 'I do sometimes think that Kevin might have given up, actually, if it wasn't for him.'

I glanced into the living room. Hawthorne was engaged in conversation with the South American man and had forgotten about me. 'But Kevin helps Hawthorne too,' I said.

'Oh yes. Mr Hawthorne is always asking for him.'

'What exactly does he do?'

I do think Lisa Chakraborty was about to tell me but at that exact moment Kenneth Brannigan put his head round the door. 'All set and ready!' he announced.

'I'll just bring the coffee.'

It was already made. Lisa brushed past me, carrying it out. I followed her, aware that I had just missed an opportunity to open a back door into Hawthorne's life. At the same time, I now knew where Kevin's room was to be found and already a plan was formulating in my mind. The evening wasn't over yet.

Everyone had sat down in a rough circle around the coffee table, which was now scattered with copies of A Study in Scarlet that had appeared from nowhere. There weren't quite enough seats so several of the guests were crushed together on the sofas while the twins were cross-legged, in identical positions, on the floor. An upright chair had been left free for me, next to Hawthorne. I went over to it and sat down.

'Where were you?' he asked.

'I was in the kitchen. With Lisa. I met Kevin.' I watched his eyes when I said that but he showed no interest.

'Don't talk about the case,' he muttered darkly.

'Do you mean the murder of Enoch Drebber in Lauriston Gardens?' I asked.

'You know what I mean.'

'I'll do my best.'

Lisa Chakraborty opened the proceedings before Hawthorne could say anything more. 'Good evening, everybody. I am very happy to welcome you to my apartment tonight as we discuss *A Study in Scarlet*, written in 1886 by Sir Arthur Ignatius Conan Doyle. Before we begin our discussion, let me say how fortunate we are to have a very famous writer with us. Tony has worked on *Agatha Christie's Poirot*, *Midsomer Murders* and *Foyle's War*. He has also written many detective stories of his own, for adults and for children. I'm sure Anthony has many interesting insights he can share with us and I do hope we'll have time to hear him speak.

But let's all begin by giving him a River Court Book Club welcome!'

There was a patter of applause, which was embarrassing with so few people in the room, but I smiled gamely. Hawthorne did not join in.

'And so let's move straight away to the adventure that has brought us all together . . .'

I had realised by now that I had no interest whatsoever in what anyone in the room thought of *A Study in Scarlet* and somehow I wasn't at all surprised that although they had all enjoyed the BBC television series, and despite what Lisa had said, not a single one of them seemed to like the source material.

'I was disappointed . . . it's so clumsily written!' This was Kenneth Brannigan, kicking off the proceedings. 'It's meant to be narrated by Dr Watson. He's set up as the narrator but halfway through you suddenly find yourself transported to the Sierra Blanco in North America and before you know it, you've gone back thirty years before the story even began and you've got this ridiculous gang of Mormons—'

'Doyle really doesn't like Mormons, does he! I would say his depiction is actually quite racist.'

'The book was very short. At least it had that going for it.'

'I didn't understand the end at all. Why are the last two lines written in Latin?'

'I didn't believe a single word of it . . .'

A *Study in Scarlet* is a book I've always loved and I only half listened to the group as, one after another, they weighed in with their opinions. Curiously, having invited me to join the group, no one seemed to notice I was in the room – but that suited me fine. My mind was elsewhere.

Kevin and Hawthorne. The snatch of conversation I'd heard on the twelfth floor: *I couldn't do it without you.* What couldn't he do? Why had Kevin even been in Hawthorne's flat? I had to know.

About forty minutes into the conversation, and still without having contributed anything, I leaned over to Hawthorne and whispered, 'Where's the toilet?'

Lisa Chakraborty had overheard me. 'It's down the corridor, second on the left,' she announced loudly, so that everyone in the room could hear. Silence fell as I got up and left the room. I felt the entire group watching me.

'That clue on the wall,' I heard someone say. 'The word "RACHE" painted in blood. That's silly really. That would never happen in real life . . .'

I continued down the corridor and the voices faded

away, swallowed up by the thick walls and carpets and the excess of furniture. I wasn't going to the toilet. I was a little ashamed of myself, intruding this way – but I'd made up my mind. I almost certainly wouldn't be invited back to Lisa's flat so I would never get another chance like this. I continued past the toilet to the room I had seen Kevin entering from the kitchen. I stood there for a moment, with my ear pressed against the wood. There was no sound coming from inside. Gently, I turned the handle. Somewhere in my head a voice was telling me that this was a terrible thing to be doing. But another voice was already practising my excuse. *So sorry. I got the wrong door.*

I looked inside.

It might have been a typical teenager's bedroom apart from the hospital-style bed with the hoist standing next to it, the extra-wide doorway into the bathroom and the strange smell of medicine and disinfectant. It was messy. The lights were low. I might have noticed posters from *Star Wars* and *The Matrix* on the walls, piles of books and magazines. But instead my eyes were drawn, first to Kevin, who was sitting at a table with his back to me and who hadn't heard me come in, and then to the screen of the industrial-sized computer that was in front of him. The computer wasn't an Apple or any make I recognised. It was about five

or six metres away from me and if it had been display-
ing written data, I would have been unable to read it.
Even an image would have been hard to identify. But
what was on the screen was obvious to me and it was so
unexpected, so bewildering, that for a moment I forgot
everything else.

I was looking at a photograph of myself.

Actually, it was me and my younger son, Cassian.
At the time, he was twenty-two years old and was just
finishing a journalism course at City University. I remembered the picture being taken a couple of days
before; it showed the two of us having a drink at the
Jerusalem Tavern, a pub close to where I live. But what
was so shocking was that it had never been published. I
hadn't sent it to anyone. So how could it possibly be on
Kevin's screen?

'Kevin . . . ?' I couldn't stop myself. I hadn't gone
into the room. I spoke to him from the door.

He looked over his shoulder and realised who it was.
I saw the panic in his eyes. At the same time, his hand
scrabbled for the mouse and a moment later the screen
went black. 'What are you doing here?' he demanded.
Kevin liked a joke but he was utterly serious now.

'Where did you get that photograph?' I asked.

'What are you doing here? This is my room!'

'I was looking for the toilet.'

'Do you mind leaving?'

'I'm not leaving until you tell me how you got that picture.' I was already aware that I was behaving badly, that I shouldn't be speaking to him in this way. Is it ever acceptable to lose your temper with someone who is in a wheelchair? But I was truly shocked by what I had just seen. Kevin had been spying not just on me but on my son. 'You've hacked into my computer!' I exclaimed. It was the only way it could have got there.

'No!' He squirmed in his seat.

'Yes!' Looking past him, I saw that the entire surface of his desk was littered with complicated electrical equipment, strange black boxes with antennae and keyboards connected to a labyrinth of wires. I pointed at the screen. 'That was my son. That was me!'

He searched for an explanation, couldn't find one and miserably folded in on himself.

'It wasn't your computer. It was your phone.'

I didn't even try to counter that. 'How did you do that?' I demanded. 'Why did you do that?' And then the next thought hit me. 'Does Hawthorne know about this?'

Of course he did. That was how Kevin helped him. Suddenly I saw it all, perfectly clearly. The automatic number-plate recognition that proved Akira Anno had never driven through Hampshire. The CCTV footage that had been taken from the Welcome Break service station at Fleet. I had wondered why Cara Grunshaw had shown them to Hawthorne but she never had! He had simply stolen them, hacking into the police computer systems with assistance from his brilliant young friend on the third floor.

Kevin was staring at me, aghast. His whole body seemed to have become more twisted and out of control. 'You can't tell Mr Hawthorne you know,' he said.

'Why were you looking at my personal data?' I insisted.

'Because I like you.'

'That's a funny way to show it.'

'I'm interested in you. I read your books.'

Well, that was very flattering. But it didn't mean I liked the idea of Kevin gazing out at me through the camera in my computer or perhaps listening to me, via my iPhone, when I was in the bath. I would have been furious but, given his condition, I was forcing myself to stay calm.

'What exactly do you do for Hawthorne?' I asked.

'I don't do anything. If he knew about this, he'd kill me!'

'Don't lie to me, Kevin . . .'

'I can't tell you. I can't talk about him. Please . . .'

I don't know if he was acting but suddenly there were

tears in his eyes and that simply made me feel like the worst bully in the world. Also, I had been away from the book group for quite some time and I didn't like the idea of Kevin's mother or even Hawthorne himself coming out and finding me here. I didn't know which would have been worse.

I drew a breath and tried to sound reasonable. 'I won't say anything to Hawthorne,' I said. 'But this isn't the end of it, Kevin. I'm going to have to talk to you again.'

'You can't.'

'Yes, I can. And don't try to avoid me.'

'I'm not running anywhere.' Despite everything, his morbid sense of humour was still in play.

'And I want you to stay out of my phone! In fact, I'm going to buy a new phone.'

'Actually, that won't help.'

'For heaven's sake!' I thought I heard someone coming. I waved a finger in Kevin's direction. 'Just stay out of my iPhone, my computer, my iPad . . . even the phone on my front door. Promise me!'

'I promise.' He was looking ill. I couldn't push him any further.

'We're going to talk more about this another time. Do you understand? This isn't over!'

I backed out, closing the door behind me.

'I don't believe Sherlock Holmes for a single minute. I mean, on page thirty-two, he says he's made a study of cigar ashes and he can tell the brand of a cigar just from one glance at the ash.'

I heard Hawthorne's voice as I entered the room and sure enough the entire book group was focused on what he was saying. I took my place and pretended to listen as he continued.

'I can tell you, they've recently tried that in America. They dissolve the ash with a mixture of nitric and hydrochloric acids and then they analyse the results using plasma mass spectrometry.' He shook his head. 'Even then they only get about sixty per cent accuracy so I don't know what Holmes is going on about.'

Hawthorne paused for a moment, then began to talk about the correlation between a suspect's height and the length of his stride – dismissing another of the fictitious detective's theories. But I didn't listen to him. His words simply floated somewhere in the air. I was thinking about Kevin, who had somehow hacked into my phone without even touching it, and I was wondering how Hawthorne could operate as a private detective working for Scotland Yard when he was actually using methods that were quite probably criminal. Certainly, it put him in a very different light.

The rest of the evening went by in a sort of daze.

Someone brought up *The House of Silk* and although it turned out that only a couple of people – the identical twins – had actually read it, I was asked to talk about writing in the style of Conan Doyle. I managed to ramble on for a few minutes before Lisa Chakraborty cut me short.

'Well, thank you so much for that, Anthony,' she said. 'That was a very interesting contribution and a lovely way to round off this evening's discussion. And now all that's left for me to do is to hand over to Christine, who has chosen our next book for the New Year. I'll let her introduce it.'

Christine – spectacles, grey hair, loose-fitting cardigan – got to her feet. 'I've chosen a modern work,' she said. 'And I believe something of a masterpiece. It's *A Multitude of Gods*, the first published novel by Akira Anno.'

Well, it would be, wouldn't it! I could actually feel the warmth and enthusiasm in the room.

'Wonderful!'

'She's such a tremendously powerful writer.'

'I read *The Temizu Basin* three times. It made me cry.'

'What a lovely choice, Christine!'

There was a patter of applause.

I couldn't wait to get out. Hawthorne came with

me but I was just as keen to get away from him. We barely spoke as we walked back down the corridor and as I watched him disappear into the lift, I wondered if I should admire or despise him for using a seriously handicapped young man to help him break the law.

One thing was becoming clear. The more I learned about him, the less I actually knew.

17

The Chase

I slept badly that night. I had a bad dream that turned the book group into something out of *Rosemary's Baby* – which actually wasn't too much of a transformation. Hawthorne and Kevin were at the centre of it, crouched over a computer screen that was running a compilation of all the worst moments of my life. Even while I was asleep, I was surprised how many of them there were.

I was woken by the sound of my mobile phone ringing and was grateful to find myself in bed, in my own room. Jill had already gone. I reached out and answered it, thinking it would be Hawthorne, and I half groaned when I heard Cara Grunshaw's voice at the other end.

'Did I wake you up?' she asked, with mock concern.

It was a little after seven o'clock, the sun struggling to make itself known.

'No,' I said.

'I thought you'd like to know. I've spoken to Daunt's. They don't want to press charges.'

'That's good news.'

'I'm trying to persuade them otherwise.' She paused. 'Nothing personal. I just don't think we should be encouraging petty crime.'

I closed my eyes, my head sinking back into the pillows. 'What do you want?' I asked.

'You know what I want.'

I took a breath. 'Hawthorne is going back to see Adrian Lockwood today,' I said. I knew that because he'd texted me before I got home. There had been a name, an address in Curzon Street and a time. Nothing more. No question that I wouldn't be there. As much as I disliked sharing the information with Grunshaw, I couldn't see any harm in it. After all, Hawthorne had given me permission.

'We've already spoken to him twice,' Grunshaw said. 'He didn't have any reason to kill his lawyer.'

'Yes, he did, as a matter of fact.'

'What?'

Maybe it was because I had just woken up or maybe

it was just my deep fear of annoying Grunshaw, but suddenly the answer came to me. Was this the 'shape' that Hawthorne had been talking about? Even as I blurted out the words, I knew they made sense.

'Richard Pryce was known as the Blunt Razor because he was completely honest,' I began. 'He was worried about Akira Anno because he thought she was concealing part of her income.'

'I know that.' Grunshaw sounded bored again.

'Wait a minute. It's possible that Pryce had got fresh information about Akira. He was going to ring the Law Society. According to Stephen Spencer, she might even have been involved in something illegal.'

'So what?'

'So if she was, Richard wouldn't have hesitated. He'd have upturned the entire judgement even though it would have harmed his own client. Adrian Lockwood wasn't going to allow that to happen. He hated Akira and he didn't want anything more to do with her. He may not have gone to the house meaning to kill Richard Pryce. The two of them could have had an argument. Akira told us he was violent. He could have picked up the bottle and—'

'Wait a minute,' Grunshaw cut in. 'Lockwood had an alibi. He was with Davina Richardson in Highgate.'

'He was only a few minutes away in a fast car.'

There was a brief silence at the end. Then: 'Adrian Lockwood didn't kill Richard Pryce,' Cara said, flatly.

'Do you know who did?'

'I'm close. I could be making an arrest any time.'

Hawthorne had told me that he had narrowed the identity of the killer down to two possible suspects but I didn't tell her that. Nor did I mention that I had myself narrowed it down to a possible five. DI Grunshaw had set this up as a race to the truth and she had decided to cheat every step of the way.

'Keep in touch,' she said and rang off.

I slunk out of bed and got into the shower. The conversation with Cara Grunshaw had unnerved me. As I stood there with the water hammering down, it all seemed so unfair. I had managed to spend fifty years without ever encountering people like her and now, suddenly, I was being threatened and roughed up in my own home. I was also seriously worried about Daunt's. I had told Hawthorne that the story could destroy my career and it was true. For twenty years, the press had ignored me. Then, when Alex Rider began to sell in large numbers, and particularly after the film, they had been broadly supportive. But more recently it was as if someone had decided I had got too big for my boots and I had noticed my name turning up in diary pieces that were half true and resolutely hostile. A children's author caught stealing from a much-loved bookshop would be more than a diary piece. This was 2013 and we were already moving towards the atmosphere of the bear pit where anyone who was even slightly in the public spotlight could find themselves torn down on the strength of a single accusation long before the allegations could actually be disproved.

Perhaps Grunshaw had been lying. It might be that the whole thing would go away, but in the end I decided I couldn't take that chance. I got out of the shower, dried myself and got dressed. Then I went to see Hilda Starke.

Hilda had been my literary agent for about two years. It was she who had sold my novel *The House of Silk* to Orion Books as part of a three-book deal. A small, grey-haired woman with beady eyes and a fondness for quite masculine clothes, she ran her own agency with offices in Greek Street, Soho. I had only been there a couple of times – we usually met at restaurants or at my publishers – and I hadn't been too impressed. Hilda occupied the third and fourth floors of a building above an Italian café, reached by a narrow and uneven flight of stairs. Today, there were no more than half a dozen

people in the office, including two junior agents, a receptionist and a couple of assistants – but with small
rooms and little light it still felt crowded.

I had rung ahead, of course, but she seemed surprised to see me. 'What are you doing here? How's the
next book?'

For someone so petite, she had an extraordinary
presence. I found her wearing a double-breasted jacket
and wide-collared shirt, hunched over her desk, gazing
into a laptop computer like a fortune-teller with a crys-
tal ball – and I wouldn't have put it past her to divine
the future with her exhaustive knowledge of past deals,
Nielsen charts and international trends. Ask her how
many copies the last Harlan Coben has sold or what
titles are trending on Amazon and she would have the
answer without so much as touching the keypad. If
Hilda was married – and she had never told me – her
husband wouldn't have got a word in edgeways. This
was a woman who didn't just go to bed with a book.
She went to bed with a library.

I sat down opposite her. 'I may have a problem.'

'Have you started the next Sherlock Holmes?'

'No.'

'That *is* a problem. You know that Orion wants
it by March. *The House of Silk* is doing well. You've
slipped off the bestseller list but it's a very crowded

week.' There was always a reason for a fall in sales: the weather, the time of year, other writers. I was still disappointed.

'I'm writing another book about Hawthorne,' I said.

She glared at me. She hadn't actually been too pleased when I had told her the idea in the first place and she had only come round when she had managed to get a contract with Penguin Random House. 'Why are you doing that?' she asked. 'They haven't even published the first one yet.'

'I didn't really have any choice,' I said. 'Someone got killed.'

'Who?'

'His name was Richard Pryce. He was a divorce lawyer.'

She didn't like the sound of that. 'I don't think readers will give a damn about a divorce lawyer,' she said. 'Can't you make him something more interesting . . . like an actor or a musician?'

'It was an actor who got killed last time,' I reminded her. 'And anyway it doesn't work like that. I don't have any choice in the matter. I'm just writing what happens.'

'Oh yes.' She was gloomy. And in a hurry to get on with whatever she was doing. 'So what's the problem?'

I told her what had happened at Daunt's bookshop.

'Oh for Christ's sake, Anthony. You could have stolen something a bit classier. The Doomworld series is complete crap – even if it has sold fifty-three million copies. Lucky Dawn Adams is all I can say. Kingston Press was about to go out of business before she stumbled onto that one. But it's not the sort of thing I'd expect to find up your sleeve.'

'It never was up my sleeve, Hilda. I just explained to you. The police framed me.'

'That's not going to make any difference, I'm afraid. It's your word against a respected police officer and you know which side the papers are going to take.'

'I'm not even sure anyone respects Detective Inspector Cara Grunshaw.'

'Well, I'd be very careful before you write anything derogatory about her. You don't want to get yourself sued.'

'I'm the one who's being victimised!' I was about to storm out of the room – not something I'm very good at doing, incidentally – but then I played back what Hilda had just said. 'Dawn Adams,' I muttered. 'She published Doomworld.'

'What about it?'

From the very start, I'd known the name. Dawn Adams was the publisher Akira Anno had been having dinner with on the night she had threatened Richard

Pryce. She had also been with Dawn (or so she claimed) on the night he was killed. And Akira had told us that Dawn had come up against Richard Pryce at the time of her own divorce. Forget the fact that Gregory Taylor had bought the third volume just before he died. He had simply wanted a long book for a long journey. But I suddenly saw that Dawn Adams had to be part of Hawthorne's investigation, even though he hadn't yet said he intended to see her.

Well, at least something good had come out of my turning up here. And there was more to come. Hilda relented. 'I suppose I can have a word with James,' she said.

'James?'

'James Daunt of Daunt Books. He knows your work and maybe we can persuade him that there was a misunderstanding.'

'It wasn't a misunderstanding!'

'Whatever. In the meantime, you really ought to be getting on with that second book for Orion. What happened to that idea of yours about Moriarty?'

'I'm thinking about it.'

'Well if I were you, I'd stop thinking and start writing.'

'Thanks, Hilda.'

'You know the way out . . .'

He had been riding for three days, his proud, black destrier picking its way between the Wilder flowers, the twisting thorns and the dense, black forests of the Lands Beyond Time. A silver moon had beckoned him on and the soft breeze from the north had whispered constantly in his ear. He was hungry. He had not eaten since that last feast at the court of King Pellam. But now it was a deeper, more primal hunger that devoured him and his journey was forgotten, the faithful stallion standing idly by.

The girl could only have been twelve or thirteen and yet already she had blossomed into a desirable woman. She had been leaning over a bubbling stream with cupped hands when he had found her but now she lay on her back on the soft grass, exactly where he had thrown her. He leaned down and tore open her woollen shift to reveal her ripe, curvaceous breasts with nipples that matched the delicious red of her lips. The sight of her skin and of the pubic hair just visible above the edge of her shift turned his bowels to water.

'You are mine,' he muttered. 'By the law of the great Table and the might of the magician, Merlin, I claim you as my own.'

'Yes, my lord.' She stretched out her arms and her whole body shuddered, waiting to receive him.

Barely able to control himself, he jerked off his gambeson, his belt and then everything else until he stood naked, towering over her.

I had stopped at Waterstones Piccadilly on the way to meet Hawthorne and had picked up a copy of *Prisoners of Blood*, the third book in the Doomworld series. Mark Belladonna had been given pride of place on one of the tables in the circular entrance hall and, standing there, I read a few pages. I wanted to remind myself just how terrible it was: the awful language, the use of clichés, its near-pornographic relish. The books must have made Dawn Adams a ton of money, and as I'd learned from my time with Hawthorne, money and murder have a way of going hand in hand. I was certain that he would want to interrogate the publisher soon. She was, after all, Akira's only alibi – and also lingering in my mind was the question of what the two women might have in common. After all, their literary tastes could hardly have been further apart. I had dipped back into *Prisoners of Blood* in the hope that it might answer, at least in part, some of that question. It hadn't.

I put the book down, then walked the short distance to Green Park station, thinking about the theory I had outlined to Cara Grunshaw. It was becoming ever more likely that Adrian Lockwood could be the killer. What I had told her was true. He had a motive and according to Akira, he had known haiku 182. I had actually seen a copy of the book in his house. Could he have painted the number on the wall at Heron's Wake as some bizarre statement of revenge?

Hawthorne was waiting at the station and seeing him I was tempted to ask about his relationship with Kevin, how the two of them had met and what exactly was the arrangement they had made between them. Was he paying the teenager for his work or was it just something Kevin did for fun? And there were wider implications. He always seemed to know where I was and what I was doing. Was this down to brilliant detective work or was he simply hacking into my emails?

I wanted to confront him but decided against it. I could use Kevin to find out about Hawthorne. It would be much easier than the other way round.

We set off together, walking up towards Hyde Park Corner. It wasn't quite raining but there was a fine mist hanging in the air. This was that dead time of the year, after the summer holidays and before the excitement of Guy Fawkes Night, with the Christmas decorations waiting just round the corner to go up. Every year, they seemed to come sooner.

'I read what you gave me,' he said, affably.

It took me a moment to realise that he was talking about the pages I had given him describing my meeting with Davina Richardson and my discovery of the haiku.

'Oh,' I said, carefully. 'Were they helpful?'

'You seem a bit nervous of me, mate, if you don't mind my saying so.' He thought for a moment, then quoted an extract almost word for word: '*He wouldn't be too happy, me being here without him. He hated me asking questions even when he was in the room . . .*'

'It's absolutely true!' I replied. 'Every time I open my mouth you stare at me as if I'm a badly behaved schoolboy.'

'It's not that.' He was offended. 'I just don't like you interrupting my train of thought. And you have to be careful what you say in front of suspects. You don't want to give stuff away.'

'I haven't done that.'

Hawthorne grimaced.

'Have I?' I was alarmed.

'I hope not. But actually, what you wrote was pretty helpful. The thing about you, Tony, is you write stuff down without even realising its significance. You're a bit like a travel writer who doesn't know quite where he is.'

'That's not true!'

'Yeah. It's like you're in Paris and you write how you've seen this big, tall building made of metal but you forget to mention that it might be worth a visit.'

This was completely unfair. I wrote what I saw and almost everything that Hawthorne said. Of course, I had to choose which details I chose to describe – otherwise the book would run into thousands of pages. Take Adrian Lockwood's house, for example. I had mentioned the bilberries he was eating not because they necessarily had anything to do with the crime – they almost certainly didn't – but because they were there and seemed vaguely noteworthy. At the same time, I hadn't mentioned that he had cut himself shaving that morning. There had been a nick on the side of his chin. Of course, if it turned out to be significant, if his hand had been trembling after he murdered Richard Pryce, then I would go back and put it in the second draft. This is how it all works.

'So how did I help you?' I asked. 'Maybe you can let me know which Eiffel Tower I managed to describe without actually knowing it was there?'

'Well, Davina went on at you about all the things she couldn't do without a man in her life. I thought that was interesting.'

'She's a single mother with a teenaged son.'

'That's not what I'm talking about.'

We had crossed Piccadilly and continued up to Curzon Street, heading for Adrian Lockwood's office. I suddenly became aware that Hawthorne had stopped. He was staring straight ahead of him at a wide corner on the edge of a modern, six-storey building. I could see the name above the front door. Leconfield House. This was where Lockwood had his office suite.

There was a man standing there, smoking a cigarette. I saw hair hanging in damp strands, a flapping, stone-coloured raincoat, some sort of marking on the side of his face. But more prominent than all of these, particularly with the distance between us, were his bright blue spectacles. They were like something a child might wear. They didn't even look real.

The man had been looking up at the third floor but as he lowered his head, his eyes locked onto mine. Neither of us knew who the other was but we immediately recognised the connection. I sprang forward. The man dropped his cigarette, turned and ran. Before I knew quite what I was doing, I was chasing him.

I have written a great many chases in my time. They are, after all, a staple of television drama. There are only so many scenes you can have with your characters talking to each other in a room. Eventually, you have to break into some piece of action and the most popular choices are: a murder, a fight, an explosion or a chase.

Of these, the chase is probably the most expensive. A fight, unless it's on the roof of a moving bus or involves an entire gang, is usually fairly self-contained and explosions these days are quite easy to achieve. Almost everything you see is a simple blast of compressed air, some dust and a few scraps of paper. The sound is added later and even the flames can be computer-generated. But a chase is all about movement. The characters move. The cameras move. The entire unit has to move. Worse than that, it's not enough for two actors to go haring after each other. That soon becomes boring. You have to throw in some action. A near miss in front of a car. A few punches thrown. An old woman shoved out of the way.

All of which is an apology for what I must now describe.

I was in my fifties, on foot, and although I think I'm fairly fit, I was no action hero. The man I was chasing was younger and skinnier than me but his smoking habit had played havoc with his health. From the very start, he didn't run so much as limp and it would have taken a director with incredible talent, even with all the money in the world, to make the next few minutes remotely watchable.

The man with blue glasses crossed the road and although a white van did hoot at him, it came nowhere close. I looked left and right before I went after him. He reached the other pavement and pushed past a few pedestrians, although there was no actual bodily contact. I already had a stitch and paused to catch my breath. I glanced back, expecting to see Hawthorne right behind me, but he hadn't even moved. He was standing there, holding his mobile phone. I found that extraordinary and also quite annoying. My quarry had ducked down one of the passageways leading into Shepherd Market, a charming enclave of narrow streets and squares that dates back to the eighteenth century. I saw him hurry past a pub on a corner – Ye Grapes – and I went after him. He must have been running at about 7 mph, although his raincoat was flapping behind him in quite a dramatic way.

He disappeared down another alleyway, past dustbins which he did not knock over. I followed, my feet stamping on the pavement, but I was already falling behind and I was some distance from him when I saw him reach the main road and flag down a taxi. I was sweating. A thin sheen of drizzle was clinging to my face. I arrived and would have jumped into a second taxi if there had been one but there wasn't. I had to wait about a minute before one mercifully appeared, heading down towards Piccadilly Circus. I hailed it. The driver seemed to take for ever to pull over. I yanked open the door and climbed into the back.

I could still make out the taxi with Blue Spectacles. Because of the heavy traffic, he was only a short distance away.

'Where to?' the driver asked.

'Follow that cab!' Even as the words left my mouth I realised that I had uttered a cliché more grotesque and overused than anything I would have found in the Doomworld trilogy. 'Please!' I added.

Ahead of us, a set of lights changed to green. The taxi we were following indicated and swung right along St James's Street. We crept towards the same turning but before we could reach them, the lights changed back to red. My driver didn't perform a breakneck U-turn and find another way. He didn't cut across the traffic with tyres screeching.

'Sorry, mate,' he said, as we came to a gentle halt.

18
The Dustbin Diver

Hawthorne didn't seem to have moved. He was still standing there, waiting for me outside Leconfield House when I finally arrived back in the taxi, which had charged me £10 for a circular journey that had got me precisely nowhere. He watched me as I got out and crossed over to him.

'You didn't catch him then,' he observed.

'No. He got away.' I was in a bad mood. The rain had stopped but I was damp all over. 'You weren't much help,' I muttered. 'You could have at least tried to catch him.'

'There was no need to.'

'Why not?'

'I know who he is.'

I stared at him. 'Then why didn't you stop me?'

'I shouted out to you but you didn't hear me. You went off like a bloody stampeding bull and you didn't give me a chance.'

'So who was he?'

Hawthorne took pity on me. 'You can't go into Lockwood looking like that,' he said. 'Let's get you a cup of coffee.'

We walked down to a Costa at the bottom end of Curzon Street and I went into the toilet while Hawthorne ordered the cappuccinos. Looking into the mirror, I saw that he was right. The short burst of activity had left me flushed, my hair bedraggled and damp from the rain and the exertion. I made myself as presentable as I could and by the time I came out Hawthorne had chosen a table with, I noticed, three chairs.

'Are we waiting for someone?' I asked.

'We might be.'

'Who?'

'You'll see.'

Something had amused him and it was all the more hilarious because he wasn't going to share it with me. I understood why a few minutes later when the door opened and someone walked in. He cast around nervously, then saw us and came over. I scowled. It was the man in blue spectacles whom I'd last seen fleeing down St James's Street in a cab.

'Hawthorne—' I began.

But Hawthorne was looking past me. 'Hello, Lofty,' he said.

'Hello, Hawthorne.'

'You want a coffee?'

'Not really.'

'Get yourself one anyway and bring it over.'

Lofty wasn't his real name, of course, and – equally obviously – it was the last word I would have used to describe the small, lightweight man who had appeared. He couldn't have been more than five foot three or four, with sandy-coloured hair hanging limply down to his collar, an upturned nose and the pallid skin of someone who didn't get out often or who ate unhealthily or perhaps both. As he had come towards us, he had taken off the spectacles to reveal frightened eyes that twitched and flickered around him constantly. The skin condition which both Adrian Lockwood's receptionist and Colin Richardson had mentioned – I was assuming this was the same man – was actually nothing more than a bit of scarring from acne he must have had as a teenager.

'Lofty?' I asked as he ordered himself a drink.

'Lenny Pinkerman. That's his real name. But we always called him Lofty.'

'I get that. Is he a policeman?'

'He used to be.'

'So what's he doing here?' I stopped, remembering my last sighting of Hawthorne as I set off on the chase. He'd been on his mobile. 'You called him!'

'That's right. I've got his mobile number. I asked him to join us.'

'So who is he? What's he got to do with all this?'

'He'll tell you . . .'

Lofty had ordered tea. He sat down at the table and tore open four sachets of sugar which he added to the cup. He stirred it with a plastic spoon. All this happened in a silence that was finally broken by Hawthorne.

'Nice to see you, Lofty.'

'No, it's not. It's not nice to see you at all, Hawthorne.' Lofty had a whiney voice and crooked teeth. I think he wanted to sound angry but the best he could manage was petulant. He put the glasses down on the table and looking at them closely, I saw that they were clearly fake with no magnification. He had also taken off the raincoat. He was wearing shapeless corduroy trousers and a paisley shirt, buttoned up to the neck. If he sat on a pavement, people would have been quick to give him their spare change.

'It's been a while.'

'Not bloody long enough, mate.' He looked balefully

across the table, clearly afraid of Hawthorne and disliking him in equal measure.

'Are you going to tell me what you were doing outside Leconfield House?' Hawthorne asked.

'None of your business.'

'Lofty . . . !'

'Why should I tell you anything?'

'Old times' sake?'

'Sod that!' He considered. 'Fifty quid. I'll talk to you for fifty quid. Fifty-three quid. You can pay for the tea as well.' He looked with disgust at the murky brown liquid in front of him. 'How can they charge three quid for a cup of tea? That's a bloody liberty.'

'You really that hard up?'

'I'm not hard up. I'm doing fine for myself if you really want to know. I'm doing brilliantly. But if you think I'm going to spend one minute with you without being paid for it, you can go take a flying jump. You're a miserable bastard, Hawthorne. You always were and you still are. That business with Abbott. I shouldn't have had to take the rap for that. You screwed me over and I'm only doing this fucking job now because of you.'

Do all policemen swear? Hawthorne, Grunshaw and now Lofty all had an issue with the English language that bordered on Tourette's. My ears had pricked up, however. Derek Abbott was the suspected child pornographer that Hawthorne had pushed down a flight of stairs.

'It was an accident.' Hawthorne spread his hands and gave him a beatific smile. 'These things happen.'

'You were the one who told me to nip out for a cigarette. I thought you were being friendly but you knew what you were doing all along. One fucking smoke and it cost me my job, my pension, my marriage, my whole fucking life.'

'Marge not with you, then?'

'Marge dumped me. She went off with a fireman.'

Hawthorne had taken Derek Abbott down to the interview room because he had been in the custody office at the time and there was no one else around. That was when the accident had happened. Abbott had fallen down fourteen concrete steps with his hands cuffed behind him – a flying jump indeed – and as a result Hawthorne had been thrown out of the police force. Lofty was the one who should have escorted Abbott to the interview room. And he had lost his job too.

'So are you going to tell me about Adrian Lockwood?' Hawthorne asked.

'Fifty quid! And if you don't get a move on, I might change my mind and make it a ton.'

Hawthorne glanced at me. 'All right. Pay him.'

'Me?' But I had no choice in the matter. I took out my wallet. Fortunately, I had just enough cash. I set five £10 notes down on the table and added some change. Lofty swept it all towards him and folded it away.

'I'm guessing you work for Graham Hain,' Hawthorne went on.

'You know him?'

'We haven't met – but I know who he is.'

Graham Hain was the forensic accountant who had been hired by Richard Pryce. Stephen Spencer had mentioned him to us. But there was something I didn't understand. According to Spencer, Hain had been investigating Akira Anno, trying to find the secret income stream that she had refused to declare. In other words, in the Lockwood/Anno divorce, he had been very much on the Lockwood side of the proceedings. So what was Lofty doing, breaking into Lockwood's office and now lurking outside Leconfield House? Why was he spying on his own client?

'Lofty is a dustbin diver,' Hawthorne explained. He glanced across the table. 'Tell him what that means.'

Lofty was offended. 'That's not a term I use,' he muttered, indignantly. 'It says "asset trader" on my business card.'

'You've got a business card? You're definitely going up in the world.'

'Faster than you, mate.'

'What's an asset trader?' I asked. I was getting a little tired of all this banter.

Lofty took another sip of tea. When he spoke again, he was more authoritative. He might be a wreck of a human being, and I wouldn't have wanted to enquire into his private life with or without Marge, but he knew what he was talking about. 'These big divorces, rich bastards, you've got no idea! They put their money away all over the place. Jersey and the British Virgin Islands. They've got trusts and shell companies and offshore companies full of shadow directors and it's impossible to work out who owns what. People like me – asset traders, which is what we're called – help to sort it all out. We find out what's what.'

'Ex-cops,' Hawthorne said. 'Ex-journalists. Ex-security service. Funny how it always starts with an ex.'

'I do all right,' Lofty snapped. 'I earn a ton more than when I was with your lot.'

'So tell us about Adrian Lockwood.'

Lofty hesitated, already wishing he'd asked for more money. I could see it in his eyes.

'You really make me sick, do you know that?' he said to Hawthorne. Having got that out of his system, he continued more pleasantly: 'I did some work on the Lockwood divorce. That wife of his, Akira Anno . . .

she knew we were on to her. The moment we started sniffing round her finances she got nervous and' – he flicked his fingers – 'just like that she rolled over and gave Mr Lockwood everything he wanted. She was terrified we were going to find out just how much money she had in the bank . . . and that bank was probably in Panama or Liechtenstein or somewhere. So it all went hunky-dory. Mr Lockwood was happy. The courts were happy. Job done.

'Only then something happened. All along, Mr Pryce had been having doubts about his client . . . like he wasn't being straight with him. And he wasn't happy about that. Not at all.'

'You're talking about Adrian Lockwood,' I said.

'That's right. Mr Pryce knew straight off Mr Lockwood was a villain. I bet half his clients were as crooked as the A157.'

'The A157? What are you talking about, Lofty?' Hawthorne said.

'It's the road from Louth to Mablethorpe. It's got a lot of bends.'

I wanted to laugh but Hawthorne just sighed. 'Get on with it.'

'The thing about Mr Pryce was that he always was a bit prissy, coming over all vicar's daughter at the best of times. Anyway, the case is finished. Akira has pissed off and everyone's smiling, but suddenly he's talking to the people I work for, Navigant, and he's asking them, very discreetly, to take a quick look at Lockwood's assets.' He paused, rolling his eyes. 'He was very specific. He wanted to know about expensive wine.'

'Wine.' Hawthorne repeated the word.

'That's right. He wanted to know if Lockwood liked the stuff . . . I mean, really liked it. How much of it he drank. What vintages. All that sort of thing. How many bottles he had stashed away. That made it a lot easier for me, narrowing the field. And it didn't take me very long to find what he wanted.

'To say that Adrian Lockwood is into wine is putting it mildly. He's a bleeding fanatic. I've seen his credit card slips from the Ritz and from Annabel's. An Éche-zeaux Grand Cru at £3,250. A Bollinger Vielles Vignes at £2,000 . . .' Lofty mangled the French but not the prices. 'And that was just the start of it. I took a look in the basement of his home in Antibes . . .'

'How did you get in there, Lofty?'

'That's my business, Hawthorne. It's what I do. And the amount of booze I found underneath all that dust? You wouldn't believe it! I had to look some of the names up. I'd never heard of them. And the prices! They were fucking incredible. I mean, you're only talking about a mashed-up grape!

'So one thing led to another and I found my way to Octavian. You ever heard of it?'

I shook my head. Hawthorne said nothing.

'Octavian wine cellarage in Corsham. They're a company. They store wine for hedge-fund managers and people like that. It's a funny thing. Even people who live nearby don't know much about it but you go in there, you'll find some of the best wines in the world – millions of quids' worth – tucked away in the darkness, a hundred feet under the Wiltshire hills. And of course there are all sorts of tax advantages. It's a bonded ware-house. No VAT. And no capital gains tax either because you're talking about a wasting chattel.'

I wasn't quite sure what that meant but I didn't in-terrupt. Lofty was in full flow.

'It was easy enough to find out that Mr Lockwood was one of their clients,' he went on. 'But finding out what he had there was the devil's own business. They're not stupid and they've got a lot of security. I went down to Corsham and had a sniff around but that wasn't going to work . . .'

'So you broke into his office,' Hawthorne said.

'I didn't break in.' Lenny was offended again. 'I just waited until Mr Lockwood went for lunch and walked in off the street. Easiest thing in the world. Told them I was from the IT company. The receptionist showed me into Lockwood's office and even gave me the password for his computer, silly bitch. That way I was able to access his account at Octavian and find out how much capital he had invested.'

'And how much was that?'

'Just shy of three million quid, all paid for by one of his companies working out of BVI. Of course, Mr Pryce hit the bloody roof when he heard that. I don't suppose any of it had ever shown up on his Form E.'

All along we had assumed that Richard Pryce had been investigating Akira Anno and that when he had rung up his partner, Oliver Masefield, on the day of his death, muttering about the Law Society, he had been thinking of her. But that wasn't the case. It was his own client, Adrian Lockwood, who had rung the alarm bells. Lockwood was the one who had concealed his wealth, lying to his solicitor – not a great idea when the solicitor was known as the Blunt Razor.

Why wasn't Hawthorne more excited? As far as I could see, this blew the entire case to smithereens. But he had just finished his coffee and had taken out a cigarette, which he was rolling back and forth along the table. 'Two more questions, Lofty,' he said. 'What were you doing at Leconfield House just now? And why did you run off like that?'

'What do you think?' Lofty sneered. 'Mr Pryce was

my client. I liked him and I feel responsible for him. I'm quite interested to know who killed him and I'm wondering if Lockwood was responsible.'

'That's not possible,' I said. 'He was with someone on the Sunday evening at exactly the time Pryce was killed.'

'Who says they didn't both do it? Anyway, I've been keeping an eye on him just in case he meets someone or does something that blows the lid off what actually happened.'

'And you ran . . . ?'

'Because there's been a murder and funnily enough I worry about my health. It's often necessary in my line of work. When I see someone I've never met before running towards me, I generally turn and run the other way. Of course, as soon as I got your call, I realised there was no need for it. Not that I ever wanted to see you again, Hawthorne, just so you know.'

Hawthorne considered. 'So you've been watching him,' he said. 'Found anything yet?'

Lofty slid his chair back and stood up. He had left half the tea. 'If I had, I wouldn't tell you,' he said.

'You're still upset!'

'Yes. I am still upset. Bloody upset. That's the truth of it. You screwed up my life and I don't know why I've told you as much as I have. Anyway, that's it. You've had all you're getting for fifty quid. Fuck off and leave me alone.'

He hurried out of the coffee bar.

'Who was Abbott?' I asked. I was thinking about the child pornographer Hawthorne had pushed down the stairs, but I knew nothing about what had happened.

'Just someone I met at work. There was a health and safety issue. Lofty was a staff officer and he got the rap. I don't know why he blamed me.'

Hawthorne looked at me with eyes that could not have been more perfectly innocent but I knew he was lying to me. Just like he always did.

19
Sword and Sorcery

Adrian Lockwood was unable to see us, or so we were told by the prim young receptionist perched behind a desk shaped like a comma in a small outer office in Leconfield House. Presumably she had replaced the girl who had allowed Lofty in – and she had certainly passed an advanced class in superciliousness.

'I'm afraid he has a conference call.'

'We can wait.'

'He has another meeting straight after.'

We were forty-five minutes late so I suppose this was fair enough. But even so I wondered if Lockwood wasn't sitting quietly behind one of the closed doors, listening to us being put in our place. In the end we agreed to come back at five o'clock. That left us with a few hours to kill.

Hawthorne was on his mobile before we had even got out into the street. I heard him introducing himself and asking for a meeting with Dawn Adams – 'a police-related matter' – and the next thing I knew, we were in a taxi on our way to Kingston Books. Akira Anno had told us that her friend lived in Wimbledon, which was right next to Kingston, but her offices were in central London, in Bloomsbury as it turned out.

The worldwide success of the Doomworld series was evident before we even entered the building. The publishing house occupied a handsome four-storey office on the corner of Queen Square with prominent signage on the front door and about a dozen books on display in the window. They were the only business there and quite possibly owned the whole building. Kate Mosse, Peter James and Michael Morpurgo were just three of the big-name authors who had signed up with them.

The front door led into a generous entrance hall with original Quentin Blake artwork on the walls and a giant glass bowl of sweets and chocolates on the reception desk. The receptionist here seemed much happier to see us.

'Yes, Dawn is expecting you.'

No surnames here. A young guy, perhaps an intern, appeared and escorted us to an office on the first floor with two windows looking out over the square. There was a desk piled high with books and contracts but Dawn was waiting for us to one side, a very elegant black woman, sitting on a sofa behind a low coffee table with her knees together and her legs folded. She was in her fifties, about the same age as Akira Anno. Everything about her was impressive, from her quietly expensive clothes and the diamond ear studs to the designer glasses on a thin silver chain around her neck.

Two chairs had been placed opposite her and when, at her invitation, we sat down, we found ourselves looming over her. It was quite deliberate, a sort of reverse psychology. We would have to adjust our behaviour if we were not to seem like bullies. Sitting comfortably on her sofa, some distance below us, she had arranged things so that she was quietly in command.

I was surprised when she smiled at me. 'Anthony, how nice to see you,' she said. I had no memory of having met her. 'How are things at Orion?'

'They're fine, thank you,' I said.

'I really enjoyed *The House of Silk*. It made me wonder if you've read *Solo* yet?'

William Boyd had just published a James Bond novel – following on from Sebastian Faulks and Jeffery Deaver. 'Not yet,' I said.

'I think it would be a fantastic idea if they got you to write a Bond next. I know the Ian Fleming estate. I could have a word with them if you like . . .'

'Well, I'd certainly be interested.' I tried to sound non-equivocal when actually it was something I'd wanted to do all my life.

'I'll talk to them.' She turned to Hawthorne and now she was a little cooler. 'I'm not sure how I can help you.'

'I told you on the phone. I'm investigating the murder of Richard Pryce.'

'Yes. Well, apart from one brief encounter in a restaurant when I didn't even speak to him, I hadn't seen Mr Pryce for over a year and I had no further dealings with his practice. I only knew he was dead when I saw the story in the newspapers and I can't say I shed too many tears.'

'I can understand that, Ms Adams. You first met him at the time of your divorce.'

'I never actually met him one-to-one, Mr Hawthorne. He wrote to me. He also wrote about me. He drew a picture of me in court as a woman entirely dependent on the financial acumen of my husband, even though said husband was a drunk and a womaniser who had inherited all his wealth from his equally squalid father. At the time, I'd spent seven years putting all my efforts into building up my own publishing business and perhaps you can imagine how humiliating and offensive that depiction of me was. Or perhaps you can't.' She drew a dismissive hand across the air. 'In any event, I had absolutely nothing to do with his demise, although, as I say, it's just possible that I raised a glass of Chablis when I heard of it.'

'Well, that's not quite true, is it,' Hawthorne returned. 'You say you've got nothing to do with his "demise", but you've been involved, on the sidelines, from the very start.'

'I don't know what you mean.'

'You were with Akira Anno at The Delaunay restaurant when she threatened Mr Pryce. And you were with her a second time, as it happens, on the night of the murder. At first, Ms Anno suffered an unfortunate memory loss. She said she was at a cottage in Lyndhurst. But when that was disproved, she was forced to admit she was with you.'

I thought Dawn would fight back, but, ignoring Hawthorne, she turned to me. 'What exactly are you doing here?' she asked, quite pleasantly.

'I'm writing about him,' I replied. There seemed to be no point lying. Dawn Adams knew who I was. She might as well know what I was doing.

She was surprised. 'For the newspapers?'

'For a book.'

'True crime?'

'Yes. Well, sort of. I have to move a few things round and change some names, but it's all basically true.'

She considered for a moment. 'That's interesting. Have you got a publisher yet?'

'I've signed a three-book deal with Selina Walker at Penguin Random House.'

She nodded. 'Selina's very good. Just don't let her bully you with deadlines.' She turned back to Hawthorne. 'In response to your remarks, first of all, Akira never threatened Richard Pryce. The two of us had been having dinner together at The Delaunay and she saw him on the other side of the room. Inevitably we started talking about him and that was when we discovered that we'd both had similar experiences. It's possible we'd had a little too much to drink but Akira got it in her head to create a scene. She went over to his table – he was there with his husband. She picked up his glass of wine and poured it over his head. It was a stupid thing to do. I'd be the first to admit it. But at the same time it was deeply satisfying.'

'She threatened to hit him with a bottle.'

'No. She said he was lucky that he hadn't ordered a bottle or she would have used that, by which I assume she meant she would have emptied the entire contents over him.'

'But it's quite a coincidence, don't you think, that just a week or so later he was killed with a wine bottle.'

'It could be a coincidence, I suppose. Although have you considered the possibility that someone in the restaurant might have overheard her?'

That was a thought that hadn't occurred to me. Akira Anno could have quite accidentally suggested the murder method to someone who knew Richard and who just happened to be there. They might even have done it deliberately to frame her. I wondered if Hawthorne had checked out the names of all the patrons who had been at The Delaunay that night.

'As to Akira being at my home on Sunday night,' Dawn went on, 'there's nothing very surprising about that either. We're old friends.'

'How did you meet?'

'At a book festival. In Dubai. A week round the swimming pool at the InterContinental Hotel. It's a good place to get to know people.'

'How long was she with you?'

'Do you really consider this a line of enquiry worth pursuing, Mr Hawthorne? Very well! She came for supper at about six o'clock and once again we had rather too much to drink. You're going to get the impression that we're a couple of old soaks but it's not like that. We weren't drunk. In fact, we'd been working. But Akira had had two or three glasses with me and I thought it was more sensible if she didn't drive back so I invited her to stay the night.'

'You say you were working. What sort of work does she do for you?'

Dawn Adams hesitated just for a moment and I had a feeling that for all her bluster, whatever she was going to say next might not be completely true. 'She advises me on literary manuscripts,' she said.

'You pay her?'

'Of course.' Dawn looked at her watch, a very delicate Cartier on a thin gold strap. 'As I told you on the phone, I'm afraid I can't give you a great deal of my time.'

Hawthorne ignored this. 'Why did Akira Anno lie about being with you?' he asked. 'Having supper with an old friend, a publisher . . . you'd have thought there was nothing more innocent in the world.'

'I have no idea. You'll have to ask her that. Perhaps she found your interview methods offensive and decided to take you for a ride.'

'Lying to a police officer is an offence.'

'As I understand it, you're not a police officer.'

I had to hand it to Dawn Adams. She certainly wasn't afraid of Hawthorne. But if she'd known him better, she might have been a little less curt with him. I saw the anger stirring in his eyes and it made me think of a crocodile rising from the mud.

'You say that Ms Anno advises you on literary manuscripts,' he said. 'How many literary writers do you actually publish?'

It was a good point. In the window downstairs I had seen one or two well-respected authors, but the books on the shelves in Dawn's office were less highbrow. I ran my eyes over a children's picture book, a couple of airport thrillers, the Doomworld trilogy and a book of Greek recipes by Victoria Hislop.

Again, there was just a hint of uncertainty before she recovered. 'We don't have any. But it's an area I very much want to move into. We receive a great many submissions and Akira reads them for me.'

'Then why not publish her? Since the two of you are such good mates . . .'

'I've suggested it. But Akira has a contract with Virago. I think we're done here, aren't we?' There was a telephone on the coffee table. Dawn picked it up and dialled a single number. 'Tom,' she said. 'My guests are just leaving. Could you come up to the office . . . ?'

'Actually, I haven't finished.' Hawthorne's voice was cold.

She hesitated, the phone still in her hand. 'Actually, it's all right, Tom. I'll call you in a minute.' She put the phone down.

Hawthorne paused and I knew from experience that he was about to come out with something extraordinary. Even so, his next statement took me completely by surprise. 'I'd like to speak to one of your other writers,' he said.

'Which one is that?'

'Mark Belladonna.'

She stared at him. 'I'm afraid there's absolutely no way Mark will speak to you.'

'And why is that?'

'Well, first of all, he's got absolutely nothing to do with this. And secondly, he's very reclusive. He lives in Northumberland and he has acute agoraphobia. He never goes out.'

'But he was in The Delaunay the night when you had that dinner.'

'That's impossible.'

'It's not impossible, Ms Adams. It's true. And as it happens he was also involved in the death of a second man . . . Gregory Taylor. Taylor visited Richard Pryce on the day Taylor died. The two of them had known each other for years. And just a short while later Taylor was killed, pushed under a train. But before he died, he bought a copy of a book, the latest Mark Belladonna. He didn't buy it because he wanted to read it. He bought it to send us the message . . . which is the reason I'm here.'

All of this was news to me. If Hawthorne had checked out who was eating at The Delaunay, he had certainly never mentioned it. But it was true that he had drawn my attention to *Prisoners of Blood*, which Gregory Taylor had picked up in W. H. Smith at King's Cross. *Why did he buy that book?* That was what he had asked.

Dawn Adams had lost control of the situation. Suddenly it was as if the sofa was swallowing her whole. She was almost squirming. 'I don't know what you're talking about.'

And then, without warning, the door opened and, of all people, Akira Anno came hurrying into the room. Dawn Adams was as surprised to see her as I was. 'Akira . . . ?'

'I came straight over when I got your call.' Akira looked at us malignantly. 'I know these two men. I've already had confrontations with them. I know their methods and how they will use them to threaten and intimidate you. I didn't want you to have to see them on your own.'

So Dawn had rung her to say we were coming. It

made me think that the two of them must have been colluding . . . but in what?

'We were just talking about Mark Belladonna,' Hawthorne went on. He was utterly unfazed by the interruption. It was as if he had expected it, even welcomed it.

Akira went over to a third chair and sat down. She was as immaculate as ever but suddenly she seemed unsure of herself, perhaps even afraid.

'I want his address and his phone number,' Hawthorne said.

'I won't give them to you.'

'You can take that stand if you want to, Ms Adams. Then I'll call Detective Inspector Grunshaw and Detective Constable Mills and we'll see how you get on when you refuse to co-operate with them.'

'I can't . . .'

'Why not?'

'You don't understand. Mark never—'

And then, from the other side of the room came the two quiet words: 'He knows.' It was Akira. Her face was ghastly. She was looking down at the floor.

What did he know? And why didn't I know it too?

'Why don't you just come straight out with it?' Hawthorne exclaimed. 'Do you think I'm a complete idiot? Did you really think I wouldn't work it out?'

He paused, waiting for either of the two women to

speak, and when neither of them did, he provided the answer for them. 'Akira Anno *is* Mark Belladonna, isn't she! Mark doesn't exist.' He rounded on Akira. 'You wrote those stupid books.'

There was another silence. I don't know who was more shocked: me because I had never suspected it or Dawn because he had guessed.

'Are you going to deny it?' Hawthorne demanded.

I looked at Akira, who was sitting in her chair looking like a puppet that had been thrown aside, its limbs disconnected. On the sofa, Dawn Adams looked genuinely afraid. 'You can't tell anybody,' she whispered.

'Wait a minute!' I exclaimed. 'Akira Anno wrote *Excalibur Rising* and *Prisoners of Blood* and . . .' I'd forgotten the title of the first one.

'*The Twelve Men of Steel*,' Akira muttered, still not meeting my eyes.

'But that's impossible. They're full of pornography.' I searched for the worst thing I could say about them. 'They objectify women!'

'They sell millions of copies.' Despite everything, Dawn had leapt to the defence of her friend. Now she got to her feet and walked over to her desk, taking her place on the other side. That put her closer to Akira, back in control. 'It was my idea. I met Akira at Dubai, just like I told you. She's a wonderful writer. Her books have won a great many prizes and there was even a film. But you know the market for literary fiction, Anthony. It's tiny, almost non-existent.'

There was a bottle of water on the desk. She poured herself a glass. 'This wasn't Akira's idea. It was mine. I had to persuade her, but I knew there was a huge market in sword and sorcery.'

'And sex,' I added.

'Whatever you want to call it. *Game of Thrones* was already huge . . . before the TV series. The two of us were having a cocktail by the pool and I suggested it to Akira almost as a joke, really. If someone like George R. R. Martin could make a fortune out of fantasy fiction then it would be easy for a writer as talented as her.'

'But it's everything she despises!' I insisted. It was almost as if Akira wasn't in the room. She had been banished, replaced by Mark Belladonna who had come down from Northumberland, somehow overcoming his phobia.

'There isn't a writer in the world who doesn't want to sell!' Dawn countered.

'Of course that's true!' I agreed. 'But she . . . !' I pointed at Akira. 'She's a complete hypocrite!'

Akira looked up. 'Nobody must know,' she whispered and even behind the tinted glasses I could see the panic in her eyes. 'You can't tell them! It will finish me!'

Dawn nodded. 'If people found out that Akira was the author, it could do enormous damage to her reputation. And it certainly wouldn't help my business either!' She was more reasonable than Akira, more pragmatic. But then she was a publisher, not a writer. 'You don't know how hard we've had to work to keep Mark Belladonna out of the public eye,' she went on. 'It's true that Akira, in her other work, has a completely different profile but lots of writers have used an alias.' She sighed. 'When I suggested the idea, it was just a joke. Neither of us had any idea how huge the series would become.'

So this was the income stream that Stephen Spencer had mentioned, the earnings that Akira had kept from Richard Pryce. Dawn was right, of course. Once the public found out how they had been tricked, Akira, Mark and Kingston Books might well be finished.

But Hawthorne was in an unforgiving mood. 'I don't know,' he said. 'I think it's going to be very difficult to keep this from Detective Inspector Grunshaw.'

Akira said nothing.

'Anthony, I'm sure you understand the situation here.' Dawn had decided to bypass Hawthorne and appeal directly to me. 'I've put my life into this business and Doomworld is what holds it all together. And Akira hasn't done anything wrong.' She leaned forward. 'Her series is loved. It's being filmed for TV. Why ruin her life?'

'That's a haiku!' I exclaimed.

'I'm sorry?'

'What you just said.' I glanced at Akira, who had folded herself up, in the depths of misery. Despite everything, I felt sorry for her. 'I'll do what I can.'

Next to me, Hawthorne stirred. 'That's not usually very much,' he said.

He was actually laughing when we went back out into the street. I'd seen Hawthorne's sense of humour, which was subtle and a little devious. But I don't think I'd ever heard him laugh.

'How did you know?' I asked. 'About Akira Anno and Mark Belladonna?'

'It's pretty straightforward.' He took out a cigarette and we set off, walking back towards Holborn station. 'To start with, we knew Akira was hiding money. Stephen Spencer had told us. How else could she have been earning it apart from writing? And then there was the way she lied about meeting Dawn Adams. Why make up all that crap about a cottage in the middle of nowhere? Having dinner with a publisher is about the most natural thing in the world for a writer – unless they're up to something pretty unusual together.

'But what really did it for me was that moment at Daunt's. Didn't you see the look on her face when you were caught nicking *Prisoners of Blood*? She was horrified. I thought she was going to be sick. But it wasn't just because you'd stolen a book, it was because you'd chosen *that* book. She thought you must have rumbled her.'

It was true. She had said nothing. She hadn't even looked at me. Her eyes had been glued to the book.

'It still seems quite a leap,' I said.

'Not really. She's a writer and like all writers she's a bit of an egotist so she couldn't completely abandon authorship of her crap stories. The last four letters of Belladonna are her own name backwards. And three of the letters in Akira turn up in Mark. I'm surprised you didn't see that, mate.'

I was surprised too. I do the *Times* crossword every day. I love anagrams, codes, acronyms . . .

I was still trying to piece it all together. 'What you said about King's Cross just now. Was that true? Was Gregory Taylor trying to send a message?'

'Yes, he was. Just not the message you think.'

What message was that? And had we just eliminated

Akira Anno from our enquiries? Both she and Dawn Adams had been insulted by Richard Pryce and they had provided each other with an alibi on the night of the murder. Added to which, Pryce had been investigating Akira's income. Suppose he had stumbled onto the truth about Mark Belladonna? That would have given them both a powerful incentive to kill him.

I thought I'd narrowed the list of suspects down to one of five. Now it had slipped back up to half a dozen.

20
Green Smoke

'You do realise that Akira is trying to land me in it. There's nothing she'd like more than to see me arrested for something I didn't do. I mean, all that stuff she said about me. I don't have a violent temper! If I did, I can tell you, I'd have done her in years ago. She was the most annoying person I ever met. She'd have tried the patience of a Shinto saint – and probably did, for all I know.

'As for that bloody haiku of hers, yes, she showed it to me. She seemed to think it was terribly clever but I'm afraid it went right over my head. *The sentence is death*? What's that meant to mean exactly? She took a great deal of pleasure in reading it to me but she might as well have been quoting from a Japanese washing-machine manual for all the sense it made.'

The strange thing about Adrian Lockwood was that even when he was in a bad mood, as he was now, he still seemed quite laid-back and jovial. The sunglasses and ponytail were still in place, along with the white shirt splayed open at the neck. His office was less extravagant than his house, a utilitarian set of suites so lacking in style that it could have belonged to one of those management companies that lease space by the month, and I suspected that he didn't come here very often. The laptop that Lofty Pinkerman had hacked into was on the desk in front of him. He was in a padded leather chair, bent several ways to follow the contours of his body. He was sitting with his hands folded behind his head.

'And if either of us was going to paint that number on the wall, it would have been her. What did you say it was? A hundred and eighty-two? Do you really think I'd have been able to remember that? It could just as easily have been the one about the flower blossoming in the car park or the sparrowhawk losing its feathers or any of the other rubbish she saw fit to print.'

'The haiku was about you,' Hawthorne said.

'Was it?'

'Akira told you so. And anyway, you'd have remembered the number quite easily.'

'Why?'

'Because it's the date of your marriage! You told us you got married just after your birthday – on the eighteenth of February.' Hawthorne gave Lockwood one of his dangerous smiles: '18/2.'

I should have seen it for myself. I had been in the room when Lockwood told us the date. I had even made a note of it. But once again I had missed the connection.

'Look!' Lockwood spread his hands, metaphysically embracing us, man to man. 'The marriage was a bloody disaster. I've already told you that—'

'It was your second marriage to end in disaster,' Hawthorne interrupted. 'Your first wife, Stephanie Brook—'

'You can leave her out of this!' Lockwood was redfaced. This was a side of him I hadn't seen before. 'That's completely out of order. The fact is, you're as bad as some of those scum journalists who reported it. Stephanie was a lovely girl, lovely, and for a time we were happy together. But she was a mess. She drank and she took recreational drugs and in the end she died in Barbados. But I wasn't even on the boat when it happened. It was a tragic accident. Maybe she killed herself, like they said. I don't know. I don't think it makes much difference when you fool around with that stuff. At any event, it's got nothing to do with what happened to Richard.'

'Except that in both instances, you were involved.'

'I wasn't anywhere near Richard either.'

'You were in Highgate. Not so far.'

Lockwood hesitated, knowing where this was heading. 'That's right. I was there.'

'With Davina Richardson.'

Lockwood sighed loudly. 'Yes. I told you . . . I went round for a drink.'

'Just a drink?'

'I don't quite understand what you're implying.'

'Then let me put it more simply, Mr Lockwood. Were you and Mrs Richardson going to bed together?'

'That's an extremely impertinent question. Just because you're a detective – or an ex-detective, rather – does that give you the right to poke around in my private life?'

Hawthorne looked bored. 'It's a yes or no question. We're all grown-ups here.'

'What possible difference does it make?'

'It might tell me if she was prepared to lie to protect you.' Hawthorne paused. 'Or the other way round.'

Lockwood considered, but not for long. 'All right, damn you. Yes. We'd been sleeping together for a while.'

'While you were still married?'

'Yes.' He took a deep breath. 'It wasn't as easy as you might think. You may say we're all adults but you're forgetting she had a teenager in the house: her son, Colin. Obviously, we couldn't go canoodling while he was around and I couldn't bring her back to Edwardes Square while Akira was there. Anyway, Akira had a nose like a bloodhound. She'd have known if there had been another woman in the house. So we went to hotels – which I didn't much care for, if you want the truth. It just felt shabby.'

'Did Akira ever discover you were having an affair?'

'No.'

'How about Richard Pryce? Did you tell him?'

'Why would I have told Richard? Do you think I had to put that in my Form E? Nobody knew.'

'And now that you're a free man, is she going to move in?'

Lockwood laughed out loud. 'You've got to be joking. Davina's an attractive woman, perfect for a quick squeeze. But there's no way I'm jumping through that hoop again. My first marriage . . . well, I just told you. It was a tragedy. My second was a farce. I think that's enough drama in one life.'

He'd had enough. I saw his mood change as abruptly as if a switch had been thrown. 'I think I've told you everything you need to know,' he said. 'So if you don't have any further questions . . .'

'Actually, I have some information for you.' Hawthorne was in no hurry to leave. 'The person who broke into your office . . .'

'Yes?'

'We found him.'

By now, Lockwood had learned not to trust Hawthorne, particularly when he was at his most co-operative. 'And . . . ?'

'His name is Leonard Pinkerman. It turns out he's a private investigator of sorts. You might be interested to hear that he was working for Richard Pryce.'

'I'm sorry? He was working for *Richard*?'

'You gave Mr Pryce a bottle of wine. Is that right?'

'I already told you that.'

'And of course you know that a bottle of wine was used to kill Mr Pryce, that he was bludgeoned to death with it.'

Lockwood was stunned. Any trace of the conviviality with which he had greeted us had been completely stripped away. 'Are you saying it was the same bottle?'

'A 1982 Château Lafite Rothschild, Pauillac.' I wasn't surprised that Hawthorne had remembered the marque and the date.

'Yes. I gave him that.' It took Lockwood a few moments to realise that nobody was speaking, that he was expected to offer more. 'Richard had done an exceptional job on my behalf and I wanted to thank him. I'd paid his fees, of course, and they were considerable. But not having to go to court obviously saved me a small fortune and I thought I'd show my appreciation.'

'With a £2,000 bottle of wine?'

'I have a lot of wine.'

'How much exactly?'

'I'm sorry?'

'You keep your wine at a company called Octavian in Corsham, in Wiltshire. How much wine do you actually have?'

A slow smile spread across Lockwood's face but it wasn't a pleasant one. 'You have been busy, haven't you, Mr Hawthorne?'

Hawthorne waited for the answer.

'I have a collection of mainly French wine and champagne which has a market value of around two and a half million pounds. You're going to ask me why I didn't declare it, and obviously poor Richard was worried about it if he sent his man round to break into my office . . . Hardly very ethical, I must say!

'Well, I didn't declare it because the wine was actually purchased by a company of mine and can no longer be classed as an asset as I've used it as collateral against a very large loan. This is for a project of mine, a new housing development in Battersea. It's all perfectly straightforward and if Richard had ever asked me about it, I'd have been happy to tell him, but I can assure you I had absolutely no idea he was concerned. He never said anything to me.' He laid his hands, palms down, on the desk. 'Now, is there anything else?'

This time, Hawthorne stood up. I did the same. 'You've been very helpful, Mr Lockwood.'

'I won't say it's been a pleasure.' The words were carefully measured.

Hawthorne took a step towards the door, then seemed to remember something. 'One last thing. You said you left Davina Richardson's house at around eight fifteen. How can you be so sure of the time?'

'I suppose I must have looked at my watch.'

'There's a clock in the kitchen.'

'We weren't in the kitchen. We were in her bedroom. I got dressed and I left. Maybe she mentioned the time. I honestly can't remember.'

Hawthorne smiled. 'Thank you.'

It was the gesture that gave him away. As Adrian Lockwood talked about his watch, he raised his hand to show off the heavy-duty Rolex that he had strapped on his wrist. And that was when I saw it. Not on the watch but on the sleeve of his shirt, very small, half concealed by the cufflink: a spot of green paint.

And I knew exactly what shade of green it was. I remembered the fancy name that Davina had chosen from Farrow & Ball.

Green Smoke.

It had to be.

I arrived home that evening at the same time as Jill, who came in weighed down by problems from the set. Another location had fallen through. We were now two full days behind schedule. Nothing seemed to be going right.

We had dinner together, not that you could actually call it that. Jill had a salad with a tin of tuna fish. I scouted around in the fridge but all I could find was a bottle of champagne that had been given to me by Orion when I got into the top ten, and two eggs. I scrambled the eggs and ate them with Ryvita as there wasn't any bread.

'So how was your day?' Jill asked.

'It was OK.'

'Have you finished the rewrites?'

'I'll finish them tonight.'

It was quite normal for the two of us to start work

again after dinner. We have a shared office and we'll often find ourselves sitting side by side well on the way to midnight. Jill is the only person I know who works harder than me, running the company, overseeing the productions, organising our social life, managing the flat. We actually met working together in advertising. She was the account director. I was the copywriter. Two days after meeting me she asked – pleaded – to be moved to any other account in the building but somehow we began a relationship and twenty-five years later we are still together. I had written four shows for her: *Foyle's War, Injustice, Collision* and *Menace*. She was the first person to read my books, even before Hilda Starke. It feels odd to be writing about her and the truth is she has made it clear that she's uncomfortable being a character in my book. Unfortunately, truth is what it's all about. She is the main character in my life.

'You're working with that detective again, aren't you?' she said as we sat there, eating.

'Yes.' I hadn't wanted her to know but I never tell her lies. She can see right through me.

'Is that a good idea?'

'Not really. But I have a three-book deal and a case came up.' I felt guilty. I knew she was waiting for my script. 'I think it's over anyway,' I went on. 'Hawthorne knows who did it.'

He hadn't said as much but I could tell. There was something quite animalistic about Hawthorne. The closer he got to the truth, the more you could see it in his eyes, in the way he sat, in the very contours of his skin. He really was the dog with the bone. I'd hoped we might have a drink after our meeting with Adrian Lockwood but he couldn't wait to get back home. I could imagine him sitting at his table, assembling his Westland Sea King with the same voracious attention to detail he brought to the solving of crime.

'Do *you* know?' she asked.

It was a depressing question. I felt sure that the solution must be obvious by now. All along, it had been my hope that I would actually work it out before Hawthorne. And yet, I was still nowhere near. It really wasn't fair. How could I even call myself an author if I had no connection to the last chapter – the whole point of the book?

'No,' I admitted, then added, hopefully, 'Not yet.'

After dinner, I went up to the office, which Jill had actually constructed for me on the roof of the flat. It's about fifteen metres long and quite narrow with uninterrupted views towards the Old Bailey and St Paul's. At the time, a new building was rising up, adding a streak of silver to the skyscape and completely changing my view. It would become known as the Shard. I sat at my desk, gazing out at the evening sky. Despite what I had said, I wasn't in the mood for scriptwriting. Instead, I drew out a notepad and began to think about the case.

If Hawthorne could solve it, I could solve it. I was as clever as him. The answer was right in front of me. I went through it all one last time.

Adrian Lockwood.

He was the most obvious suspect. Despite what he'd said, it was possible that he knew Pryce was investigating his secret wine stash and might have overturned the divorce as a result.

According to Akira Anno, he had a temper. His first wife had died. And then there was the spot of green paint I had seen on his shirt. Was it the same green as the number on the wall at the scene of the crime? Of course it was, which meant that he had painted it, although I couldn't quite see why.

The trouble was, he had a solid alibi for the time of the murder. He had been with . . .

Davina Richardson.

She couldn't blame Pryce for her husband's death in Long Way Hole. It had happened too long ago, he had supported her ever since, and – anyway – Gregory Taylor had accepted the responsibility.

But she and Lockwood were lovers. And what had

Pryce's husband, Stephen Spencer, told us? Pryce had got fed up with her. *She was bleeding him dry.* Suppose Pryce had finally pulled the financial plug on her, sending her into a murderous rage? She could have talked to Adrian Lockwood, who had his own reasons for wanting Pryce dead. They could have planned it together.

Akira Anno.

She was still my main suspect – after her ex-husband. She was the start of everything that had happened with the threat she had made in the restaurant and she had written a haiku that suggested she had murder in mind, even if she insisted it had been addressed to Adrian Lockwood. I could easily believe that she was vengeful enough to kill Richard Pryce and it wasn't much of a stretch to see her daubing the number 182 on the wall either. It somehow reminded me of Japanese murals with their attendant calligraphy. It suited her. And yet she had an alibi too.

Dawn Adams.

Two women, both divorced, both with a grudge against the smooth-talking solicitor who had humiliated them. More than that, if Richard had discovered the truth about Mark Belladonna and Doomworld, he could have ruined both of them. Now that I thought about it, there was something quite literary about writing a message, leaving a mark at the scene of the crime. In a way, Dawn and Akira mirrored Adrian and Davina. Two sets of people with similar aims, working together.

Stephen Spencer.

He didn't look like a murderer to me, but I couldn't rule him out. He had lied about visiting his mother and he might well have lied about the state of his marriage. The fact was that he was being unfaithful. Richard Pryce knew and had discussed his will with one of the partners at Masefield Pryce Turnbull. If Spencer was about to lose his marriage, the house and the inheritance, he certainly had the most straightforward motive for murder.

Susan Taylor.

Nor had I forgotten Gregory Taylor's widow. Her husband had died one day before Richard Pryce and she had actually come down to London on the day of the murder. Nobody had asked her to account for her movements but had she really been on her own, just sitting there in a cheap hotel? I remembered the curious glint of cruelty in her eyes as she had spoken: *What do you think I did?* Was there something about Long Way Hole that she hadn't told us? Richard, Charles and Gregory – all stuck underground with the water rising. All three were now dead. There had to be a connection.

It had to be one of them.

One in six. But which one?

Jill came into the office and, seeing me deep in thought, slid the partition across, closing off her side. We call it the divorce door. I turned another page and began to think of all the clues that I had noted as I accompanied Hawthorne – from the broken bulrushes next to Pryce's front door to the book that Gregory Taylor had bought at King's Cross station to the splash of green paint on Adrian Lockwood's sleeve. I remembered Hawthorne talking about the number painted on the wall and Richard Pryce's last words: *What are you doing here? It's a bit late.* I wrote them down and drew a circle round them. It didn't help.

What else was there? Hawthorne had gone on about the shape of the crime. We had been sitting in his flat, talking over that glass of rum and Coke. I went back through my notes and found his exact words.

It's not like that, Tony. You've got to find the shape. That's all.

But if there was a shape, I couldn't see it. I was still convinced that the answer must be found in a single clue, something that had been right in front of me but the significance of which I had missed.

I cast my mind back to the visit we had made to Adrian Lockwood's house: the umbrella by the door, the vitamin pills, the bilberries. I tried to remember why I had written them down in my notes. Why had I mentioned them at all?

That was my eureka moment.

I fired up my computer and went on the internet. What a wonderful device . . . a gift to writers and detectives alike! In seconds I had the answer I needed and at that moment everything came together in a rush and I suddenly saw with blinding clarity exactly who had killed Richard Pryce. It was something I had never thought I would experience. Agatha Christie never described it, nor did any other mystery writer I can think of: that moment when the detective works it out and the truth makes itself known. Why did Poirot never twirl his moustache? Why didn't Lord Peter Wimsey dance in the air? I would have.

I spent another hour thinking it through. I saw Jill turn off the light and heard her go to bed. I made more notes. Then I rang Hawthorne. I didn't care that it was late.

'Tony?' It was almost midnight but he didn't sound upset to hear from me.

'I know who did it,' I said.

There was an empty silence at the other end of the telephone. Of course he didn't believe me. 'Tell me,' he said, eventually.

So I did.

21

The Solution to the Crime

It was with a mixture of excitement and dread that I made my way back up the steps and into the police station at the corner of Ladbroke Grove where I had first attended the interview with Akira Anno. The memory of my conversation with Hawthorne was still buzzing in my head.

'Tell me I've got it right.'

'You've nailed it, mate. More or less . . .'

'Hawthorne . . . !'

'You've got it right.'

From the start I had known that it was possible to get there ahead of him, but I was disappointed that he was so grudging in his respect for what I'd done. Maybe he was a little peeved. To be fair to him, he had corrected me on a few points where I had got things confused.

More importantly, he had agreed to the course of action I was taking now, although I wasn't going to let Cara Grunshaw know that.

I had to share what I knew with her and her unpleasant sidekick, DC Mills. I didn't want either of them to get the credit but I owed it to Jill and the series. I was still certain that Grunshaw was behind many of the problems that the production team was facing and it was the only way I could get her off our backs. It didn't matter that much to Hawthorne. He was paid by the day; one of the reasons he was so painstaking in his enquiries. He didn't seem to be particularly interested in taking the credit. Even so, he had chosen not to come with me. I didn't blame him. I wasn't looking forward to seeing Grunshaw myself.

She was waiting in the same dingy interrogation room where we had met before. She was wearing a bright orange jersey and a multi-coloured bead necklace, but they contrasted with the sourness of her expression, her refusal to smile or to look anything but threatening. Darren Mills was looking jaunty in a sports jacket and trousers with a very slight flare. Generally, I have quite a lot of admiration for the British police. They're always extremely helpful to writers, giving us access to operations, control rooms and all the rest of it. They must get fed up always being depicted as aggressive or corrupt – but where these two are concerned, I have no regrets.

'So what do you want?' Grunshaw asked. She was sitting at the table with Mills leaning against the wall behind her. She hadn't offered me a cup of coffee. She didn't look at all pleased to see me.

'You wanted information,' I said. 'We know who killed Richard Pryce.'

'You mean, Hawthorne worked it out?'

'We worked it out together.' That wasn't strictly true but I needed his authority.

'Does he know you're here?'

'No. I didn't tell him.'

I was worried for a moment but she didn't see through the lie. 'Well, go on then.'

'Can I have a glass of water?'

'No. You can't have a fucking glass of water. And get on with it. We haven't got all day.'

I was tempted to turn my back on her and walk out. But it was too late for that now. This was my moment. I plunged in.

'This has been an investigation into not one death but two,' I began. 'There was the murder of Richard Pryce at his home in Fitzroy Park—'

'Yes, yes, yes,' Grunshaw interrupted. 'We know where he lived.'

I held my ground. 'Forgive me, Detective Inspector, but if I'm going to tell you this, I'm going to tell it my way.'

'Whatever you say.' She scowled. 'But it had better be good.'

Behind her, Mills crossed his arms and his legs, using his shoulder blades to stay upright against the wall.

'There was the killing of Richard Pryce and there was the death of Gregory Taylor just twenty-four hours before. What's made this investigation difficult has been working out the connection between them – if there was one at all. Was Gregory's death murder? Was it suicide? Was it an accident? Let's take them one at a time.

'It couldn't have been murder. Only two people knew he was in London. Richard Pryce, the man he had come to see, and his wife. It's just possible that Richard could have followed him to King's Cross and pushed him under a train, but why would he do that? Gregory Taylor had a terminal illness and Richard had just agreed to pay for the operation that might save him. If he wanted to kill Gregory, all he had to do was refuse. And Susan Taylor had no reason to kill her husband either. Their marriage was happy enough and she'd been the one who'd sent him to London to get help. There was only one other person who might have had a grudge against him – Davina Richardson could have blamed him for the death of her husband. He had been the team leader at Long Way Hole. But she didn't know he was coming to London and although it's true he was close to Highgate station, there's no evidence that the two of them met.

'So was it suicide? That doesn't make any sense either. Gregory Taylor came to London to get money for his operation and he rang his wife. We've heard the message and he's ecstatic. Richard Pryce isn't just going to pay £20,000 or £30,000, he's going to pay the whole thing. Of course, Gregory could still be depressed. The operation may not succeed. He's still ill. But everything in his behaviour suggests that this is a man who wants to live. He's going to take his wife out to dinner to celebrate. He's arranged to meet an old friend, Dave Gallivan, to talk about Long Way Hole . . . I suppose we'll never know what he was going to say. He even buys a paperback with six hundred pages to read on the train!

'It had to be an accident. It's the only explanation that works. I'm sure you've seen the CCTV footage. He's in a hurry. He wants to get home to celebrate with his wife. There's a crowd of football supporters and someone pushes into him. He shouts, "Look out!" and he falls.' I paused. 'If he'd wanted to kill himself, would he have done it inside a station, with the train moving so slowly? The transport police didn't think so and nor do I.'

Grunshaw and Mills were silent, gazing at me sullenly. At least I had their full attention.

'There are only really six suspects in the murder of Richard Pryce,' I went on. 'And I'm not going to go through them all. The point is this. If Gregory Taylor had been murdered, then maybe Richard's death would have been connected to what had happened at Long Way Hole all those years ago. But if you accept that it was an accident, then there's a whole different shape that presents itself and that's got to relate to Adrian Lockwood and Akira Anno and their divorce. That was where this all started – a threat in a restaurant. Akira couldn't have made herself clearer. She despised Richard Pryce and she wanted to hurt him with a bottle of wine.

'More than that, Akira was afraid of him because he was investigating her finances. She had a secret income stream that she hadn't told anyone about. If Pryce had found out how she was earning her money that would have been a good reason to kill him. Of course, she'd had to have known he'd found out and that's a problem because as far as we know, she had no idea.'

'How was she earning the money?' Mills asked.

I didn't answer.

'Let's get to the night of the murder. These are the facts. It had been raining and there were a few puddles on the ground but otherwise it was dry. It wasn't particularly dark – there was a full moon that night – but just before eight o'clock, one of the residents in Fitzroy Park, a man called Henry Fairchild, saw someone coming off Hampstead Heath, carrying a torch. That person rang the doorbell of Heron's Wake and Richard let them in. But something else happened. They stepped off the path and into the flower bed, breaking some of the bulrushes and leaving a small indentation in the earth. There's one other thing we need to remember. When Richard opened the door, he was talking to Stephen Spencer on his mobile phone. "What are you doing here?" he asked his visitor, which means he knew who it was. "It's a bit late."

'That last remark is rather strange. It's eight o'clock on a Sunday evening. True, winter time has just begun. But it's not really very late at all. What does he mean?

'I have to admit, I've thought about this for a long time. It puzzled Hawthorne too. But then I remembered something I'd seen when I was at Adrian Lockwood's house. It was just a small detail but it somehow caught my eye. He was eating bilberries.'

'This had better be going somewhere,' Cara growled.

I ignored her.

'Bilberries are rich in antioxidants known as an-thocyanins,' I explained. 'They're said to improve the health of your eyes – particularly if you suffer from nyctalopia, or night blindness. RAF pilots used to eat bilberries when they were flying night missions during the war.' I was quite proud of that. It was something I had learned researching *Foyle's War*. 'Night blindness is caused by the failure of the photoreceptors in the retina and there's no real cure. But bilberries help. You can also take vitamin A – it's the reason why mothers tell their children to eat carrots. And why some peo-ple choose to wear sunglasses during the day. Adrian Lockwood wears sunglasses. He has a bottle of vitamin A in his kitchen.'

I waited for all this to sink in. Mills used his shoul-ders to shift himself forward and sat down in a chair, Christine Keeler-like, with his knees spreading out on either side of the chair back.

'You're saying that Adrian Lockwood killed Pryce,' Cara said.

'Pryce was investigating him. The fact was that Lockwood had lied during his divorce proceedings. He had hidden assets – vintage wine – adding up to £3 mil-lion and against all the rules he'd kept it concealed. Then he'd made a stupid mistake. He'd given Pryce an insanely expensive bottle as a thank-you present after the trial.

Maybe he was showing off. But Pryce got suspicious and asked an investigator to look into it. The investigator, a man called Leonard Pinkerman, discovered the truth – and Richard Pryce was furious. He was well known for being a hundred per cent scrupulous. Even though the legal proceedings were over and he'd won his case, he wasn't going to let the matter rest. It went against everything he believed in. On that Sunday, the day he died, he called his partner and told him that he wanted to consult the Law Society. Now do you see how it works?

'Adrian Lockwood loathes his ex-wife and he'll do anything to stop the verdict being overturned. If he goes back into court he may have to pay out a whole load more. He's lied to his solicitor. And the taxman may be interested to learn that he's sitting on an asset that's worth a small fortune. But he has a plan to deal with the whole situation. He spends the early part of the evening with his lover, Davina Richardson, and leaves her house at around seven o'clock.'

'Wait a minute,' Mills cut in. He didn't speak often but when he did he was as snarky as possible. 'Mrs Richardson told us that he left at eight o'clock! She was quite sure of it.'

That was what I had thought too, but looking back through my notes I had finally seen the truth. My Eiffel Tower moment.

'Yes,' I said. 'But she also told me that she was use-less without a man around the house. She said there was a whole string of things she couldn't do. She couldn't park the car. She couldn't work the TV remote control. And she always forgot to change the clocks. Richard Pryce was killed on the Sunday after the clocks had gone back! At least, they were meant to have but Da-vina had forgotten. It was seven o'clock when he left the house. Not eight o'clock as she thought.

'Lockwood drove himself to the top of Hampstead Heath but he couldn't risk driving into Fitzroy Park. It's a private road and it would be easy to notice – and remember – any car that turned up on a quiet Sun-day night, particularly if it had a personalised num-ber plate. Lockwood happens to drive a silver Lexus with the number plate RJL 1. So he walked down from Hampstead Lane. There was a full moon but with his poor night vision he still needed a torch. He was also carrying an umbrella. Mr Fairchild didn't see it against the beam of light but I noticed it when I was in his home. As he approached the door he stumbled, again because of his eyesight. He trampled the bulrushes but steadied himself using the umbrella, making a mark in the soil.

'Richard Pryce was on the telephone when he opened the door and he must have been surprised to see his client. "What are you doing here?" he asked. And then he added: "It's a bit late." Don't you see? It was a bit late because only that afternoon he'd telephoned his partner, telling him what action he was going to take. He'd already made his decision. It was a bit late to argue.

'Even so, Lockwood persuaded Pryce to let him in and they went into the study. Pryce must have taken out the bottle of wine to show to him, or maybe Lockwood asked to see it because it was essential to his plan. You see, he had heard what had happened at The Delaunay. He knew that his ex-wife had seemingly threatened Pryce in front of a crowd of witnesses. We don't know her exact words but whatever they were, they were close enough. She had threatened him with a bottle and now he would be killed with a bottle. It must have amused him to know that she would get the blame.'

'And what about the number on the wall?' Grunshaw asked.

'It was exactly the same reason,' I said. 'He might not have planned it originally but he got the idea seeing the paint pots in the hallway. He knew that Akira had written a poem about murder . . . a haiku. He remembered the number because it was the same date as his second marriage. Incidentally, you might like to look into what happened to his first wife in Barbados.

This isn't the first time he's been involved in a violent death. Anyway, he was very happy to tell us that Akira was unstable, that she wasn't afraid to kill. He wrote the number knowing it would lead us eventually to the words she had written: *The sentence is death.* He wanted us to believe that she was exulting in what she'd done.'

There was a long silence.

I was very much enjoying the sight of Grunshaw and Mills as they took this all in. It was my moment in the sun. I tried to remember if I had left anything out. But no, it was all there.

'Have you told anyone else about this?' Grunshaw asked.

'Only Hawthorne. I've told him, of course.'

'Have either of you approached Lockwood?'

'No.'

'Don't.' She glanced at Mills, who nodded as if at some unspoken thought. 'We'll take it from here,' she went on. 'I'm not saying your theory is correct. There may be one or two holes in it.' I knew she was lying when she said that. I had gone over the whole thing several times through the night and Hawthorne had corrected me on a few points. It was watertight. 'But we'll interview Mr Lockwood and see what he has to say.'

'Fine.' I stood up. 'But now I hope you'll leave

Foyle's War alone. And for what it's worth, it would be nice if you gave Hawthorne a little credit.'

Cara Grunshaw looked at me almost with pity. 'Just for your information, I haven't gone anywhere near your stupid television series,' she said. 'As to what I'm going to do or what I'm not going to do, you can piss off, all right? And if you want my advice, you'll steer clear of Hawthorne. He's trouble. Everyone knows that. You stick around with him, you're going to get hurt.'

I was a little deflated as I left Notting Hill police station but I had cheered up by the time I got home. I would have preferred it if Lockwood hadn't been the killer – at the end of the day, it had been extremely likely from the start – but what did it matter? The case was over. I had enough material for a book. Now all I had to do was write it.

I'd found a new lease on life and quickly dealt with the script revisions for *Foyle's War*. I finished them by the middle of the afternoon and emailed them to the office. I tried ringing Hawthorne a couple of times but only got his voicemail. At four o'clock, I decided to go out. There was an exhibition of paintings by Daumier at the Royal Academy which I'd heard was worth seeing. I could pop in there for an hour and then see a film and have dinner with Jill.

The doorbell rang. I picked up the intercom. It was Hawthorne. 'Can I come up?' he asked.

I buzzed and let him in.

It was only the second time he had been to my flat. For different reasons, we were both eager to keep each other out of the places where we lived. When he stepped out of the lift, he was looking very pleased with himself. 'So you saw Cara Grunshaw,' he said.

I was already on the defensive. 'You said you didn't mind.'

'I don't.'

'Did she call you?'

'No.' He was carrying an edition of the *Evening Standard*, which he unfolded and spread out on my table. I put on my glasses and read a small article at the bottom of page two:

POLICE MAKE ARREST
IN HAMPSTEAD MURDER

This morning police have arrested a 58-year-old male in connection with the murder of divorce lawyer Richard Pryce who was found dead in his Hampstead home last week. Detective Inspector Cara Grunshaw said: 'This was a particularly brutal murder but after a meticulous and wide-ranging police investigation, we are very glad to bring the perpetrator to justice.' No further details have been released.

I finished reading, then glanced up at Hawthorne. He was leaning over the newspaper, smiling. Something inside me went cold. I read the article a second time. Hawthorne was still smiling. It was a grin that went almost from ear to ear.

I knew.

'I got it wrong, didn't I,' I said. I was feeling sick.

He nodded.

'It wasn't Adrian Lockwood.'

He shook his head. 'Poor Cara,' he muttered. 'She's only gone and arrested the wrong man.'

22
One Hundred Minutes

'You really are a complete bastard, Hawthorne,' I said. He was still so pleased with himself that he seemed indifferent to my comment. 'You knew I was wrong all the time. You used me to get back at Grunshaw.'

'I thought you'd be pleased, mate. She's going to have egg all over her face. The Assistant Commissioner isn't going to be pleased.'

'But she'll destroy me! She'll hurt the production—'

'She won't do anything. Cara is all mouth and no trousers. Believe me. You won't hear from her again. She's made so many mistakes in her career that after this little mishap they may even boot her out. I told you. She's thick! Everyone knows it.'

'Not as thick as me,' I said. I was depressed. It wasn't just that my moment of glory had been snatched away from me. I still didn't see how I had got it so wrong.

Hawthorne and I were sitting together in a taxi, crawling through the rush-hour traffic. London has a congestion charge but it clearly doesn't work as most of the time you could limp faster than you can drive. I've often walked from my flat to the Old Vic without being overtaken by a single bus and generally I go everywhere on foot. Just for once, though, I didn't mind being stuck, even if the meter was ramping up the fare. I wanted time alone with Hawthorne. I needed him to explain.

'You weren't thick,' he said and just for once he sounded almost sympathetic. 'You just didn't think it all through.'

'I looked at every angle,' I insisted. 'The pills. The bilberries. The glasses. The bottle. If there was a single flaw in my thinking, where was it?'

'Well, I could mention a couple,' Hawthorne replied.

'Go on!'

He pursed his lips like a doctor about to deliver bad news. 'All right. Let's start with this eye disease of his. What did you call it?'

'Nyctalopia.'

'You got that off the internet.'

'Yes.'

He shook his head. 'Maybe he has got it. I don't know. He could have been eating those bilberries because he likes bilberries. And people take vitamin A for all kinds of things: it's good for the teeth, the skin, for fertility . . .'

'Did you get that off the net?'

'No. I just know. And maybe he wears sunglasses because he thinks they look trendy – like the ponytail and the Chelsea boots. But the thing is, if he couldn't see in the dark, do you really think he would have walked all the way across Hampstead Heath, even with a torch? He could have parked the car in Highgate and walked down the hill. There are street lights all the way. Or he could have taken a cab.'

There was, I suppose, some truth in that. 'What else?' I asked.

'The motive – or what you think is the motive. Adrian Lockwood had three million quid's worth of wine hidden away in Wiltshire. But according to him, Richard Pryce never said anything about it. Yes, he discovered it was there. Yes, he was unhappy about it. But they'd never actually come to blows.'

'He would say that,' I insisted. 'He didn't want us to know Pryce had been investigating him. He was lying!'

'In that case, why would he tell us that someone had

broken into his office and hacked into his computer? Think about it, Tony. He knew Pryce had forensic accountants working for him. He probably even knew about Lofty. After all, Lofty had been spying on Akira too. So if he'd known he was being investigated, he would never have shared that information with us. It was the last thing he'd want us to know.'

Again, I couldn't deny Hawthorne's logic.

'What about the umbrella? What about the hole in the flower bed?'

'Lots of people have umbrellas, but it's irrelevant because it wasn't made by an umbrella in the first place. And for that matter, Henry Fairchild got it wrong. It wasn't a torch.'

'Then what—'

Hawthorne held up a hand. 'I don't want to have to say it all twice, mate. Let's wait until we get there.'

I hadn't heard Hawthorne tell the driver our destination but had noticed that we had crossed the Euston Road and were heading north. I assumed that we were going back to Pryce's house in Fitzroy Park . . . full circle, as it were. But we went up Archway and turned right on to Shepherds Hill and when I paid the fare – a £30 journey, including tip – I was somehow unsurprised.

Davina Richardson opened the door to us. She

looked very anxious. 'I hear they've arrested Adrian. Is it true?' she demanded.

Hawthorne nodded. 'I'm afraid so.'

'But that's ridiculous. Adrian would never have hurt anyone. He's just not that sort of person. And anyway, he couldn't have. I told you. He was here with me!'

'Do you think we could come in, Mrs Richardson?'

'Yes. Of course. I'm sorry . . .'

We followed her back through the kaleidoscopic interior and into the kitchen where we had first sat together. She was already hitting the wine. There was a bottle of rosé and a glass out on the table and next to it a packet of cigarettes. She had also been munching her way through a tube of Pringles. She looked even more of a mess than she had on the last two occasions. It had been a while since her husband had died, but this had been followed by the loss of her closest friend and now her lover was in jail. She was surrounding herself with anything she could use to prop herself up.

'Is Colin in the house?' Hawthorne asked.

'Yes. He's upstairs. Don't worry – he won't disturb us. He's plugged into his computer.'

We arranged ourselves around the table. Davina took out a cigarette and lit it. 'I'll do anything I can to help you,' she said. 'I know it's a mistake about Adrian. I've told everyone. He was here that evening with me.'

'Are you quite sure about that, Mrs Richardson?'
Hawthorne locked into her in the way he did so well,
leaving her no room for manoeuvre. 'We're talking
about the evening of Sunday the twenty-seventh of October. That was the day after the clocks had gone back
to winter time.' He glanced at the grandmother clock
beside the door. 'Are you sure you remembered to
change them on Saturday night?'

'Of course I did!' She stared at the clock, then
brought her cigarette up to her mouth, unable to dis-
guise the shake in her hand. 'I'm sure I did!'

'But you did mention to my friend here that you might
have forgotten.' *My friend.* Hawthorne meant me.

'Did I say that?' Everything about Davina – her long
chestnut hair, her scarf, her sparkly jersey, her entire
frame – seemed to be collapsing in on itself.

'That's what I thought you said.'

'Well, maybe you're right. Maybe I left them until
Monday. I really don't remember.'

I wasn't quite sure what was going on. I thought
Hawthorne had dismissed out of hand everything I
had told Cara Grunshaw. That included the breakdown
of Lockwood's alibi. But now it seemed that he was
agreeing with at least that part of what I'd said, getting Davina to admit what I had already worked out for

myself, meaning that Lockwood could have committed the crime after all.

'I can't help you,' Davina wailed. She looked exhausted, close to tears. 'Yes. I did forget the clocks. I always forget them and Colin shouts at me when he's late for school. But what difference does it make? Adrian went straight home. He called me later.'

'When was that?'

'About an hour after he'd gone.'

'On your mobile or on your landline?' Hawthorne was still at his most aggressive. 'You know that we'll check?'

'Maybe he called me the next day. I can't tell you. I don't know anything any more.' She poured herself some more wine and took a large swig.

Hawthorne allowed a brief pause. When he continued, he was a little gentler. 'The reason we're here, Mrs Richardson, is to help Mr Lockwood. He's been arrested by DI Grunshaw but I don't think he did it.'

'You don't?' Something between hope and fear stirred in her eyes.

'Would you like me to explain to you what I think happened . . . the way I see it? Then there'll be a few questions and I can leave you alone.'

'Yes.' She nodded. 'I'd like that.'

'Right.'

He glanced at me, then began.

'I don't want to upset you any more than you've been upset already, Mrs Richardson, but this all starts with your husband's death at Long Way Hole all those years ago. You've got to admit, it's quite a coincidence, isn't it? Gregory Taylor travels two hundred miles from Ribblehead in Yorkshire. He hasn't been to London for years. He meets up with his old mate, Richard. And little more than twenty-four hours later, they're both dead in mysterious circumstances. Now, you're not going to tell me there's no connection, are you? I mean, what would be the odds of that happening?'

'I read about Gregory in the newspapers,' Davina said. 'It was an accident.'

'I don't think it was an accident,' Hawthorne said.

'You mean . . . he was murdered?' I said. Again, I was confused. I was sure we had both dismissed the idea.

'No, Tony. He didn't fall. He wasn't pushed. He killed himself. I would have thought that had been obvious all along.'

'But . . . why?'

'I'll have a cigarette, if you don't mind,' Hawthorne said, helping himself to one of Davina's. He went through the ritual: taking one out, rolling it through his fingers, lighting it. The air was full of smoke. 'I've kept saying to you, you've got to find the pattern that works,' he said, addressing me. 'It doesn't work if he was murdered. It doesn't work if he tripped up and lopped his own head off. But if you start with suicide, everything falls neatly into place.'

'He had no reason to commit suicide!'

'If you believe what he told his wife, that's true. But let's start with the idea that he might have been lying.'

Hawthorne blew out smoke and watched it disperse in the air in front of him.

'This is my version of events,' he said. 'Gregory Taylor has been diagnosed with Ehlers-Danlos syndrome, which is about as bad as it gets. He needs an operation or his brain is going to shut down. He's broke, living in Yorkshire, but he has got one rich friend – Richard Pryce. The two haven't seen each other for six years. They've barely spoken since the day they managed to get another mate of theirs killed, but even so, Gregory, urged on by his wife, gets it into his head that now, in his hour of need, Richard will help him.

'Now let's suppose what really happened was that Richard Pryce told him to sod off. I don't know why, but somehow that scenario doesn't seem to surprise me. Let's imagine that on the Saturday afternoon when the two of them meet at Heron's Wake – which is, incidentally, one of the stupidest names I've ever heard for a house – Richard says quite categorically that he won't help, that he doesn't want anything to do with Gregory and asks him to leave.'

'But why would he do that?' Davina asked. 'Neither of them were to blame for the accident. There was an inquest. Richard and I talked about it. The two of them did what they could to save Charles. They could have got themselves killed. They didn't see each other again because they were so upset about what had happened, but you're making it sound like they hated each other.'

'Maybe they did,' Hawthorne said. 'Because maybe they weren't telling the truth about what really happened. And let me tell you this, Mrs Richardson. When people keep secrets, those secrets have a nasty way of festering. They can turn into poison. They can kill.'

'I don't know what you're talking about.'

Hawthorne sighed and tapped ash. 'We may never know what happened at Long Way Hole because the only three witnesses are dead now, and anyway it was all a long time ago. But I can tell you for a fact that the story Gregory Taylor and Richard Pryce told doesn't add up. Their mate Dave Gallivan, the man who led the rescue attempt, knew it too. He went to the inquest but he decided not to raise his suspicions. The cause of death was clear enough and he didn't want to upset anyone's feelings.

'But here are some of the questions they could have asked. One: your husband missed Drake's Passage and continued into Spaghetti Junction, which was on higher ground. So why didn't he just wait there until the flood-water had passed? It wouldn't have been very nice, but he could have sat there for twenty-four hours until someone came and found him.

'The bigger question is number two. According to the local farmer, Chris Jackson, it started raining heavily at four o'clock. He looked out of his window and he saw a little stream just outside the house. He called it a conditions marker. And at four o'clock it wasn't a little stream, it was a gushing river, already spelling out death to anyone who was trapped under-ground. One hour later, there was a knock on his door and Gregory Taylor and Richard Pryce arrived with their tale of woe.

'According to Susan Taylor – Gregory's wife – he and Richard were trying to get out of the cave after the flood started. We know that they still had to cover another four hundred yards – which is about a quarter of a mile. But then they noticed that Charles had been left behind and being the heroes that they were, they fought their way back in. They looked for Charles. They shouted for him. But there was nothing they could do. They got out of the cave and went for help. Ing Lane Farm was almost two miles away and even though they must have been pretty exhausted they had to hike there on foot.

'So let's do the maths. Four o'clock the rain is gushing down. Let's be generous and say they continued through the cave system for fifteen minutes before they noticed Charles Richardson was missing and so they would have had to spend fifteen minutes getting back in again. Let's give them ten minutes looking for their friend. They give up and decide to go for help. It's about thirty minutes to the exit. And how long do you reckon it takes them to get to Ing Lane Farm without a car? Shall we say another thirty minutes? That adds up to one hundred minutes. But Dave Gallivan at the local cave rescue team logs the call at five past five. That's just sixty-five minutes after the flooding. In every sense, it doesn't add up!'

'I don't understand,' Davina said. She had been pulling heavily on the wine while Hawthorne talked. The bottle only had a couple of inches left.

'There was no rescue attempt,' Hawthorne said, flatly. 'Whatever happened in Long Way Hole, nobody tried any heroics and Gregory and Richard both knew it. That was why they never saw each other again. Every time they looked at each other, they had to confront the truth.'

'They killed Charlie?'

'They left him behind. They didn't even try to help him. So now let's go back to Sunday the twenty-seventh. Gregory was desperate. Without the money for his operation, he was going to die. Richard threw him out. So what did he do?'

'He killed himself!' I said. What other answer could there be?

'That's right, Tony, but first he rang his friend Dave Gallivan. He said he wanted to tell him about what had really happened at Long Way Hole, but that was just making mischief. He already knew he wasn't going to see Dave again. He had decided on his plan. You see, he had a £250,000 life insurance policy.'

Of course. Susan Taylor had told us that. She'd made a grim joke that he wouldn't be able to use the money to pay for the operation that could save him.

'Gregory was afraid that if he killed himself, he would lose out on his life insurance. Maybe there was a suicide clause in the contract. Normally there's a two-year waiting period – but who knows? He didn't want it to look like suicide in order to protect the payment, so he set about sending a series of messages that everything was fine, he was going to live and that life was a bed of roses.

'He rang his wife with a message of comfort and joy and invited her to dinner at the Marton Arms the following night. But here's the question. Why did he call her at the time when he knew she would be taking their daughter to dance class? Could it be that he didn't want her to answer? That he couldn't trust himself to lie to her and that anyway he needed the message to be recorded, so that she could play it to the police?

'He also invited Dave to have a drink with him on the Monday. He even went so far as to take a selfie of himself smiling on Hornsey Lane, one minute away from the so-called Suicide Bridge in Highgate. What's that if it isn't signalling to the world "I'm not going to commit suicide!"? And finally he buys a big, fat book at the railway station because he wants us to think that he's going to start it on the train even though it's the third part in a series he's never read . . . In fact, he doesn't read books at all because I was in his house and I saw for myself. No books. No shelves.'

'He killed himself,' Davina repeated, emptying the last of the wine.

'But before he killed himself, he pressed the self-destruct button,' Hawthorne said. 'What exactly was he doing in Hornsey Lane, five minutes from here?'

'You said! He took a selfie . . .'

'He did more than that. He came to this house. He told you the truth about Long Way Hole.'

There was a heavy silence, punctuated by the sound of movement; perhaps a breeze blowing a curtain. Hawthorne looked up briefly but there were just the three of us in the room and he dismissed it.

'You can't know that,' Davina muttered.

'When you have excluded the impossible, whatever remains, however improbable, must be the truth,' Hawthorne replied.

'He came here?' I was so stunned by this piece of information, or deduction, or whatever it was, that I blurted the words out helplessly.

'On his way back to King's Cross station. Yes. He told Mrs Richardson what had really happened to her husband. My guess is that Richard Pryce, her dearest friend and the godfather to her child, had left his friend to drown. Is that right, Mrs Richardson?'

Very slowly, Davina nodded. A single tear traced itself down the side of her cheek.

'They lied about the flood,' she said. 'Charlie never got separated from them. It was just like you said. He got stuck at the contortion and they could have easily reached him but they were too scared. Richard was the worst of them. He persuaded Greg to get out. They could actually hear my Charlie screaming but they abandoned him. They saved their own skins and he drowned.'

'I'm very sorry,' Hawthorne said and I thought that for once he actually meant it.

'Don't ask me any more questions. I'll tell you the rest.'

This was a very different Davina Richardson. It was as if something had snapped inside her. She just wanted it to be over.

'I know the truth now and it's that Richard betrayed us,' she said. 'He looked after us. He gave us money. He got me work. He pretended to be my friend. But all along he'd been lying to us. He knew perfectly well what had happened at Long Way Hole. If he hadn't been such a coward, Charlie would still be alive. I'm not stupid, Mr Hawthorne. I know that everything he did for Colin and me was an expiation. He was trying to buy his way out of his guilt. But in a way that made it worse. I think I would have respected him more if he'd simply ignored us.

'When Greg Taylor told me what he'd done, I knew I had to kill him.' She got up and went to the fridge.

She spent a moment looking for another bottle of wine but there weren't any more. She opened a cupboard and found some vodka. She brought that to the table. 'I don't think I'm an evil person. I'm just empty. Can you understand that? I've lived the past six years with a great big hole in my life and I suppose I've allowed it to consume me. I didn't want to see Greg. When he turned up at the door, I couldn't believe it was him. He was a stranger to me. After he left, I knew exactly what I was going to do.

'Adrian Lockwood was here on Sunday evening and I deliberately made sure that the clocks hadn't gone back. You see, later on I wanted him to be able to say that I'd been here when Richard died. I drove over to Fitzroy Park. I left the car at the top of the street and walked down. I had a knife with me . . . in my handbag. I was going to stab him.'

'You didn't walk across the Heath?' Hawthorne asked.

'No.'

'Was Richard Pryce on the phone when he opened the door?'

'He may have had a phone in his hand. I don't remember. He was surprised to see me but he invited me in. He pretended he was worried about me. I know

now that everything he ever said and everything he felt about me was pretence. We went into the study and he asked me if something was the matter. I hated the way he looked at me, as if he cared about me. It enraged me. I can't even tell you how I felt. That was when I saw the bottle of wine. I picked it up and hit him with it. I hit him quite a lot of times. I know the bottle smashed at one point and I used the end to cut him.'

'What about the knife?'

'I'd forgotten about it. Anyway, I didn't want to use it. I knew it could be traced back to me.' She stared into the middle distance. 'The whole thing was so strange, Mr Hawthorne. When I killed him, I felt absolutely nothing. It was as if I wasn't even in the room. It was like watching an image of myself on a television screen with the volume turned down. I didn't even feel any anger or anything. I just wanted him to be dead.'

'And what then? Why did you write the figure one eight two on the wall?'

'I remembered the poem that Adrian had shown me. The one written by Akira Anno. I don't know why – but those words spoke to me. They told the truth about Richard. He had whispered in my ear and in a way he had killed both of us. I decided I wanted to leave a message behind so I went and got a brush and painted that on the wall. It was a stupid thing to do but I wasn't in my right mind.'

Another long silence. She poured herself some vodka, using the same glass that had held the wine.

'What do you think happens now?' Hawthorne asked.

Davina shrugged. It took her a while to find the next words. 'Does anybody really need to know?' she asked. 'You're not really a detective any more. Do you need to tell anyone?'

'Adrian Lockwood has been arrested.'

'But the police will work out that he didn't do it. They'll let him go eventually. They'll have to.'

'And you'll get away with murder?' The edge had crept back into Hawthorne's voice and I knew without any doubt that he wouldn't go along with what she was suggesting. 'Do you really think I'd let that happen?'

'Why not?' For the first time, she raised her voice, challenging him. 'I'm a single mother, a widow, on my own. It wasn't my fault that my husband, the one true love in my life, was taken away from me. What good will it do, putting me in prison? What will happen to Colin? We have no close relatives. He'll have to go into care. You could just walk out of this house and say you were unable to solve the case. No one in the world would be any the wiser. Richard will have paid for what he did to Charlie and what he did to me. And that's the end of it.'

Hawthorne looked at her sadly, but also, perhaps, with respect. 'I can't do that,' he said, simply.

'Then I'll get my coat. I'll have to ask one of the neighbours to come in, but I can leave with you straight away if that's what you want. And I'll plead guilty, by the way . . . I'll make it easy for everyone. I'm sure you'll be very proud of yourself, Mr Hawthorne. Do they give you a bonus for catching criminals? Just give me a few minutes to say goodbye to my son.'

I have to say, I was completely dumbfounded. The speed of this turnaround had been so sudden, the confession so comprehensive, that I felt I had been left behind – like Charles Richardson in the cave system. On the one hand, I could see exactly why Davina had killed Richard Pryce, but on the other, I still found it hard to make sense of. She had denied coming over the Heath, so who was the man with the light (it wasn't a torch, Hawthorne had said) that Henry Fairchild had seen? And if Richard hadn't been on the phone to his husband when he opened the door, who was it that Stephen Spencer had heard? Could it be that someone else had visited the house prior to the murder?

These and a dozen other thoughts spun in a turmoil

through my head, only to be interrupted by a slow handclap. It was Hawthorne.

'You did that very well, Mrs Richardson,' he said. 'But I know you're lying.'

'I'm not!'

Hawthorne turned to the door. 'Colin – is that you outside? Why don't you come in and join us?'

Nothing. But then Davina's fifteen-year-old son appeared, this time dressed in jeans and an oversized T-shirt with BREAKING BAD on the front. It was only the second time I had seen him. He was heavier and more adult than I remembered. Perhaps it was down to the way he was scowling, his eyes dark under his tangle of curly hair. The acne spot on his chin had got worse. I wondered how much of the conversation he had overheard.

'Colin! What were you doing there?' Davina asked. She would have gone over to him but Hawthorne was in the way.

'Looks like he was listening through the doorway again,' Hawthorne said. 'He seems to make a habit of it.'

I felt I should intercede. Obviously this was no place for a teenaged boy to be. 'I'll take him upstairs,' I said. I moved towards him.

'Stay where you are, Tony!' Hawthorne called out.

'Haven't you got it? She didn't kill Richard Pryce. He did!'

It was too late. I had already reached him.

Then everything happened at once. Colin snatched something up from the kitchen surface. Davina cried out. Hawthorne started forward. Colin punched me hard in the chest. I fell back and Hawthorne grabbed hold of me. Colin turned and ran. I heard the front door open and close. And then I was looking in dismay at a kitchen knife with a six-inch blade, half of which was sticking out of my chest.

23
Partners in Crime?

It's not easy to describe what happened in the next few minutes. It may well be that I was in shock and I was certainly in no mood to take notes. I remember Davina, sitting slumped and helpless at the table, hitting the vodka while Hawthorne took out his mobile phone. He called for an ambulance but not, at this stage, the police. I kept on staring at the knife, which looked like some alien object, and I couldn't quite get my head around the fact that it was, at least for the moment, part of me. I wanted to pull it out but Hawthorne warned me not to touch it. He helped me into a chair and grabbed hold of the vodka bottle, pouring me a large shot. I needed it. I was feeling completely sick and with every minute that passed, the pain was getting worse. This wasn't, of course, the first time I had been stabbed. I suppose that, looked at another way, the scene might have had a certain comic edge – but I certainly didn't see it that way.

The ambulance arrived in less than ten minutes, although it felt a lot longer. I heard its siren as it raced towards us along Priory Gardens. I kept looking at my shirt, depressed that I had put on a new Paul Smith and it was ruined. At least there didn't seem to be a great deal of blood and there was some relief in that. I don't like the sight of blood at the best of times, particularly if it's my own. Hawthorne was sitting close to me. Am I misremembering or did he actually hold on to my arm for a time? He really did seem to be concerned.

Meanwhile, Davina was completely out of it. 'We need to find Colin!' Her words drifted across the kitchen.

'Not now,' Hawthorne said.

She stood up. 'I'm going to find him.'

Hawthorne pointed a finger at her. He didn't shout, but there was such controlled fury in his voice that there could be no argument. 'You stay right there!'

She sat down again.

And then the door opened and a team of paramedics came bursting in and hurried over to examine me. I have a feeling they took the knife out there and then, but again, I can't be sure. They injected me with something and a few minutes later I was lying on my back with an oxygen mask on my face, being loaded into the ambulance for the short journey to the Royal Free Hospital in Hampstead.

As it turned out, the wound was nowhere near as bad as it looked. It was on the other side of my chest, away from my heart and it had missed all my other vital organs too. In fact it was only two inches deep. By the time Jill came to visit me later that evening, I was already sitting up in bed with a couple of stitches and a thick wodge of bandages, watching the news on TV.

She wasn't amused. 'You can't keep ending your books with somebody trying to kill you,' she said.

'It's only the second time it's happened and anyway, he wasn't trying to kill me,' I told her. 'He was just a kid. He thought I was going to grab hold of him and he panicked.'

'Where is he now?'

'I don't know. I imagine the police will be looking for him.'

'What about his mother?'

What about her? I supposed there was every chance she would be charged as an accessory to murder. I wouldn't know until I'd spoken to Hawthorne. 'She's being questioned.'

Jill sat down on the end of the bed.

'I'm sorry,' I said.

'When are they going to let you come home?'

'Tomorrow morning.'

'Is there anything you need?'

'No. I'm fine.'

She looked at me with a mixture of worry and exasperation. 'If you want my advice, you'll leave this out of the book. People aren't going to believe it and you're going to look ridiculous.'

'I'm not even thinking about the book at the moment.'

'I wish you'd never met Hawthorne.'

'Me too.'

I said that. And I was beginning to think I meant it.

Sure enough, I was discharged from the hospital after breakfast and the first thing I did when I got home was to ring Hawthorne. He didn't ask me how I was but I got the impression he had made enquiries at the hospital and already knew. We arranged to meet at a coffee shop midway between our two flats just this side of Blackfriars Bridge.

'You're sure you're up to it?' he asked.

'I need to know what happened after I left in the ambulance.'

'Bring an umbrella. It looks like rain.'

He was right. It was pouring down by the time I set out and the weight of the umbrella pulled at my chest, making the wound throb. Farringdon Road, never handsome at the best of times, was an oily black streak with the traffic sitting, ill-tempered, at the lights and cyclists wrapped in bright plastic weaving their way through. We arrived at the same time. Hawthorne picked out a table in the window and as I took my place the rain was hammering against the glass, then sliding down in a series of oscillations like the screen of an old black-and-white TV. It wasn't winter yet. It had been warm outside and the coffee shop had a muggy feel, although we were almost alone.

Water dripped off Hawthorne's raincoat as he hung it on a hook behind his chair. Underneath, his suit was dry. The journey had worn me out and for once he bought the drinks: a double espresso for him, hot choc-olate for me. I needed the comfort. He brought them over to the table and sat down.

'How are you feeling?' he asked, at last.

'Not great,' I said. The stitches were hurting more than the original knife wound. I hadn't slept well. 'Have they found him yet?' I asked.

'Colin? Yes. He went round to a friend's house and the police picked him up this morning.'

'What will happen to him?'

'He'll be charged with murder.' Hawthorne shrugged. 'But he's under sixteen so they'll probably go easy on him.'

I waited for him to go on. 'Are you going to tell me the rest of it?' I said. 'It's the only reason I've come here. I'd have much rather stayed in bed.'

'What's the matter with you, Tony, mate? You don't need to sound so bloody miserable. We solved it!'

'You solved the crime,' I said. 'I didn't do anything. I just made a complete fool of myself.'

'I wouldn't say that.'

'Well what would you say?'

He considered. 'You put Grunshaw in her place.'

It wasn't enough. 'Just tell me,' I said. 'Colin killed Richard Pryce. How did you work it out?'

He looked at me quizzically, as if he didn't quite understand me. Then he told me what I wanted to hear.

'I said to you that I'd narrowed it down to one of two people,' he began. 'I always had a feeling that it had to be Davina Richardson or her son – but at the end of the day, the murder of Richard Pryce had the kid's fingerprints all over it. What I told Davina yesterday – the death of Charles Richardson, Gregory Taylor coming round to the house – that was all true. But she never went round to Heron's Wake with a knife. She was only saying that to protect Colin. She's a good mum. I'll say that for her. She's been protecting him all along.

'You see, what happened was that Colin must have eavesdropped on the conversation between Gregory Taylor and his mother. Don't you remember the first time we went round? She told him off for listening at the door. He did it again last night. I knew he was outside. It was a habit of his. Well, it was bad enough for Davina listening to what Gregory had to tell her about Long Way Hole. All those lies. The cowardice. But think of it from a fifteen-year-old's point of view. Richard had become a second dad to him. Of course, he didn't have any kids of his own. He put Colin through school. He bought him expensive presents – that telescope, for example. He was always there for him and when Colin finally heard the truth, what do you think he felt? It must have driven him mad.

'And the next night, he did something about it. We know Colin wasn't in the house—'

'How do we know that?' I interrupted.

'Because Davina was in bed with Adrian Lockwood. She told us they could never get up to that sort of thing when Colin was around, so he must have said he was staying with a friend or something. In fact, he cycled over to Fitzroy Park, taking a short cut across the Heath.'

I had seen the bicycle in Davina's hallway. I had walked straight past it three or four times.

'The light that Henry Fairchild saw wasn't a torch. There was no need for it with a full moon.'

'It was a bicycle light.'

'That's right. There was a big puddle by the gate so Colin had to dismount and he was pushing the bike through. He continued down to Heron's Wake and dumped the bike by the front door. My kid does that with his bike all the time. He's too lazy to prop it up against the wall, especially when he's in a hurry. He just lets it fall.'

'The bike fell onto the bulrushes.'

'That's right. And it was the pedal that made that hole in the soil. Then Colin rang the door. Richard opened it and of course he was surprised to see him. "It's a bit late." Yes, it was. Eight o'clock at night in a quiet part of Hampstead. That is late for a kid to be out on his own.

'Richard invited him in. He could probably see that Colin was upset, although he had no idea what had brought him to the house. He got them both a drink. You remember what we saw on the table in his study?'

'Two cans of Coke.'

'Exactly. There was alcohol in the house but Richard didn't drink it – and nor did his visitor. That's one of the reasons I figured it wasn't Davina. She drinks like a fish. Again, who drinks Coca-Cola at eight o'clock in the evening?'

'A child.'

'To be honest with you, Tony, there were a lot of things about this murder that struck me as childish. I mean, that number on the wall for a start! What sort of person bludgeons someone to death and then wastes time painting cryptic messages for the police to find?'

'But what did it mean? Had he read the haiku?'

'No, no, no, one eight two had nothing to do with the haiku. That was just Davina making things up. You've got to get inside Colin's head. When I first walked into that room, before we'd even heard of Akira Anno and her stupid poetry, I told you what it might mean.'

'You said it could be a bus route, the name of a restaurant . . .'

'. . . or an abbreviation used in texting. That's something a teenager would know all about, isn't it?'

'What does one eight two mean? In texting.'

'I hate you.' Hawthorne smiled. 'He couldn't really have put it more clearly, could he?'

'But why did he do that? You say you understand the way he was thinking. But I can't imagine why any kid would do a thing like that.'

'Who was Colin's favourite author – after he stopped reading your books?' Hawthorne asked. 'His mum told you. And the funny thing is, the same writer seems to have been tiptoeing along three paces behind us ever since we started this investigation.'

'Conan Doyle!'

'Sherlock bloody Holmes. That's right! Didn't the parallels jump out at you when we were reading *A Study in Scarlet* at the book group? I quite liked the book, by the way. I think the others were a bit hard on it and for what it's worth, *A Multitude of Gods* is fucking unreadable. I'm not sure I'll get to the end . . .'

'What parallels, Hawthorne?'

'The writing on the wall! Enoch Drebber is poisoned in Lauriston Gardens and the killer writes "RACHE" on the wall . . . not in paint but in blood. And then at the end of the book, in Utah, numbers keep appearing all over John Ferrier's house. It's a warning from the Mormon elders.'

'What? He copied it?'

'Or he could have been thinking of *The Sign of Four.*'

Hawthorne sighed, then began again.

'Look, maybe Colin didn't mean to kill Richard
Pryce. Maybe he went over there just to shout at him.
He probably wanted to get a bit of teenaged angst off
his chest and tell his loving godfather to fuck off out
of his life. But you can imagine it. Things get out of
hand. Colin starts by accusing him of leaving his dad
on his own in the bottom of a flooded cave. To start
with, Richard denies it, but he's smart enough to know
that the game is up. So he tries to explain himself – but
that just makes things worse. Colin is shouting at him.
Richard tries to calm him down. Maybe he even puts a
hand on him and that makes Colin think he's gay and
that he's trying it on. Anything's possible. But the point
is, he completely loses it and then he sees the bottle of
wine that Richard's got on his desk or somewhere in
the room. He doesn't know what he's doing. He picks it
up and he smashes it into his godfather's face and then
he stabs him and he stabs him and the next thing he
knows, he's standing over a dead body with blood and
wine everywhere.

'What next? Now he's scared. He's committed murder. He's got to cover his tracks and because he's a kid,
and not even a very bright kid, he thinks of Sherlock
Holmes. He remembers the paint pots he saw in the
hallway and he gets a brush and paints a number on
the wall, just like in a Sherlock Holmes story. And the

first number that comes into his head is one that he knows well and exactly expresses what he's feeling. *I hate you.*'

He stopped. I couldn't have written it any better than the way it had just been described.

'It didn't end there,' Hawthorne went on. 'When we went to see Davina Richardson, he came into the kitchen and he couldn't resist joining in. By now the cocky little sod probably thought he'd got away with it, so he decided to spin us a story, again straight out of Sherlock Holmes. Richard Pryce is being followed. And it can't be anyone normal. There's something wrong with his face. That was what he told us.'

'I thought he was talking about Lofty.'

'Lofty won't win any beauty prizes but there's nothing particularly wrong with his appearance. And also he wasn't following Richard Pryce. He was working for him! No. There's a story – 'The Yellow Face'. It starts with a client, Grant Munro, who says he's seen a ghastly face watching him from an upstairs window. You look in your notes. I think you'll find Colin used almost exactly those words.'

I was embarrassed. I should have been the one to know all this, not Hawthorne. I was the one who had written about Sherlock Holmes. His shadow had been there the whole time. I'd even spent a whole evening talking about the books. But maybe because they were written more than a century ago, I hadn't seen their relevance to the case we were pursuing.

'When did his mother know?' I asked. 'Was she protecting him all along?'

Hawthorne hesitated and I realised he wished I hadn't asked that. And suddenly I was wishing it too. 'Actually,' he said, 'she only found out when you told her.'

My wound was throbbing. I could taste the sugar in the hot chocolate sticking to my lips. 'Go on,' I said.

'I did warn you about chipping in when I'm interviewing someone,' Hawthorne said. 'And the thing is, the first time we were with Davina Richardson, without meaning to you changed everything.'

'What did I say?'

'You told her about the number written on the wall. And you said it was written in green paint.'

'What was so bad about that?'

'Do you remember what was happening in the kitchen when we were there?'

I cast my mind back. 'She was smoking. There were plates in the sink.'

'And the washing machine was on. She was washing Colin's clothes. She'd already told us that he couldn't look after himself, that he was always in a mess. My guess is that he'd come home on Sunday night with green paint on his jacket or shirt and probably quite a lot of blood and wine too. He'd have washed those out himself in the sink or covered them with mud or whatever – but the green paint he couldn't get rid of. Mum found the clothes, still stained, and put them in the wash. It explains why, the moment you mentioned green paint, she got up and stood against the washing machine and she never moved, as if she didn't want us to see what was on the other side of the round window. She also got Colin out of the room as fast as she possibly could. She'd been pleased enough to see him when he came down, but suddenly it was bath night and home-work and all the rest of it. She was terrified he would give himself away.

'That was when she started changing her story – or adapting it. All of a sudden, Colin – who's tall for his age and can certainly look after himself – is being bul-lied at school. It was darling uncle Richard who sorted it out. Richard and Colin were inseparable. He was just a sweet kid in need of a dad. No way the little chap would go round and batter him to death with a bottle.

'It didn't stop there. The next time we went round to Priory Gardens – and this time she made sure Colin wasn't there – she had it all set up. She had to divert our attention. If we weren't going to suspect her son, there had to be someone else in the frame. The person she picked was Adrian Lockwood. He might have been her lover but she would sacrifice him in the blink of an eye to save her kid. Maybe she knew the significance of one eight two. Maybe Colin had told her what it meant. Well, she'd got an answer for that too. First of all she fed you that haiku. Did you really think that book, brand new by the way, just happened to be lying there – and just one page away from the poem she wanted you to see?'

'I was the one who turned the page.'

'If you hadn't, she'd have done it for you. But you were looking at haiku 181. It was in front of your eyes. Even an idiot would have thought of seeing what came next.'

'Thank you.'

'She knew the poem connected with Adrian Lockwood because the eighteenth of February was the date of his wedding. And then she gave you that spiel about how hard it was to live alone, how she always forgot to put the clocks back. And if that wasn't enough, just in case you hadn't picked up on it the first time, she said it again while I was there. "I went out at half past four. No! I mean half past three. I keep getting confused!" Laying it on with a trowel! What she was doing, of course, was deliberately destroying Adrian Lockwood's alibi. She wanted us to believe that he had left an hour earlier, which would have given him plenty of time to pop in and murder Richard Pryce. She even mentioned he was angry with Richard, although she didn't say why. She was just feeding him to us, bit by bit.'

'And she put green paint on his sleeve.'

'I wondered if you'd noticed it. Yes. That was her – what do you call it? French word . . .'

'Her pièce de résistance.'

'That's the one.' Hawthorne smiled.

'You saw it too. You might have mentioned it.'

'It was too bloody obvious, mate. There were only two ways it could have got there. Adrian Lockwood could have killed Richard Pryce and splattered paint on his shirt when he wrote the message . . .'

'. . . or she could have put it there.'

'If they were sleeping together, she'd have had easy access to his clothes. And of course, she knew what colour to choose.'

'Because I'd told her.'

Hawthorne finished his coffee and glanced out of the window. The rain was beginning to ease off but grey pebbles of water still clung to the glass. 'You don't need to be so hard on yourself, Tony. We solved it. I get paid – and you get your book. By the way, I still haven't seen the first one. Have they sent it to you yet?'

'No. I haven't seen anything.'

'I hope it's a good cover. Nothing too arty. Maybe a bit of blood.'

'Hawthorne . . .' I began.

Somehow I had known before I even sat down that I was going to say this. I had decided that Jill was right.

'I think this is a bad idea. These books, I mean. I'm a fiction writer, not a biographer, and I don't feel comfortable doing this. I'm sorry. I'll finish this one . . . I might as well since I've got all the material. But I'm going to ring Hilda Starke and ask her to cancel the contract for the third.'

His face fell. 'Why would you do that?'

'Because of what you just said! We've investigated two cases together and both times I've said something stupid that's completely mucked it up, and both times I've almost managed to get myself killed. It doesn't make me feel any better that I made a complete fool of myself. You used me. You deliberately set me up to get back at DI Grunshaw, but it's worse than that. You actually congratulated me. You persuaded me that I'd managed to work it out when everything I'd said was wrong.'

'Not everything. I checked. Adrian Lockwood does have an eye problem.'

'Fuck off! I admit it. I'm not clever enough to be

Holmes, but if you want the truth, I don't much enjoy being Watson either. I don't think this is working. I think we'd be better off going our separate ways.'

He didn't say anything for a moment. He looked upset.

'You're just saying that because you're in pain,' he muttered eventually. 'You've been stabbed. I'm amazed they even let you out of the hospital so quickly.'

'It's not just that—'

'And it's a bloody horrible day.' He cut in quickly, not wanting me to say any more. 'If it was bright sunshine out there, that would change your mind.' He pointed. 'That's an example of that thing authors put in books when the weather makes a difference to the way people feel.'

'The pathetic fallacy,' I said.

'Exactly!' He brightened up. 'That's exactly what I'm saying. You know about that stuff. You're a writer. And I bet when you get home tonight and start doing your notes, you'll enjoy describing just how shitty it is out there. Blackfriars Bridge. Farringdon Street. You'll choose all the right words and you'll make it come to life. There's no way I could do anything like that. Which is why it's such a great partnership. I do the legwork. You do the rest.' He smiled. '*Partners in Crime*. That's what you should call the book.'

'There's already a book with that title, Hawthorne.'

'I trust you, mate. You'll think of a better one.'

I looked out of the window. I still wasn't sure. But on the other hand, the rain had finally stopped and it seemed to me that a few rays of sunlight were beginning to break through.

Appendix
A Letter from Gregory Taylor

26 October 2013

Dear Susan,

I'm writing this in a café on Hampstead Heath. I've just seen Richard and we've had our words and I've made my decisions and I want you to know right from the top that I don't feel too bad. I love you so much. I love our two little treasures, June and Maisie. I wish things could have turned out another way but they haven't and I'm not going to sit here and complain. I've bought myself a cup of tea and a giant Bakewell tart. It's not as good as yours. It was raining a bit this morning but now it's cleared up and there are kids out playing and dogs walking and all in all the world doesn't look so bad a place.

If you're reading this, it means I'm dead. That's not something I ever thought I'd find myself writing, but it's the truth and we both have to face up to it. I wish I could send this to you right away. I wish I could be with you to comfort you. But that's not possible for reasons you'll understand. It'll be six months before you get this. I'm hoping everything goes as planned. I'm sending the letter to my sister Gwendolyn with instructions not to open it but to send it on to you next April. I hope that doesn't creep you out! But I know you'll understand why I have to do it this way.

It's the insurance. You get a quarter of a million quid when I'm gone. That's a big amount of money. Enough to look after you and the girls for the rest of your lives. Enough for you to move out of Ribblehead if that's what you want. Maybe you'll go back to Leeds. It was me who dragged you into the Dales in the first place and I often think that was selfish of me and no good came of it in the end. But with the money you can make the decisions. I hope you'll be happy. That's my only thought sitting here. You and the girls.

But you have to be very careful with this letter.

You should destroy it after you finish reading it. Don't show it to anyone. Don't tell anyone . . . not even Dave. I haven't looked at the policy but these insurance companies are full of weasels and they'll find any excuse not to pay up. They've got to think I died in an accident. I'll come to that in a minute. This isn't easy for me. It's not easy for you. But it's the way it has to be.

I hope you will forgive me. You always were my one true love.

I have to take you back to April 2007. Yes, it all goes back to Long Way Hole. I have to tell you the truth. Don't be angry with me, Sue. I didn't tell you the truth then and I wanted to, but I couldn't. Part of the reason was that whichever way I tried to swing it, it was my fault. I was in charge. I planned the excursion. And I was the one who said it was all right to go ahead. When I look back, I think that the only reason I did those trips was to hang on to something that had already gone. Richard and Charlie and me. We'd been close mates at Oxford and we'd had some wild times together and every year when we met we'd try to relive what we'd had, but we all knew that as we got older it was slipping away and each year there was a bit less of it and we all had to pretend a bit more. By the end, Richard

was a big-shot lawyer. Charlie was doing all right
for himself in marketing. But I'd ended up in the
finance department of a little company nobody had
ever heard of in the back of beyond. I never really
felt comfortable when I was with them and it didn't
change no matter how much beer we drank.

I knew we shouldn't have gone down Long
Way Hole. That's the truth of it. Looking at those
clouds, cumulonimbus, I knew in my gut that we
could be in trouble. The air was unstable. I had no
doubt there was going to be a storm but I persuaded
myself it was in the distance, that it wasn't going to
come our way. Maybe it was the fact that it was the
one time I was in charge. Richard and Charlie both
trusted me. There was an 18-metre pitch next to
the waterfall. We set up the rig and went down.

We only had two miles to cover to the exit at
Drear Hill, but you know Long Way. That first
pitch to start off with and we had to set up a pull-
down system as it was a through trip and we were
coming out the bottom end. Then there's a 35-metre
waterfall pitch and a couple of awkward climbs and
all that before you even reach Drake's Passage and
Spaghetti Junction. Not for the faint-hearted. But
we were all OK as we set off. Lots of laughing and
joking. Just like old times and all that.

I'm not going to go into all the details. You're sick to death of it and I've only got so much time to finish this. But here's the bottom line. I lied to you. I lied to the inquest. Charlie Richardson never got lost and he didn't die the way we said.

What happened was that the storm hit us when we were about two-thirds of the way through. I was first, then Richard, then Charlie. We knew at once that we were in trouble. In all my years caving, I'd never experienced anything like it. First off, there was a change in air pressure. Our voices didn't come out the same any more. And we could feel this sort of throbbing inside our ears and even in our bones. All the walls were glistening and water was dripping down, making its way through. That was just the start of it. There was this echoing sound, a rumbling that seemed to come out of the bowels of the earth, and all the time it was getting louder and louder until we had to shout to make ourselves heard. You've got to remember that we were 85 metres underground, on our own, and it was like the whole world was ganging up on us. We had to make a decision and we had to do it fast.

We had two choices. We could climb up into Spaghetti Junction and that's what I would have done. We'd be on higher ground there and hopefully the floodwater would pass underneath. But the other two weren't having it. Going in there, we knew we'd get lost. We'd have to sit there in the dark waiting for cave rescue and if the whole system flooded, who knew how long that would take? And we couldn't be sure we'd be safe, even in Spaghetti Junction. If the water rose high enough, we could get trapped there. We'd have backed ourselves into a corner. We'd drown.

We only had minutes to make the decision. We knew the flood pulse was on its way. Do you have any idea of the power of the water coming through those tunnels? We could already feel it punching at us. The cave, the very air, was vibrating. Bits of stone were coming loose and raining down on us. It was terrifying.

You know what we decided. We decided to press on. If we could just get through Drake's Passage, we figured we'd be all right. If we could get to the vertical crack, we could chimney ourselves up and let the water pass underneath. We might be stuck there a while but it still seemed the better option. The main thing was, it took us nearer the exit. That was what we all wanted. All three of us.

I went first. Then Richard. It wasn't so difficult. A 3-metre drop, then a corkscrew round. The two of us made it through and now we're crouching in a low passage, no room to stand, and we realise that Charlie hasn't made it. He's stuck. He's shouting. We can hear his voice. 'Guys! Guys!' Then something else. We can't make out the words because the water is so close. I've often told you that when you're underground, water can sound like people's voices. Well, right now it's like the whole world is screaming at us.

I put my mouth right next to Richard's ear and I shout as loud as I can, 'We have to go back for him!'

'No!'

I can't believe I've heard him right.

'No!' He shouts it a second time. 'It's too dangerous.'

'But he'll die.'

'To hell with him! Leave him!'

I can't believe it. But I look at him and see that he is yellow, that he's crying like a baby. I swear at him and I crawl back towards the contortion. And there he is. Charlie. Standing up. I can't see his head. Just his feet and his legs coming out of the bottom of the tube and I guess that his cow's tail or something has got caught and he hasn't got any purchase. He needs to pull himself up to release it. And I could help him but then water starts jet-

ting through and it's black in the light of my head torch and all the walls are shuddering and I think if I wait another second I'm going to die here and I turn round and crawl away as fast as I can, leaving Charlie to stand there and drown.

That's what happened, love. I'm not saying we could have saved him, but we could have tried. Maybe we could have got him out before the main surge hit. But we didn't. We made it to the crack and waited there while the water rushed out underneath us. Then we followed it to the exit. We were both soaked and we were exhausted. We were covered in cuts, I suppose from the falling rocks. We were lucky to be alive but we didn't feel that way. We were disgusted with what we'd done, both of us. Me as much as him.

I'm not going to pretend that I was any better than Richard, but I want you to know that it was him who said what we were going to do once we got out. Once a lawyer, always a lawyer. I always heard he had a reputation for telling the truth but that wasn't what he did this time, not when it would have stayed with him for the rest of his life. And think what it would have done for his career!!! Not the Blunt Razor. The Blubbing Loser. He made up the story about Charlie getting lost in Spaghetti

Junction. We pretended we'd gone back in looking for him. In fact, we went straight up to Chris's place at Ing Lane Farm and got him to call out cave rescue.

That's half the story. My hand has already got cramp, sitting here, writing. I need to finish this and move on. So I'll be brief.

I never really spoke to Richard again after that. Of course we were both at the inquest and you saw us together once or twice. But I couldn't look him in the eye. I was disgusted with him. He made me sick. But I was also disgusted with myself. If the two of us had gone straight back together, I think we could have got Charlie out. But we left it too late. I never went caving again after that. You know that. Now you know why.

And then I got ill and the NHS couldn't help and you told me to go down to London and talk to Richard. Did you never wonder why I was so against it? Why I put my foot down every time? We had all those arguments and I know I was upsetting you, but I never wanted to see him again and anyway, I knew in my heart that he probably wouldn't help. The very sight of me would just remind him of the coward and the liar that he was. But you wouldn't take no for an answer. You more or less dragged me on to the train. And this is the result of it. Here I am.

Do you know, I very nearly didn't go to his posh house in Hampstead. I nearly rang him to say that I'd changed my mind. I was going to tell you that he'd refused to give me any money for my treatment and leave it at that. But I can't lie to you, Sue. Long Way Hole was the only time in all our years together that I lied to you and it made me sick to my stomach. I went to see him, just like you wanted. And just like I expected, he turned me down flat.

He wasn't anything like the man I remembered. Well, he was only a lad really, nineteen, when we first met. He was very polite. He invited me in. He offered me a cup of tea. But when I told him why I was there, he refused to help. He said that in view of what had happened, he didn't think it was appropriate for him to involve himself in my affairs. Words like that. The strange thing is that over the years I think he'd persuaded himself that I was to blame. Well, I'd been the one who'd seen the storm clouds. That had all come out at the inquest and it was a matter of public record that I was the one who gave the go-ahead. (He even used those words . . . I wanted to punch him when I heard them com-

ing out of his mouth.) But somehow he'd managed to conflate everything so that it was as much my decision as his to leave Charlie behind. Well, I could write more. I could write until the cows come home. But the bottom line is he threw me out.

This is the difficult part, Susan. This is the bit I don't want to write. And it's why you're going to have to wait six long months until you finally learn the truth.

I'm going to kill myself. You know I'm no good as an invalid. I don't like doctors and pills and all the hospital rubbish and I don't like you and the girls seeing me sitting there, suffering. I want you to remember me how I was – the good and the bad bits – and not as an invalid, in pain. I've worked out what I'm going to do and I'm going to make certain it looks like an accident so those insurance weasels will be sure to pay out.

But first of all I'm going to tell Davina Richardson what really happened to her husband. Richard may breathe a sigh of relief when he hears I'm gone but I don't see why he should get away with it. She doesn't live too far from here and I just called her on her home line and she's in. We didn't speak. But we will. I'm going to make her promise not to tell anyone I've been there and then she'll do the dirty work for me. Bring Richard down and wipe that lawyer's smile off his face.

I don't want to end writing about Richard. When you pulled that first pint for me back in Leeds, I knew straight off that you were the girl for me. You were beautiful then and you're beautiful now. I know we've had our ups and downs, but that's true of every marriage and, sitting here, I remember only the good bits. Our two girls, to start with. But that visit to Skye. Running the Three Peaks. Coniston Water. That weekend we had in Paris when we lost the passports. All the laughter. I hope you get married again, love. You should. You're the best. Try to forgive me for what I have to do.

Your loving husband,
Greg.

The letter was sent to Gwendolyn James in Huddersfield. She passed it on to the police. It is reproduced here by kind permission of Susan Taylor, Gregory Taylor's widow.

Acknowledgements

O ne of the stranger aspects of writing about my investigations with Daniel Hawthorne is that I end up having to thank people who actually appear in the book . . . though not all of them. As will have become clear, some of them made my life very difficult while others have demanded that I change their names or remove them altogether: one of them has even gone so far as to threaten me with lawyers, although I would say my depiction of her is entirely accurate.

It would have been impossible to write *The Sentence Is Death* without two men in particular. Dave Gallivan, who led the rescue team into Long Way Hole, spoke to me at length about his work. Chris Jackson went one stage further. He actually took me caving – an experience I enjoyed much more than I expected. We went through Drake's Passage and he showed me the actual spot where Charlie Richardson died. Later on, he read the manuscript and drew my attention to a number of technical errors. I very much enjoyed meeting both of them and won't forget our steak and kidney pie at the Station Inn in Ribblehead.

Graham Hain, the forensic accountant at Navigant, is also mentioned in the book. Although he had never met Richard Pryce, he gave me some brilliant insights into the way a high-end divorce might work. Alex Woolley, a solicitor at Winkworth Sherwood, and Ben Wooldridge, a barrister at 1 Hare Court, were both generous with their time and provided me with a complete legal backdrop. Any mistakes, of course, are mine.

Vincent O'Brien, the managing director of Octavian Vaults and Andy Wadsworth, the Vaults Custodian, introduced me to a business I didn't even know existed . . . They look after ten thousand private collectors from thirty-nine countries. I'd also like to thank Detective Constable James McCoy and everyone at Euston station's British Transport Police for allowing me to see them at work. As I say in the book, these secret worlds never fail to excite me.

A special thank you to Vivek Gohil, who lives with (rather than suffers from . . . a distinction he made clear to me) Duchenne muscular dystrophy. I wanted to write sensitively about the condition and, for obvious reasons, I couldn't really approach Kevin Chakraborty. Vivek is an incredibly inspiring young man – and he has a nice mum too. Thanks also to Jane Mathews, the Senior Press Officer at Muscular Dystrophy UK, for introducing us.

Selina Walker and the team at Penguin Random House have been a total pleasure to work with, as ever. My wonderful family, Jill Green and my sons, Nicholas and Cassian, are endlessly supportive even as they see their privacy being shredded, word by word. I have a terrific agent in Hilda Starke, helped by her assistant, Jonathan Lloyd. My own assistant, Alison Edmondson, helped organise my life and introduced me to most of the people on this acknowledgements page. And finally, I suppose, I have to thank Daniel Hawthorne, who first approached me to write this series. Perhaps it wasn't such a bad idea after all.

16 August 2018

About the Author

ANTHONY HOROWITZ, one of the UK's most prolific and successful writers, may have committed more (fictional) murders than any other living author. His novels include *Magpie Murders, Trigger Mortis, Moriarty, The House of Silk, The World Is Murder,* and the bestselling Alex Rider series for young adults. As a television screenwriter he created both *Midsomer Murders* and the BAFTA-winning *Foyle's War* on PBS. He lives in London.